MW01094675

Kill Your Darlings

ALSO BY PETER SWANSON

Kill Your Darlings

A NOVEL

Peter Swanson

WM

WILLIAM MORROW

An Imprint of HarperCollinsPublishers

This is a work of fiction. Names, characters, places, and incidents are products of the author's imagination or are used fictitiously and are not to be construed as real. Any resemblance to actual events, locales, organizations, or persons, living or dead, is entirely coincidental.

KILL YOUR DARLINGS. Copyright © 2025 by Peter Swanson. All rights reserved. Printed in the United States of America. No part of this book may be used or reproduced in any manner whatsoever without written permission except in the case of brief quotations embodied in critical articles and reviews. For information, address HarperCollins Publishers, 195 Broadway, New York, NY 10007.

HarperCollins books may be purchased for educational, business, or sales promotional use. For information, please email the Special Markets Department at SPsales@harpercollins.com.

FIRST EDITION

Designed by Kyle O'Brien

Library of Congress Cataloging-in-Publication Data has been applied for.

ISBN 978-0-06-343362-5 (hardcover)
ISBN 978-0-06-344788-2 (international trade paperback)

25 26 27 28 29 LBC 5 4 3 2 1

For Chiqui Sawyer and Jaqui DeMaio
And in memory of Tom

If once a man indulges himself in murder, very soon he comes to think little of robbing; and from robbing he comes next to drinking and Sabbath-breaking, and from that to incivility and procrastination.

—Thomas de Quincey

Blood will have blood.

—Macbeth

Kill Your Darlings

2023

i

The first attempt at killing her husband was the night of the dinner party. Wendy had been cajoled into hosting by Marcia Lever, the head of the English department. Marcia called Wendy directly, instead of going through Thom, Wendy's husband, even though he was the one who taught at New Essex State University. But Marcia and Wendy had long been friends, and Thom, especially of late, was unreliable about making plans.

"Feel free to say no," Marcia said on the phone. "But any chance you want to throw a small shindig out at Goose Neck? Just you and Thom, myself and Jim, if he doesn't get sick, and then our two new hires. You met Sally Johnson, right? She started back in the fall."

"I went to that introductory cocktail thing you threw, but I didn't talk with her. Who's the other new hire?"

"There's a new admin I thought we could invite. Emily. Has Thom mentioned her?"

He had, throwing her name out there in the awkward way he

sometimes did when talking about his current crush. His voice would get very monotone and he'd say something like, "Emily saw such-and-such movie and said it was brilliant. I've mentioned Emily before, haven't I?"

"Sure," Wendy said.

"That's six," Marcia said. "I'd invite Roger and Don, as well, but only if it's okay with you. I know this is a big ask."

"I'll do it, Marcia. I could use a boozy dinner party myself, but I'm going to make you stay late and help me clean up."

"Of course, of course. Totally. Thank you, Wendy. I owe you."

The dinner party happened two weeks later. All said, it wasn't a total disaster. Marcia's husband, Jim, not surprisingly, canceled at the last moment with a lingering cold he thought might be the flu. Roger and Don came, and Roger, in particular, made sure that the conversation never lagged. When Thom had first gotten his tenure-track position in the English department, Roger had been the old guard. Nearing seventy now, Roger was still the old guard, but Thom wasn't too far behind. Roger's husband, Don, had recently retired as the CFO of a large Boston company that did something Wendy could never remember, and it was clear that his retirement plans involved drinking himself to death in short order.

Sally Johnson, recently poached from somewhere in California with the offer of tenure, was less chilly than Wendy remembered her being at the welcome party. Still, she wasn't exactly warm, but she did bring gerbera daisies, and she did drink two glasses of wine before the meal was served, and told everyone, again, about the thesis she'd written when she got her PhD at Cornell. Wendy watched her, fascinated by her posture and how carefully she chose her words. Everyone else was simply blurting out whatever crap popped into their heads. Sally seemed rehearsed somehow. Then Wendy remembered, a few years ago, when the poet Marcus Robertson had been a visiting professor, how he'd told her that Black academics learned very early on that they had to be twice as professional as everyone else, that they could never show a chink in their armor. That there was no room for error.

But the person at the party who really interested Wendy had been Emily Majorino, hired in January after Linda, the longtime department secretary, had retired. For one, Emily was Thom's type, *exactly*, down to the old-fashioned green cardigan she was wearing and a nervous habit of chewing at her lower lip. She had brown hair, shoulder-length, large eyes set a little too far apart, and narrow shoulders. She brought a bottle of white wine, and when she handed it to Wendy in their large open kitchen, she said, "I've been looking forward to meeting you."

"Oh," Wendy said.

"I'm a fan of your poetry."

Wendy actually laughed, since it was so far from what she was expecting to hear. "Sorry," she said. "You're maybe the first person who's ever said those words to me. Out of the blue, I mean. How did you end up reading my poetry?"

"I own *Specifics Omitted*. I thought of bringing it for you to sign but didn't want to embarrass you. Maybe some other time."

"Sure," Wendy said, still a little confused. Twenty years earlier she'd won a first-book award from a university press and published her only work. She'd felt enormous pride at the time while also being cognizant of the fact that no one besides her immediate friends and family would ever read it. "Are you a poet too?" Wendy said to Emily. She'd mostly found that the only people in America who read poetry were people who also wrote it.

"No, not really. I mean, I've tried . . . unsuccessfully." Now it was Emily's turn to laugh awkwardly.

"Well, thank you. And thank you for the wine. I'm just going to put it in the fridge."

Plating the appetizers, Wendy went over the strange interaction.

There had been something oddly familiar about it, and then she realized that it had been years since someone had spoken to her in the way that Emily just had. Nervously wanting something. Eager to please. It reminded her of being courted, of boys and men from the distant past. Had Emily, this odd-duck young woman, developed some sort of faraway crush on her through her poetry? It was too ludicrous to even consider.

She kept an eye on her, though, throughout the night, partly because of the strange early conversation, and partly because there was something so familiar about her. About halfway through the party, while Emily was picking at her roast leg of lamb, Wendy blurted out, "Joan Fontaine."

"Gesundheit," Don said, and everyone laughed.

"That's who you remind me of," Wendy said to Emily.

Emily, startled, said, "Who?"

"Joan Fontaine, the actress. She played the second Mrs. de Winter in *Rebecca*."

"Oh," said Emily. She was turning a little red, probably because everyone was now looking at her.

"I suppose she does a little bit," Thom said. "But *I* think she looks like Barbara Bouchet. No one here will remember Barbara Bouchet but she played Miss Moneypenny in that terrible 1960s *Casino Royale*. That's an interesting film because—"

Wendy interrupted by asking the table if anyone had been watching *Mare of Easttown* on HBO. Everyone nodded all at once. Thom glared in her direction. Still, she'd been with him long enough to know when he was getting ready to monologue about a subject that interested only him. Honestly, though, the real reason she'd stopped him was because once upon a time, many years ago, he used to tell *her* she looked like Barbara Bouchet, something he'd probably forgotten all about.

After dinner, while Marcia cleaned the dishes, the rest of the guests, all except Sally, who'd left early, moved in front of the fire in the living room. Thom doled out drinks: whiskey for Don and Roger, a rusty nail for himself, while Wendy bailed Emily out of having to drink something so strong by suggesting they open another bottle of wine. Time sped up, the way it does at the end of a party, and suddenly Roger was doing his most famous party trick, reciting all of "The Love Song of J. Alfred Prufrock" while doing his Christopher Walken impression. Thom had managed to work his way onto the sofa next to Emily. He was very drunk, the most drunk Wendy had seen him in months, at least publicly. His voice was louder, he was swearing more. She wondered if he'd do something foolish, like make an actual pass at the thirtysomething administrative assistant, but she didn't think he would. Years of drinking and socializing had taught him what lines not to cross.

"What are you working on now, Thom?" Marcia asked, having now joined the group after finishing the dishes. She was drinking a can of grapefruit seltzer water.

"I'm writing a mystery," Thom said, then shrugged as though he'd said something ridiculous.

"Oh yeah?"

"Well, we'll see about it. I think it's a mystery story. It has a murder in it."

"Tell us about it, Thom."

Wendy listened intently as Thom explained that he wasn't willing to divulge any details yet. But even without details, gooseflesh had broken out along both her arms at this new information that Thom was writing a book. A book with a murder in it.

Wendy excused herself, knowing she wouldn't be missed, and went upstairs to their bedroom. The sweater she was looking for was draped across the chair on her side of the bed, and she wrapped it around herself. All Aprils in New England were cold but this particular one was breaking her heart; day after day of forty degrees and sporadic rain. She started back down the stairs but there was a pause in the jazz record that was playing and she could hear that Thom was still talking at length. She reversed course, deciding with sudden certainty that she needed to find out about this book.

In Thom's office she opened his laptop up and punched in his password, the same one he'd had for many years. There was an array of open browser tabs, but Wendy wasn't interested in those. She went to his writing folder and found his latest Word document, titled "WIP" for "work in progress," and opened it up. Thom had created a title page already:

Come End of Summer
a novel of suspense
by Thom Graves

Wendy scrolled to the next page and found an epigraph.

> And the thought that, after all, he had not really killed her.
> No, no. Thank God for that. He had not. And yet . . . had he?
> Or, had he not?
>
> —Theodore Dreiser, *An American Tragedy*

She didn't need to keep reading. The quote, alone, had made her instantly sober. And furious. She decided to keep scrolling and read the first paragraph of the book, enough to know that Thom was writing some version of their own story, a story they had agreed was *never* to be shared with anyone. A story the world could never know. His novel began:

> He saw her in Bryant Park, dusk of a summer night, the city parting its shoulders to facilitate her grand re-entrance into his life. She

must have seen him, as well, because before he had a chance
to extinguish his cigarette, to re-order his mind and body, she was
there in front of him, jacket collar quivering, a threat to the tranquility
he had created in the ten years since last they'd met.

"Blech," Wendy said out loud, mainly in response to the prose. For a moment Thom's words had distracted her from the realization of what he'd done, what he was doing. They'd grown apart over the years, but Wendy believed, *had* believed, that the one thing that cemented them together was a commitment to never speak of the past. Their sins were private sins. It was Thom who saw the world through books and movies, who once upon a time had said that they were like Fred MacMurray and Barbara Stanwyck in *Double Indemnity*. They had boarded a train together and there was no getting off, all the way to the final stop. Wendy had also believed that no one else would ever be allowed on that particular train, not friends or priests or other lovers. And their story wasn't for books either.

What was he thinking?

Back downstairs the album had ended, and the guests were searching for coats. Thom was at the bar, pouring himself another drink, then turned around to scowl at the deserters.

"Is he going to be all right?" Roger said to Wendy at the door, which was rich, considering his own husband was currently weaving his way toward a collision with a rosebush.

"He'll be fine. He won't remember a thing."

Wendy picked up Emily's scarf, which she'd dropped to the floor while struggling with her winter parka. "Here you go. How did you get here? Are you driving?"

"Marcia's driving me home," she said.

"Oh, good. Our only sober guest. It was nice meeting you."

"Maybe we could get together," Emily said, the words coming fast, like a Band-Aid being ripped away. "We could talk about poetry."

"Yes, I'd like that," Wendy said, wondering if her voice sounded as bemused to Emily as it did in her own head.

Everyone left, and Wendy let Thom pour her another glass of wine she wasn't planning on drinking. But they sat together and listened to side two of *Live at the Pershing*. "Party poopers," Thom said.

"It's two a.m."

"Is it?"

"Yep."

Wendy considered bringing up the book he was writing but knew it wouldn't be worth it. She hadn't been kidding when she told Roger that he wouldn't remember anything the next day. He wouldn't. She could see it in his blank eyes and the way his mouth was slightly ajar, lower lip hanging. She took a tiny sip of her wine. He had put his empty glass down and was mimicking playing the piano along with Ahmad Jamal. God, she despised him. It was a new realization. For a long time she'd known she disliked him, known that the thought of spending the remainder of her years in his company filled her with a kind of dread. She'd also known that he was never going to change, but she hadn't admitted to herself yet that she truly hated him. That she wanted him gone.

I should just kill him, she thought.

"What are you smiling about?" Thom said.

"Just murder," she said back. "Your murder."

He laughed and moved his hands along the imaginary keys.

But twenty minutes later he was standing at the top of the stairs on the second-floor landing, a hand loosely on the banister, a confused look on his face. Wendy was passing from the bedroom to the bathroom but stopped to ask him what was wrong.

"I thought I'd forgotten something downstairs and now I can't remember what it was."

He really was drunk, his head drooping, his free hand waggling a finger.

"Your glasses, maybe," Wendy said.

Then, without really thinking about it, or rather, as though she'd planned this very maneuver before, she reached out toward the front pocket of his shirt and gently pushed him in the chest. "Jesus," he said, tottering backward then righting himself, but he was wearing socks and one of his legs gave way and he fell down the stairs, hard, spinning all the way over then thudding to a halt at the bottom landing. The violence of it was extraordinary.

"Thom!" Wendy yelled, then followed him carefully down the steps. He was silent except for a low purr that reminded her of a cat. But when she'd reached him, he suddenly came to, springing back onto his feet as though he'd simply fallen onto a couch and was now getting up again.

"Fuck," he said. "What just happened?"

"You fell down the stairs, Thom," she said. "You're drunk."

He asked again in the morning, when he'd found the bruises on his body. "I don't know how you fell," Wendy said. "I was brushing my teeth. Anything broken?"

"My last shred of dignity," he said, and went downstairs to start the coffee.

ii

Thom checked the weather app on his phone; it told him it was currently raining in New Essex. He looked outside but saw no sign of rain, even though the dark, swollen sky was threatening. He felt terrible, having drunk far too much the night before, and he'd woken up with about five mysterious bruises down one side of his body (Wendy had gleefully informed him he'd fallen down the stairs). Still, he was determined to ignore the pain, to get outside and take a walk, try to stretch his muscles, clear his head a little. He stared at the app again, then out through the window that looked onto Naumkeag Cove, now at low tide, gulls and crows hovering overhead. Goose Neck was a small, rocky peninsula that jutted into the outer harbor of New Essex, and for whatever reason it had its own weather patterns, ignoring all forecasts. He decided to risk it and went to get his coat.

He was halfway through the circling walk that would take him along most of the perimeter of Goose Neck when the rain started up. He didn't mind. It was a misty kind of rain, and he was planning on showering anyway when he got back, so what difference did it make if he got wet? He buttoned the top button of his coat and kept walking, still trying to pick apart the chronology of the dinner party the night before.

It had started fine, Roger and Don in good form, Marcia jumpy as always, Wendy's roast lamb a huge hit. Sally Johnson hadn't wanted to be there, but he wasn't sure Sally wanted to be anywhere, except for maybe alone with a book. She was a true academic, that one, almost as though she'd gotten into the field out of a love for literature instead of the desire to only have classes on Tuesdays and Thursdays and the chance to take sabbaticals every five years.

He was surprised that Marcia had invited Emily Majorino. Pleased too. When she'd first been brought on, back in January, he'd been entranced by her quiet beauty. She'd mesmerized him, but not in any lustful way. Something about her stillness, her quiet voice, her mysterious life. (She was much younger than he was, but as far as he could tell she had absolutely zero social-media presence. He'd looked.) He imagined them talking to each other, confiding in each other. He imagined giving her advice. Sometimes, oddly, these fantasies would warp into her pressing a cold washcloth against his head, the way his mother used to do. Or else he imagined her cooking him a meal, telling him everything was going to be okay. He supposed he was getting old.

The mist was being replaced by actual rain, and Thom sped up, lowering his head, and still picking away at the memories from the previous night. He knew that Roger had done his party trick— his J. Alfred Walken—and that the drinks had flowed. Sally had left early. No surprise there. And he knew that he'd sat next to Emily for some time and that they'd been talking passionately, or maybe it had just been he who was doing the talking. But the words were gone. He also had no memory of how the evening had ended, just that he'd been downstairs by the fire and the next thing he knew he'd woken up in the morning, his mouth dry, his forehead damp, and his body aching as though he'd been beaten with a croquet mallet.

He turned onto Jewett Lane and stopped for a moment to look across the harbor, pocked with rain. He rubbed at his ribs and a memory from the night before, a fragment of a memory, pricked at his mind. The upstairs hallway. Wendy's face. A look of revulsion. Then it was gone.

"Okay there, Thom?"

It was one of his neighbors, Fred, out walking his dog. Thom blinked in Fred's direction. "Oh hey, Fred," he said. "Just thinking about going for a swim."

"Ha-ha."

Back at home, Thom felt worse than he had before his walk. The cold had gotten into his bones, and the partial memory from the night before, his wife's face, was haunting him.

"How'd I fall down the goddamn stairs?" he said to Wendy, who was putting together some kind of casserole in the kitchen.

"I pushed you, naturally," she said.

Wendy had a morbid sense of humor, she always had, and he sometimes wondered if it was because of what the two of them had done in the past. Or was it in spite of it?

"No, really, you must have heard me fall."

"I did. I was brushing my teeth. For a moment I thought you were dead."

"And how did that make you feel?" Thom was pouring himself coffee and noticed a slight tremor in the hand that held the cup. It was worrying.

"In the time it took me to walk down the stairs and check on you I'd already spent the life insurance."

"Oh yeah? What on?"

"A couple trips to France. A new downstairs bathroom. Maybe a Birkin bag."

"You *did* think about it."

She smiled, and Thom felt colder.

"You read the text from Jason?"

"No," Thom said, pulling out his phone.

Their son had planned a visit for the weekend, and Thom assumed that the text was a cancellation, but instead he'd texted to remind them that he was now completely vegetarian and then he'd asked if he could bring a friend along, some girl named Ashtyn.

Thom nearly asked who Ashtyn was, because he couldn't remember, but something told him not to ask, something told him that, once again, he'd forgotten some crucial information about his family's life. "I think I'll go read," he said, and took himself to his office.

He lay down on the couch across from his desk, looked at his phone a little, checking his son's Instagram to see if there was a picture of this girl he was bringing. They'd only just gotten used to the previous girlfriend, Tonya, who had been eerily uncommunicative but whom Jason seemed to genuinely love. And now he was dating someone called Ashtyn. He put his phone down and picked up his book—*Lying to Doctors* by Catalina Soto—reading just a few pages before shutting his eyes, hoping to get some sleep. But images kept appearing and disappearing in his mind. His wife's face in the dim hallway light, her eyes cold and unloving. Emily's face in the firelight as he spoke words at her, words that he couldn't conjure up. What had they been talking about? He felt deep shame that he couldn't remember. And then all he could think about was the coldness in his bones. He turned onto his side, tucked his knees up. Something flickered in the corner of his attic office, and for a moment he thought it was his cat, Samsa, skirting the baseboards. But Samsa had been dead for six months. And for a terrible moment Thom thought he might cry, something he hadn't done in years. Instead, he sat up, rubbed at his ribs again, and wondered how long Wendy would be in the kitchen. He wanted a beer but didn't want her to see him get one.

iii

The weather had cleared by Sunday morning and they all took a walk, Wendy and Thom; their son, Jason; and his new girlfriend, Ashtyn, who had turned out to be the exact opposite of his last girlfriend. Blond instead of dark, inquisitive and talkative instead of standoffish. In fact, she'd barely stopped talking since arriving late on Friday evening. She was talking now—she just couldn't get *over* how beautiful it was on Goose Neck, and she couldn't believe she'd never been here, but she was really more of a South-Shore girl, having grown up in Wareham.

"You'll have to switch your allegiance," Thom said.

"What, South Shore to North Shore? I'm a Cape girl; you're kidding, right?"

Wendy watched as Thom sped up ahead of them so that he was just with Ashtyn. He liked her, she could tell. Well, Wendy liked Ashtyn as well. She wasn't intellectual, exactly, but she seemed to exude some joy, a character trait not usually shared by Jason's string of moody girlfriends. Wendy slowed her pace, Jason beside her, so that she could talk privately to her son.

"So?" Jason said.

"So what?"

"What do you think of Ashtyn? You were just watching her and analyzing. I could tell."

"She's lovely. So different from Tonya."

"You didn't think Tonya was lovely?"

"Lovely to look at, but she wasn't exactly a conversationalist, was she?"

Jason kicked at a horse chestnut, knocking it a few feet ahead of him. She'd taken enough walks with him, ever since he'd been a boy, to know that he would keep kicking that particular chestnut for as long as he could keep it in front of him. "No, she was difficult. Ashtyn's easy, although she's smarter than she looks."

"Did I say she didn't look smart?"

"You probably thought it. She went to school on a full scholarship, you know."

Up ahead, Thom and Ashtyn had stopped walking so that Thom could point out the city hall across the harbor. Wendy and Jason stopped as well. "Yes, she told me. What are her parents like?"

"Nice, I think. Different. Neither of them went to college. She's the first in her family—"

"She has two older brothers, though."

"They're both plumbers, like their father."

"Smart boys."

Wendy took a look at her son's profile as he squinted toward the water. He'd had sort of a hipster mustache that he'd recently removed from his upper lip, and he looked so similar to the way Thom had looked at the same age. Dark-brown eyes, full brows, that beautiful rosebud mouth that was almost girlish. But he wasn't like Thom, Wendy thought. He wasn't a striver, wasn't someone who cared what others thought of him, despite the ill-fated mustache. He seemed mostly happy in his own skin.

"How are you and Dad?" he asked. They were walking again.

"How do *you* think we are?"

"Dad's drinking a lot."

"That's not exactly a new thing, is it?"

"No, I suppose not. Does it worry you?"

Instead of answering right away, Wendy thought about the question. "Ten years ago it did. I thought he'd do something to wreck his career or else he'd wreck the car, end up killing himself, or worse, someone else. But now it's just part of our life, I guess. He drinks more when people are visiting. I don't know what to say. Does it worry you?"

"Yes," Jason said emphatically. "It makes me crazy that he's always telling me we don't spend enough time together, and then when we do get together, he's so drunk he probably doesn't even remember it."

"I hear you, Jason, you're preaching to the choir."

That night, after her son and his girlfriend had left, and after Thom had fallen asleep in front of a hockey game, Wendy sat in the living room with a blanket around her, and her book in her lap, just thinking. What would she be doing right now if Thom's fall on Thursday night had broken his neck and killed him? He'd be dead three days. Jason would have come earlier, and he'd still be here. What else? The neighbors would have made casseroles, and old friends would have called or sent text messages. And she'd be planning a funeral.

It would be a lot, those first few weeks, but once Thom was in the ground, then the next phase of her life could begin. She'd delete that novel he had begun work on, make sure it never saw the light of day. And then she'd be free to do what she wanted, not just for the remainder of her life but for every day of that life. The house would be hers, and the garden, and even the television remote. She could cook more fish. Maybe even one day she could form a new relationship. Not another husband. She would never have one of those again. But maybe a painter who only came to New Essex in the summers, some uncomplicated man who was good in bed and knew how to fix tricky sump pumps and failing gutters.

Wendy realized she was smiling while she thought of this new life, then told herself to think of the alternative. What would the next thirty years be like with Thom in them? Would it be possible to get back to the kind of relationship they'd had for the first half of their married life? The feeling that they were an exclusive club of two, with their own jokes and rules? A bubble that was both exciting and comforting and only for them. In the old days when they'd started to drift apart they always managed to find each other again, remind each other that they had authored their own existence, that they were special. Plus, they'd raised Jason, someone better than either of them. In that, they were in agreement.

But now, ever since Thom started having the bad dreams and the black moods, then the affairs and the drinking, it had all gone wrong. And it wasn't going to get better. Thirty more years with Thom was not going to make either of them happy. And there was no such thing as divorce, not for them. They were together forever all the way to the end of the line, just like in *Double Indemnity*.

She sipped her tea, gone cold. Without moving from her seat she made a decision. Life would be better without Thom in it. Far better.

Another movie quote went through her mind and made her smile again. It was a shame she couldn't share it with Thom, because she thought it was quite clever.

I'm going to need a bigger set of stairs.

iv

Thom was walking across campus when he got the phone call from Wendy. She usually texted so he answered quickly. "What's wrong?"

"Why do you say that?"

"Because you're calling me."

"Oh, nothing's wrong. It's just that I've done something impulsive and now I need you to look at your calendar."

"What have you done?"

"I booked a trip."

"Oh yeah?"

"It's just a long weekend. In D.C. I thought we could take the train."

"To D.C.?"

"Georgetown, really. That's where the Airbnb is. I booked it for the first weekend in May, and then I remembered that you'd mentioned something about Peter coming to visit—"

"Oh, that's not happening," Thom said. Peter was his closest friend from college, and notorious about making plans and then canceling them.

"It isn't?"

"No, sorry, I forgot to tell you. He canceled, the fucker."

"Good. You're free for a trip, then?"

"Probably. Is it this weekend?"

"No, next one. Just three nights. A Thursday through a Sunday."

"D.C., huh?"

"It will feel like actual spring there. And if the weather's not great, there are all the free museums, and the apartment I rented is adorable. I don't know why I'm trying to sell you on this, I've already booked it. You're coming whether you like it or not."

Back in his office, Thom checked his email and saw that Wendy had sent a link to the Airbnb that she'd booked. He clicked on it. It was something called an English basement apartment. It looked cozy, had a fireplace and hardwood floors, and boasted that it was in walking distance of Georgetown Cupcake. Thom brought up a map. It looked like a cool area, and he began to check out nearby pubs. Maybe it would be a nice trip. Things had been a little chilly between

Wendy and him of late, and maybe she was genuinely hoping for a romantic weekend. And it might be a good time to tell her about the book he was working on. He didn't want it to be a secret, his mystery novel, but he knew if he brought it up that she would be upset. He just needed to convince her that it really wasn't autobiographical. *She* might read something into it, but no one else would.

Thom looked at the map some more, using two fingers on his trackpad to check out the area. It was only when he saw the link for the Exorcist Steps just down from their rental that he suddenly understood the real reason why Wendy had booked this trip. Why hadn't he thought of it immediately? Washington, D.C., and especially Georgetown, had been the site of the very beginning of their romance. Two lifetimes ago, really. Thom and Wendy, in their eighth-grade year, had gone on the three-day school trip down to D.C. They'd sat next to each other on the bus ride down, talking mostly about horror movies, and how *The Exorcist* had been filmed in Georgetown. And it was there, in Georgetown, on the last night of the trip, that Thom and Wendy had kissed by the steps that were featured in that film. Thom's first kiss ever, and Wendy's as well, or at least that was what she'd told him. And even though he hadn't thought of that school trip for many years, he remembered it now with startling clarity. It had been spring, as well, the air smelling of flowers and rain. They'd eaten one of their meals at an old-timey Italian restaurant with red-and-white check tablecloths, and he'd dropped a meatball down the front of his shirt. D.C. had been all right, but it really just seemed like one big museum, every element some sort of ode to history. Georgetown had felt alive, though. All these town houses tight together. College students strolling by. For some reason he also remembered the smell of clove cigarettes in the air. To him it was the smell of sophistication.

Suddenly he was excited to return. For some time now, it had been clear that everything he did seemed to disappoint his wife. He drank too much and talked too much and slept too late. Sometimes he caught her looking at him with true disgust in her eyes. The problem was that he believed he deserved it. His whole life he'd been waiting to be punished, always thinking that it would arrive in the form of a catastrophe. Something Old Testament. A debilitating disease. Chronic pain. The deaths of loved ones. Something awful happening to Jason. But Wendy and he had had a successful life. They both had good jobs. They had more than enough money. They had their lovely, kind son. They surely didn't deserve happiness in marriage as well. They didn't deserve love. Despite that, the thought of returning to Georgetown for a weekend, his wife having made the arrangements, filled Thom with something he hadn't felt for a long time. A sense of hope.

At the end of his office hours Emily knocked at his open door.

"Come in, come in," he said, a little bit in a daze. He'd been reading lists of the best restaurants in Georgetown and D.C.

"First of all," Emily said, a file folder hugged to her chest, "thanks for such a nice time last week at your house. Your wife is a very good cook."

"She is," Thom said.

"Did she tell you that we talked about her poetry?"

Thom was confused, but because he was used to not remembering the details of his life, he said, "She did mention it, I think."

"I'm a huge fan."

"Of Wendy's poetry?"

"Yes. She's good, don't you think?"

Thom, still a little confused, said, "Of course. When did you come across her work?"

"A while ago, I think. I don't really remember. She wrote a poem called 'The Coyote Watches Me Watching Him.' It's one of my—"

"Yes, I remember that one. Do you know she made it up? I remember after reading it that I asked her when she had a stare-off with a coyote, and she told me she was just imagining what it would be like if she had. It's funny. For some reason I always imagine that fiction is truly fictional, and that poetry is always somehow the truth, but I don't think I'm right about that."

Emily was quiet for a moment, so Thom quickly said, "Is that for me?"

She remembered the file folder she had brought into his office and pulled it away from her chest, saying, "Oh, it is. I just need your signature on this purchase order. It's the books you requested for the fall semester."

"Right."

She moved around to his side of the desk and put the order in front of him. Her proximity made him feel that odd mix of attraction and solace, as though he might at any moment bury his head against her shoulder. She handed him a pen and pointed to where he needed to sign.

"Who's Annabel Majorino?" he said, seeing the name of the person who'd initiated the order.

"Oh, me. That's my real first name. Annabel. Emily's my middle name and the one I use."

"Annabel," Thom said aloud, and Emily took a step back from him.

"Yes, just hearing you say that name aloud has reinforced my decision," she said, laughing, then coughing.

"What decision?"

"Oh, to change my name. I mean, to use a different name."

Before she left the office, she said, "Thank Wendy again for me for dinner."

"I will," he said, and watched her depart, her toes pointing inward, and spent about thirty seconds trying to remember what that was called, before coming up finally with that odd phrase "pigeon-toed."

That night, after dinner, Thom went out onto the porch with a whiskey. There was still some light in the sky and even though the temperature had dipped, Thom was comfortable in his jeans and cotton sweater. Wendy stepped out to join him, and Thom said, "Summer's coming."

"You call this summer?"

"Well . . ." Thom said. He'd grown up in New England, while Wendy had mostly lived out west, leaving her in a constant dispute with Massachusetts's weather patterns. "Grab a sweater and come join me. Maybe a drink as well."

She said something he didn't quite listen to, then retreated into the house. He assumed she'd told him that she was going to watch television but was surprised when she returned with not only a sweater but half a glass of red wine.

"Oh," he said.

"You sound surprised."

"Usually when I suggest something, you do the opposite."

"Is that really true?"

"I don't know," Thom said. It was his new answer to everything. He was in his fifties and somehow felt like the world had become a bigger mystery to him as he got older.

"Are you excited for our trip?" Wendy said, settling down onto the metal spring chair that Thom was convinced was about to break.

"I am," Thom said. "What made you think of booking it?"

"Remember when Jason was young and we used to always say how much we missed taking spontaneous weekend trips? Well, now he's gone, and we don't even have a cat anymore, so what's stopping us?"

Thom sipped at his whiskey and considered asking Wendy if the trip was to commemorate where their love story had begun. But he couldn't quite bring himself to ask that question. Maybe it was the fear that she'd look at him blankly, having forgotten all about that part of their life. Instead, he said, "You have a fan, you know, of your poetry."

"Do I?"

"You know Emily, the new secretary?"

"Yes, I know her. She had dinner here."

"Oh, yeah, yeah. Of course. Did you know she's read your poetry?"

"She mentioned it that night. She read *Specifics Omitted*."

Thom wondered if they'd already talked about this but didn't want to ask. Instead, he said, "Her real name is Annabel."

"What do you mean?" Wendy said, straightening up a little in her chair.

"Emily is her middle name. She told me today. I was thinking about it because . . . Well, it's a poetic name. Your favorite poem, right?"

"Not quite my favorite poem, but yes."

Thom watched Wendy turn her head to look out through the screened porch toward the cove. There was a tiny scrap of light left in the sky and he could just make out her profile, the slope of her nose, her pursed lips, the jut of her chin. She was deep in thought, and Thom had a familiar feeling—at least it was familiar of late—that he had missed something important. "Are you thinking of getting in touch with Judy while we're there?" he said, to change the subject.

"Who's Judy?"

"Your friend Judy, from work. Didn't she move to D. C.?"

"God, I haven't thought about her in years. No, I hadn't planned on it. I don't even know if she's still there."

"Sorry for asking," Thom said.

"Oh no, did I sound . . . You just took me by surprise."

They were quiet for a moment. Thom's drink was gone and he was starting to get cold. "Well," he said, and put his hands on his knees.

"About Emily, that woman you work with," his wife said.

"Uh-huh."

"You don't have something going on with her, do you?"

"With Emily? No, she's, like, half my age. I mean, not that if she was older . . . You know what I mean."

"You promise me?"

"Promise you what?"

Wendy was looking at Thom, but her face was in shadow, her body rigid. "Promise me you're not lying about this. You haven't done anything stupid, have you?"

"Plenty of stupidity, but nothing stupid with Emily. She's a sweet kid. I haven't even thought of her that way."

"Okay," Wendy said, turning her head to look toward the kitchen. Her shoulders had relaxed.

Thom decided to try a joke, and said, "Want her all to herself, do you?"

"Something like that," Wendy said. "It's not every day I meet a fan."

Later, in bed, Thom thought about the conversation with Wendy, how strongly she'd reacted. She had genuine cause to be concerned. He'd given her reasons throughout the years to not trust him. Maybe there really was some jealousy involved, that Emily/Annabel had shown interest in Wendy and she didn't want him to screw it up. Fair enough, he thought, and began to doze off, but kept thinking about Emily's real name, and about that poem by Poe. How'd that go again? Wendy had it memorized, he knew that much. He'd tried, as well, but it somehow hadn't stuck. All he could remember now was the first two lines, and he whispered them to himself now: "It was many and many a year ago, in a kingdom by the sea."

V

The Airbnb was smaller than it had looked in the pictures, but it was very clean, and the owners had left a gift basket with a bottle of red wine and a small box of chocolate truffles from some local candy shop.

Wendy opened the front-facing window of their apartment to let the air in. They'd gotten onto their Amtrak train that morning at South Station in Boston, each wrapped in scarves and fleece coats, and they'd disembarked at Union Station into an altogether different climate. Balmy air, even a hint of humidity. She was determined to enjoy herself a little, and to see that Thom enjoyed himself as well. She knew that other people would see that as horrific, but she didn't, exactly. If Thom were dying of cancer and had only months to live, then bringing him down here for one last hurrah would be seen as something kind, as life-affirming. And Thom did have a cancer rotting him. A lifetime of guilt and shame had metastasized into something uncontrollable. Before leaving on this trip, Wendy had steeled herself and read the first forty pages of his "mystery" novel. It was worse than she'd thought it would be. It was a confession badly disguised as fiction.

"Open this wine now, or go out and find a place to have a drink?" It was Thom, standing behind her. He'd spent the train ride studying what pubs and restaurants they should eat at during their trip. He hadn't mentioned once, not since she'd first told him about the trip, how Georgetown was a return to the place where it all began. And he hadn't mentioned the Exorcist Steps.

"I need to take a shower after that train ride. Why don't you go find a place for a drink and text me where you are and I'll meet you?"

"Mission accepted," he said, and saluted her.

She made a face, and he added, "Sorry, Jesus. Something about this trip has me on edge."

In her shower she thought about what he'd said, hoping that what was making him nervous was the fact that he hadn't yet had a drink by midafternoon, and not that he'd cottoned on to her reason for taking him on this trip. For some reason she thought about Samsa, their old cat, and how when they'd made the decision to have the vet put him down they'd both been relieved to find out that vets made house visits these days to perform that particular service. As it was, Samsa's last moments had been stretching in a bar of sunlight on the second-floor deck and not shaking uncontrollably at the animal hospital. If Thom turned out to be miserable on this trip, she didn't know if she could go through with it.

By the time she got to the Tombs, the bar he'd picked for an afternoon drink, she'd walked in out of the sunshine, her eyes taking a long time to adjust, and watched Thom come into focus. He was in his element, one elbow on the bar, a pint glass in his hand, talking to a much younger woman, who was looking at him with some interest. Not a lot of interest, but not revulsion either. Thom, naturally, had no idea that Wendy had entered the bar; he was far too focused on the pretty girl and whatever story he was spinning. Wendy stood for a moment and watched. Over the past few years, she'd felt herself becoming invisible to the world around her—it was a cliché, she knew, but one she happened to be living. Thom, on the other hand, had attained some second age of attractiveness, or maybe it was just a fairly interesting style, in his fifties. He'd let his thinning hair grow out just a bit over the ears, brushing it back, and he'd started wearing black-rimmed eyeglasses. Wendy didn't imagine he was in any way sexually appealing to the young woman he was talking to, but he had *something* going on. Maybe he'd mentioned his recently published piece on John Cheever called "Lear in Suburbia," and how it had been nominated for an obscure academic prize, and he was definitely footing the young woman's bill. Wendy made her way slowly to the bar.

"Ah, my wife," Thom said theatrically, and Wendy wondered how many drinks he'd managed to consume already. She hadn't taken that long in the shower.

The woman's name was Alice Something and she was a grad student in Georgetown's Department of English, out celebrating the completion of a final draft of her thesis. She was interesting, actually, and just when Wendy was beginning to wonder if they'd be stuck with her for the evening, two of her friends showed up and whisked her to a table.

"Having fun?" Wendy said.

"I am," he said, "but we don't have to stay. I do realize I found the darkest bar to come to on this beautiful afternoon."

"Yes, how did you find this place?"

"It's famous, and it's named after one of Eliot's cat poems."

"And they have alcoholic milkshakes," Wendy said, reading the menu.

"Let's go walk around the campus," Thom said, "then find a place for dinner."

It wasn't until it was dark and they were slowly meandering their way back to their Airbnb from the Vietnamese restaurant they'd eaten at that Thom mentioned the significance of where they were.

"Is this really the first time we've been back here since . . . ?"

"I think so," Wendy said.

"How old were we?"

"It was eighth grade, so I think we were probably both fourteen."

"God, time is strange." Thom was speaking too loud, a sure sign that he'd had too much drink. At one point during the meal she'd gone to the restroom, noticing that his gin and tonic was half-empty. When she'd returned, it was three-quarters full. Either she was losing her mind or he had quickly sucked down his drink, flagged a waiter to bring him a new one, then had two big swallows of the new drink. All in the time it had taken her to pee, and then reapply her lipstick.

"Meaning what?"

"I don't know. Meaning we were here in this same place, younger versions of ourselves, without any idea of all the things that were going to happen. And it was a different time back then, wasn't it? I mean, we were fourteen and on our own at night, running around. Goddamn freedom."

"We weren't on our own," Wendy said.

"Not on the trip, we weren't, but the night you took me to the steps."

"I don't think so," Wendy said. "That's not how I remember it. We told Miss Ackles that we wanted to look at the Exorcist Steps, and *she* brought us down there."

"No, I don't think so," Thom said.

"She hung back, a little. I mean, I don't think she was standing right next to us when we kissed. But she was nearby. I'm sure of it."

"It's coming back to me. A little. She tried to scare us, tell us how we were being watched."

"That part I don't remember."

"Maybe it was just me."

"It doesn't matter anyway. We both know we were there. At the top of the steps."

"You mean the bottom."

"Now you're just being contrary on purpose," Wendy said.

"I am. But we did go to the bottom of the steps. We started up top, and you and I ran all the way down and then back up. I remember being out of breath."

"I don't remember that part at all. Maybe you ran down the steps and I stayed at the top."

"Sensible even at fourteen."

"I was."

"Oh, here they are."

They both stopped at the top of the narrow stairs that ran down between a painted brick building and a stone wall. Streetlights illuminated the steep steps so that it almost looked like a tunnel carved out of the dark night. Wendy had read or heard somewhere that these days the steps were mostly used as a makeshift gym, runners sprinting up and down them for some inexplicable reason. But it was late, and the night had turned cold, and no one was around except for the two of them. Thom stepped forward, standing on the top step, his hand on the metal handrail.

"Where exactly were we standing when we kissed? This isn't quite how I pictured it," Thom said.

"Right here, right at the top, where you're standing now."

"Who kissed whom?"

"I think it was kind of a mutual kiss, because if I recall it started off more like a headbutt."

"Yes, that I do remember."

Thom turned around, his back to the steps. The wind was kicking up but Wendy thought that Thom was swaying more from the effects of the gin. It's a perfect murder, she thought, not for the first time. Even if she were suspected, there was no way to prove that he hadn't fallen down the stairs on his own. He'd been publicly drinking all night. In fact, he'd probably told some friends and colleagues that he'd fallen down the stairs in his own house. And it was a perfect murder because his last moments, besides the moment that would involve careening down a hundred concrete steps, would have been a great meal in a beautiful city on a cool, spring night. She took a step toward her husband.

vi

Thom felt unwell. Maybe it was the somewhat fiery food they'd eaten for dinner, or maybe it was the brandy he'd ordered for dessert that he definitely didn't need. But standing at the top of the steps from that movie that Wendy loved so much, he was a little queasy. Sad as well.

It had started with the girl he'd met at the Tombs earlier. He'd been drinking his first beer of the day with half an eye on the baseball highlights on the television above the bar when she'd stood two stools over from him and ordered a glass of Champagne.

"Celebrating?" Thom had said automatically.

She'd turned and faced him, less pretty, he thought, than she'd looked in profile. "I finished a first draft of my thesis paper this afternoon."

"Oh, congrats," he said. "What's your discipline?"

"I'm getting an MA in English lit."

"Here at Georgetown?"

"Yes."

He was about to tell her that he was an English professor himself, maybe even mention his recent publication, but he could hear Wendy in his ear telling him that he didn't need to try to impress the entire female species *all* the time. Instead, he said, "What was the subject?"

"Punishment in Victorian literature. I mean, a little more specific than that, but that was the general gist."

"Oh," Thom said, pursing his lips and nodding.

"You're either baffled or you're confused."

"No, I'm neither. I'm interested. I'm an English professor myself—not here at Georgetown—and I've long been interested in punishment. In fact, I'm writing a book right now, sort of a mystery novel, and I'd say that punishment is its central theme."

The young woman's Champagne had arrived, poured into a wineglass instead of a proper tulip, and Thom watched her flick her eyes toward the front door of the bar.

"Sorry. Ignore me," Thom said. "The last thing you probably want to talk about is the fucking paper you just finished writing. And you must be . . . waiting for someone?"

"I'm expecting friends. And yes, no more talk of punishment."

"You've been punished by it," Thom said, and he felt the imagined presence of Wendy at his shoulder groaning at his bad joke.

"It feels like it," the woman said, and then slid onto the stool, a commitment that Thom guessed was an even toss-up between her being slightly intrigued by him and her deciding that this old man with the dad jokes was not an actual threat of any kind.

"I'm Alice," she said.

Thom introduced himself as well, then said, "And that Champagne is on me, by the way. I insist."

She looked less than pleased, so Thom awkwardly mentioned that he was waiting for his wife, due any moment.

"Tell me about your novel," Alice said, taking a tentative sip from her glass.

"Well, it's actually about *not* being punished, my novel. The main character commits a crime and then he spends his whole life waiting to pay for it, but it never happens."

"Oh, that's interesting. How does it end?"

"I don't know yet," Thom said. "Honestly, I've only written the first few chapters."

Then Alice had parted her lips to ask some follow-up question, but Wendy was already there, smelling of lavender, probably from the strange soap at the rental. Thom made the introductions, surprising himself by remembering his new friend's name. A brief memory flashed in his mind from years ago, the time he'd introduced his wife to a visiting writer he was enamored with, and for a terrifying five seconds he'd actually forgotten Wendy's name. He'd just stood there, mouth open, both women watching him in alarm. Had he actually forgotten his own wife's name? Then it leapt into his head, and everyone pretended it hadn't happened. He'd been reliving that humiliating moment on and off for ten years, but lately the memory of it filled him with a cold desolation, as though it were a premonition.

After the student was reunited with friends her own age to celebrate with, Thom and Wendy decided on one more drink while consulting phone maps for nearby restaurants. They agreed on Vietnamese, with the proviso that the following evening they would go to the chophouse that Thom had picked, an old politicians' restaurant famous for its lamb.

Decision made, they finished their drinks. The coldness that Thom had felt with the arrival of his wife was ballooning into something more alarming. It was a feeling he'd had on occasion during the last year or so, the feeling that he had disappointed Wendy so many times in the course of their marriage that all the love was well and truly gone. That even when she laughed at one of his jokes, or listened to one of his stories, she was doing it with absolutely no love at all. Thom went to the restroom and told himself that Wendy was the one who'd planned the trip, after all, that some part of her wanted him there with her. He told himself to breathe while looking into the slightly warped mirror above the bathroom sink, then went back out to the bar. Wendy's coat was on.

After they'd finished eating, Thom found himself saying, "I've decided to quit writing the book I started."

"Was that the mystery novel?"

"Yes, did I . . . ?"

"You mentioned it to Marcia, I think, when she was over for dinner."

"Oh, right."

"But you're quitting it?"

"I think so. Maybe I was only writing it in the first place just to see if I could write a novel."

"You've written a few half-novels in your time," Wendy said.

"Yes, exactly my point. *Come End of Summer* will enter the pantheon of Thom Graves's half-finished novels."

"*Come End of Summer* is the title?"

"Oh, I didn't tell you that? The working title anyway."

Wendy's lower lip slid a little ways forward, as it often did when she was forming an opinion. But nothing came. The subject changed to their plans for the following day.

When they were walking back to their rental apartment, Wendy mentioned the Exorcist Steps, the first time she'd referenced the fact that once upon a time they'd been children in this part of the world, and that this was where their story began. "Let's go look at them before heading back."

Thom almost made a joke that they could re-create their kiss, but instead found himself talking about time, and how strange it was, and all the while he was speaking, he was telling himself to shut up, that the last thing Wendy wanted to hear was some cheap philosophy about growing old. She'd told him numerous times that he talked too much about it. Still, he kept talking, and that palpable dread he'd felt earlier in the afternoon had returned, the feeling that Wendy was no longer by his side. Well, by his side physically, but not by his side in any metaphorical way at all. He was all alone in an empty universe.

They reached the steps, not quite how he remembered them. When they'd first been there, more than forty years ago, the steps were imbued with a mythic quality, probably because he'd only ever heard about *The Exorcist*, first from his older sister, Janice, who had watched it at her friend Karen's sleepover party. The following night Janice had sat on his bed, a ghoulish smile on her face, and told him every gross moment from the film, including a scene with a crucifix that Thom didn't really believe could actually have been in the movie. Or any movie. His sister was prone to exaggeration, both then and now.

Still, the unseen film grew in Thom's mind, haunting him. He was both desperate to find a way to see it and terrified at that very prospect. He actually had dreams about it, the first of a lifetime of dreams in which films and reality blended together.

When he'd boarded the bus that was bringing the eighth graders down to D.C., the only free seat had been next to Wendy Eastman. He didn't really know Wendy; no one did, since she'd only arrived at the beginning of that year, having moved from somewhere out west.

He couldn't believe he'd wound up next to her on the bus, especially since the ride to D.C. was about eight hours total. He'd have been happy with just about any member of his class except for Wendy. In the end, though, it had gone okay. They'd made decent small talk, with Wendy listing all the places she'd lived in her life, and then, as they'd neared D.C., she mentioned that she hoped to go see the Exorcist Steps while they were there. That it was a location from her favorite movie.

Thom, who hadn't even known that *The Exorcist* took place in D.C., told her all about what his sister had relayed to him from the sleepover, and how he'd become obsessed with a film he hadn't seen. So Wendy told him the entire plot, not just the icky parts, and by the time they'd finally arrived at their hotel they were both determined to find the long, narrow steps down which the priest had fallen to his death.

Thom remembered that on the final night of the three-day trip their teachers had taken them to eat in Georgetown and then Wendy and he had snuck off to find the steps. Bringing it up to Wendy now, she had a very different memory—that they hadn't snuck off at all but that Miss Ackles was with them. And when she'd said it a memory came back to him, vague and unformed, Miss Ackles telling him how they were always being watched. She'd done it in a spooky voice, like something from a *Scooby-Doo* cartoon. Still, they both agreed that they'd kissed. And now he was standing at those steps again. They were unchanged, he thought, while he and Wendy had completely changed. They'd grown old—older, maybe, was the better description—and they were no longer children. He'd been looking down the steps, steep and narrow and impersonal, then turned to look at his wife.

She stepped toward him, her eyes not quite meeting his. "Strange, isn't it?" he said.

After she placed a hand flat across his chest, a memory tried to surface. It was from a few weeks ago, that drunken party at their house, when he'd fallen down the stairs. The memory was Wendy's face, and now that her face was close to his again, he was filled with a deep, unnerving sense of déjà vu. *Here it comes,* he said to himself, *the end of the story.*

He opened his mouth to say something to Wendy, immediately forgetting what it was he needed to say. But still he spoke. Thom said, "Go ahead, I'm ready," not knowing if he was making a joke or not.

She smiled in the moonlight.

vii

Thom fell almost slowly at first. For one moment Wendy thought he might come to rest just a few steps down, but then gravity went to work, his legs going over his head as if he were a child doing a slow-motion somersault, picking up speed, bouncing down the remaining steps until he came to a stop at the bottom, just a dark, shadowy mass in the lamplight.

She let out a long, hissing breath. Her legs felt watery and she took hold of the railing and lowered herself so that she was sitting on the top step. It felt strange that nothing momentous had occurred to mark her husband's fall. No one had screamed. No sirens had sounded. No dogs had barked in the distance. It was quiet.

She unclasped her purse and took out her phone, dialing 911.

After being asked for her emergency, she broke into the breathless words that she'd already planned.

"My husband, I think he was drunk, he just fell down the steps."

"What steps?" came a voice that was so regulated that for a brief moment Wendy wondered if she was talking to a real person.

"I don't know what they're really called, but they're the Exorcist Steps. From the movie."

"Are you in Georgetown?"

"Yes."

"Okay. I'm sending people your way right now. Are you near your husband's body?"

"No, he's . . . down at the bottom, and I'm up . . ."

"That's okay. Can you be very careful and walk down to the bottom of the steps toward your husband?"

"Okay," Wendy said, and ended the call. She knew she wasn't supposed to, but she needed a moment to think. For one terrible moment she thought she was being watched, and turned around to look back at the dark buildings. There was no one there, just her alone. The 911 operator had told her to go down the steps, and that was what she did, climbing down them now, one hand still holding her phone, and one on the handrail. It was still quiet and her shoes made clacking sounds on the concrete.

When she got to the bottom and saw the way that Thom was lying, she knew he was dead. It would have been surprising if he wasn't. He'd fallen so violently.

She sat down again, on the second step from the bottom, about a yard away from Thom's body. He was cast in a sickly yellow light from a streetlamp. One arm was up and over his head as though he were attempting to answer a question in class. There was less blood than she thought there would be, but his head was at an unnatural angle. She thought there might be some blood on his neck, but then she realized she was looking at a sharp bump under his skin that was causing a shadow to fall where there shouldn't be one. Something had snapped in his neck.

She turned and looked down the street instead. Someone was on a bike, pedaling past on the other side of the nearest road, but Wendy kept quiet. She had already heard the sirens in the distance.

Sitting still on the step, Wendy worked on her breathing, not knowing if she was scared or if the walk down the steps had taken it out of her. She repeated some of the lines she'd been telling herself the past several days. This is what's best for her. And this is what's best for Thom. But it still felt momentous, like she'd cracked her world in two. There was the world she had five minutes before, Thom still alive, and now there was this world, and who knew what that was going to bring.

The sirens were closer now. She took another look at her husband, all of his angles wrong. Darling, darling, she thought, and almost looked away. But she kept her eyes on him, forming a memory she would one day push to the very back of her mind. It would go into a room with other memories. Not gone forever, of course. But the room had a door and she knew how to shut it.

Blue lights flooded the scene and she turned away from her husband to the arriving ambulance.

2018

i

"It's the only thing we have in common," Thom said, a joke he'd made . . . how many times?

"We can't be the only ones, of course," Wendy said. "But I've, we've, never met anyone else with the same—"

"With the same nightmare," Thom said.

"Why do you call it a nightmare?" This was from Louise Holly. She and her husband, Mike, were over for dinner. It was the first time just the four of them had socialized together. Mike and Louise were a recently retired couple who had moved to Goose Neck a year and a half earlier. It was such a small community that Thom and Wendy had seen them often enough, but had never felt the need to have dinner with just them until Thom had discovered that he and Louise shared a love for jazz trumpet. So, Mike and Louise were over for lasagna and to listen to Thom's vinyl collection of Miles Davis and Chet Baker records. And now Thom was opening another bottle of wine even though Mike and Louise were drinking decaf coffee, and they were all talking about the upcoming shared fiftieth birthday party that Thom and Wendy were throwing.

"It's a nightmare because your birthday is supposed to be a day just for yourself, and I have to share it with my wife. And she doesn't even care about her birthday."

"When I heard you two were doing a shared fiftieth," Mike said, "I naturally assumed you were combining them because they were close together, not that you had the exact same birthday."

"It *is* strange," Wendy said.

Mike asked, "When did you realize?" at the same time as Louise said, "Who was born first?"

These were all questions they'd been asked before, of course, multiple times. Whenever anyone learned they were born on the same day it became the most interesting thing about them.

"I was born close to noon and Thom was born . . ." She turned her head and looked at him, even though she knew.

"At seventeen minutes past eleven at night. I'm almost a half day younger."

"God, that's amazing," Louise said, sitting up in her chair as though she'd been watching a dull movie and something exciting had just happened. "I don't suppose either of you are interested in astrology, are you?"

"That's my cue to clean up," Wendy said, rising.

"Wendy is an astrology atheist, and I'm agnostic. You a believer, Louise?"

"Not really, but I read my horoscope daily."

Still standing, Wendy said, "Thom and I are living proof that it's all bullshit. We're astrology twins and totally different."

"You can't be completely different," Mike said. "You share enough in common that you've stayed married for . . ."

"We're not completely different, of course," Thom said, "but like I was saying, I quite like my birthday. It feels like a day that you are allowed to do whatever you want. You know, without guilt. It's all about you. If you want that third martini, then who's going to say anything about it?"

Wendy, having sat back down again, watched Thom talk about birthdays. It was funny how he always said the same things in the same way. She was reminded of her mother, who had finally died the previous year after suffering from five years of escalating dementia. Toward the end she could only ever really talk about things from the past, either her childhood or her own children's childhoods, and when she talked about these memories, she'd recount them using the exact same phrases with the exact same intonations. Wendy's brother, Alan, always sentimental, found these conversations comforting, as though proof that humans are made up of memories, while Wendy was secretly alarmed, her mother's deterioration convincing her that humans were nothing more than robotic machines, devoid of free will. She'd found it hard to spend time with her mother over the last two years, so it was a good thing that Alan lived so close. Wendy had done her part by paying for the twenty-four-hour care that Rose needed in order to stay at home and with her dogs.

"The other thing is," Thom continued, "Wendy is absolutely overjoyed, because it means one less party per year, aren't you, Wen?"

"I do like parties, actually. I'm just not fond of parties that come with a reason."

"Don't all parties have reasons?" Mike said. He was either older than his wife, Louise, or else just aging faster. He was slumped on the sofa in a way that looked like he might need help getting off of it, and he had crumbs in his lap from the plate of cookies that they'd brought from the dining table to the living room.

"Well, the usual reason is to eat and drink and socialize. The parties I dislike are birthdays and anniversaries and going-away parties. That kind of thing."

"What about Valentine's Day?" Louise said.

"Well," Thom said, pouring more wine for himself, "since our birthdays are February thirteenth, Valentine's Day just gets thrown into the mix, and as one of the only men who actually likes that holiday, I lose again."

"Now I *am* going to start cleaning up," Wendy said.

After the Hollys had left, Thom came into the kitchen to offer help just as Wendy had almost finished loading the dishwasher. "You have fun?" he said.

"They're nice," she said.

"But dull."

"A bit dull."

In bed Wendy was starting the new Jane Austen biography she'd been gifted at Christmas when Thom, undressing, said, "You do know that it's not the only thing we have in common?"

"What is?"

"Our birthdays."

"I know. We have lots in common."

"Do we?" Thom sounded genuinely surprised. Wendy laughed.

"Our lovely son," she said.

"Having a child together doesn't mean that we have something in common."

"If you want to be pedantic about it, I suppose not. But I was thinking that we both love him. That's something we have in common."

Thom, wearing only a T-shirt and socks, was thinking. Wendy was about to return to her book when he said, "We love him differently, though."

"Do we? How so?"

"I think that you love him in a healthy way. You want him to do well in life and succeed and fly the coop and all that."

"You don't want that?"

"No, I do, in theory, but I think . . . down deep, that I love him sometimes so much that I want him to break his back or something and then he'd live forever with us. He'd never leave."

Wendy started to laugh, but Thom, now naked, actually had a serious look in his eyes. "I just want him safe here, with us."

"With a broken back?"

"Well, no. I was being extreme. But my love feels almost psychotic sometimes. Like a combination of fear and madness. And, no, I don't want him to get hurt, but I think I grieve sometimes that we no longer take care of him the way we did when he was younger. I miss his helplessness."

"We have Samsa," Wendy said.

"Samsa's not helpless exactly," and their cat, sleeping on the extreme corner of their king-sized bed, twitched an ear at the sound of his name.

"No, but he needs to be fed and he likes to be picked up."

Getting into bed on his side, his reading glasses in one hand and his own book—a paperback copy of *A Little Life*—in the other, Thom said, "When I was little, I did have this fantasy that I would find a bird with a broken wing and that I would take care of it and it would become attached to me. It didn't need to be a bird, I guess, it could be a sick squirrel. Any small animal."

"You didn't go out and break a bird's wing to make it come true, did you?"

"My father made that joke at the time and I remember considering it, like maybe it wasn't such a bad idea after all. I think I'm too drunk to read."

Thom turned to his side, bringing the duvet with him, in order to put his book and reading glasses on the bedside table, then curled up, facing away from Wendy.

"I'll read a little more," she said, returning to the sentence she'd marked with a finger. But she'd read less than thirty seconds when Thom said, his voice muffled by the pillow, "You called us twins to the Hollys."

"Did I?"

"I think so."

"No, I just said we were astrological twins."

"I guess you're right. Still . . ."

Wendy, angered slightly, didn't immediately respond, knowing that another thirty seconds of silence would ensure that her husband would be asleep. A short, guttural snore indicated that he was. She tried to return to her book but kept thinking about his twin comment. Yes, that was one of their rules, one of their secrets. For almost as many years as they'd known each other, they'd been referring to each other as twins. It had started as a joke, not just because of their shared birthday but the fact that they looked a little bit alike. They each had large dark-brown eyes and high hairlines and compact mouths that seemed a little too close to their noses. Their skin was the same hue as well, pale as skim milk in wintertime, although Thom could actually get a tan in summertime, while Wendy burned. "We're twins, you know, not actual twins, but cosmic ones." That had been Thom, years ago. She'd probably grimaced and told him that she'd rather not think of him as a sibling. But it had stuck, this idea that they were connected in ways far more significant than marriage or parenthood or even love. This twindom, or twinhood, whatever you wanted to call it, became one of their secrets. It was never to be spoken out loud to anyone else, in the same way that so many things were never to be spoken out loud to anyone else. They didn't talk about Wendy's first marriage, or the fact that they re-met at that conference in Ohio in 1991, or anything else that happened that following year. They didn't talk about guilt or regrets. The past was the past.

It was Thom, though, who most often broke these rules, especially lately, so Wendy seethed a little that he'd dared to call her out on referring to them as astrological twins. She composed a speech in her mind, telling him all the times in the past couple of years when he'd drunk too much and made jokes about his and Wendy's dark history, or given speeches about how the guilty were never truly punished. Then she threw the speech away. In the morning this would all be forgotten, and they had a party to plan, and according to the latest weather reports, a storm moving in. There would be things to do. Wendy closed her own book and turned off her reading lamp.

ii

"What do you think?" Jason said. Five minutes earlier he'd handed his father a printed list of possible songs for that night's birthday bash. Thom was at the kitchen island, slowly working his way through a dry ham sandwich, and even though he'd been staring at the list his son had produced, his mind had been elsewhere.

"Etta James?" Thom said, picking the first track his eyes landed on. "How old do you think your mother and I are?"

"Mom said it was one of her favorites."

"I can't even remember how it goes."

Jason sang "At Last" in his shaky baritone. He'd been late to puberty, and Thom sometimes found himself shocked by his son's altered voice, even though he was now seventeen, waiting to hear from colleges he'd applied to, and with a serious girlfriend to boot, one he was almost certainly having sex with.

"Oh, right. Scratch that one out. Your mom will never notice. Besides, this is a dance party."

"Scratch Etta James," Jason said, swinging the list toward him and producing a pen. When Wendy and Thom had agreed to let him DJ the event, neither had been really prepared for how seriously he would take the task. He'd strategically divided the playlist between songs that would set the proper mood, songs that would get the fifty-year-olds onto the dance floor, and songs that "were so banging they could simply not be ignored."

"No wedding songs," Thom said.

"Define a wedding song."

"I'll know it when I hear it. No chicken dance, no Meat Loaf."

"Dad, have you met me?"

Thom went over the list, made a few suggestions (more Prince), then finished his ham sandwich, resisting the urge to wash it down with a beer. It was going to be a long day and an even longer night. They'd rented the VFW hall downtown and hired a catering company plus a bartender who could stick around until one a.m. After that they'd be on their own. It was strange to be throwing a party not happening at their own house. Normally, on the day of a party he'd be frantically preparing for the onslaught. But they were full-on adults now, he supposed, and had their parties catered.

After lunch he put on his winter boots, plus a light jacket, and went outside to work on the driveway. There had been a major storm a week earlier that dumped nearly two feet of snow across the region, but the last two days had been unseasonably warm, turning that snow into a heavy, waterlogged slush from which streamed rivulets that froze into black ice overnight. The day was insufferably bright and Thom squinted while pushing waves of icy muck into the road that fronted his house. One of his neighbors, Larry, swung by to ask him if he needed to bring anything to the VFW hall that night, code for wanting to know if he needed to bring a flask of whiskey, as he usually did to beer and wine parties. "It's a full bar, Larry, courtesy of us."

"That's what I heard. Mighty generous."

"Janine coming as well?"

"Ah, probably not, I'm sorry to say. Another round yesterday and she's not feeling her best."

"Sorry to hear that, Larry."

The other neighbor he spoke with was Ellen Larson, out pushing her newborn. She wished Thom a happy birthday and since he couldn't remember whether they'd invited her and her husband to the party, Thom didn't ask if he'd see her later. Instead, he gushed at the baby girl, her name temporarily forgotten, and avoided looking directly at Ellen, who was so pretty that Thom sometimes believed she caused him actual physical pain.

After an hour of on-and-off shoveling, there was no visual evidence that the driveway had changed in appearance or reality, so Thom quit, plunging his shovel into a pile of grimy snow that had been created by the plow, then walking around to the back of the house to lean against one of the large boulders that marked the edge of their tiny backyard. He thought of going inside, getting both his sunglasses and maybe a light beer, and returning to his sunny perch, but told himself that the night ahead required some sort of drinking plan. Maybe one beer while getting dressed, then a strong drink upon arrival at the hall—a Manhattan, maybe—then back to beer for the remainder of the evening, making sure to alternate beers with full glasses of water or seltzer. The most important thing was not to switch over to whiskey later in the evening, or to not switch over to whiskey until he was safely back at home, fireside with Wendy.

He wasn't worried about bad behavior so much as he was worried about having a blackout, a period of time with no recall. He'd had a number of these in the last few years and they'd filled him with such a sense of fear, almost as though they represented brief glimpses of his death to come. He mentioned it only once to his wife, and she told him that she already knew he was having blackouts (of course she did), and that her fear was that in one of them he'd tell one of the young women he was infatuated with all about what they'd done years earlier.

"That will never happen," he said. "I promise."

But leaning against the boulder now Thom wondered, not for the first time, if he could somehow fictionalize what he and Wendy had achieved twenty-five years ago. Wendy wouldn't like it, but it *was* half his story to tell. And now, on the day he turned fifty, he realized that maybe it was the only thing that made him special, this story of transgression, and his firsthand knowledge of it. It would make a great novel, a kind of American *Crime and Punishment*. No, that wasn't right. More like a modern take on Dreiser's *An American Tragedy*. He'd read that in high school, and it had stayed with him throughout the years. But his story would be different. It would be about punishment, what happens when someone waits their whole life for it and it never comes. A tingling feeling crept over his skin that maybe this novel was a good idea. An opening line even occurred to him. Was this the book that he was meant to finally write? Of course, Wendy would be furious. Maybe not furious, but she'd be worried that he would be putting them in danger somehow. But that was ridiculous. Crime novels with outlandish murders were published all the time. No one went around assuming that the authors of these novels were basing them on actual events.

A sudden, jarring flutter went through his chest, not for the first time, but this one was accompanied by a tightening of his throat that made him think he might suddenly be sick. He placed a hand against the cool surface of the rock and thought to himself, Jesus, I'm dying on my birthday, dying before I get a chance to finally write the great American novel. He breathed deeply through his nostrils, telling himself to calm down. The fluttering stopped, but his throat was still tight. He swallowed several times, remembering that his phone was inside. Should he call 911? Should he tell Jason, no doubt back in his room perfecting the set list? Wendy was out to a birthday lunch with two of her friends. Regardless, he needed to make his way back to the house, unless he really was dying, in which case maybe this rock was an excellent spot. He flexed his jaw several times, then walked on stiff legs up onto the deck and through the sliding-glass doors into the kitchen. All of his symptoms had disappeared, and he felt fine, except for a slightly racing heart and a fuzzy mind. He poured himself a glass of water from the tap and consumed it in one long swallow. From upstairs he heard the sound of music, a bass line he recognized as belonging to a song by the Talking Heads. It was a song whose title he could never remember, a song about being already at home. Not great for dancing, Thom thought, refilling his water glass.

iii

The party was in full swing, and Wendy had begun to have fun. There had only been one toast, delivered by Larry Bathurst, while everyone was sitting down to eat the prime rib and baked potatoes that Thom had insisted on serving ("we're old folk now and need to eat like it"). Larry, despite his circumstances, had delivered a toast that was funny rather than sentimental, and for that, Wendy was grateful.

And now the buffet was closed, the tables cleared, the dance party happening. The song was "Tempted" by Squeeze. Despite their turning fifty, most of Wendy and Thom's friends on Goose Neck were ten years older at least, and the spectacle of them cutting moves on the VFW dance floor was mostly horrifying. She sipped her white wine and watched from a distance. Why was it that perfectly good dancers started to look ridiculous once they hit a certain age? Her oldest friend, Daniela, had come up from New York for this party. The two of them had spent their college years in Houston, hitting clubs, staying up till dawn. Daniela had been a tireless and sexy dancer. And she wasn't a bad dancer now, but she just looked like . . . like a mom, Wendy supposed, since she was one, three times over. But still, it was a depressing sight. Thom, on the other hand, had always been a spectacle on the dance floor, all quick pivots and flailing elbows. He was dancing now with Laura Ferreira, Jason's girlfriend, who seemed only mildly embarrassed by his gyrations. Laura was two years younger than Jason, not a big difference except for maybe in high school, especially with Jason leaving for college soon. Laura was quiet, studious, arty, and rather beautiful, and Wendy hoped that when Jason broke her heart he would be kind about it. She thought he would be.

The song ended and something new began that Wendy didn't immediately recognize, some recent bass-heavy hit. No one left the dance floor.

She finished her wine and was trying to figure out what to do next when Walter Johnson approached, bringing her a fresh glass.

"Saw you were getting low," he said.

Walter was a watercolor artist who had moved to Goose Neck two years earlier. Wendy knew him because he volunteered to work events at the Saltwick Institute, the nonprofit writers' residency where Wendy worked as the director of retreat and operations. Thom had become convinced that Walter only volunteered in order to spend time with Wendy. She scoffed whenever he'd say this, but secretly believed he was probably right. He was not a particularly attractive man, with thinning hair and deep-set eyes and that body shape particular to certain men, all their weight in their stomach, so that their pants were always drooping a little off their hipless frames. But he was the only man who ever made a point of seeking her out at parties and art openings, and he always asked her questions about herself. Wendy had no interest in him—why would she want another fragile, middle-aged man in her life?—but she appreciated his interest.

While she gossiped with Walter, Thom danced over and said they should join him on the dance floor. His forehead was sweaty, and he was breathing heavily.

"Maybe you should take a break, darling," Wendy said.

"'Fifty-year-old man dies on dance floor. Story at eleven.'"

"What song do you think you'd like to die dancing to?" Walter said.

"That's a good question. Let me think for a moment."

Wendy watched Thom as he pondered. He loved this type of thing, making lists of favorite songs, movies, books. Talking about the best sandwich he'd ever had.

"It would have to be New Order, I think."

"Which song?"

"'Blue Monday'?"

Walter was nodding, reverently. Wendy's annoyance grew.

"Ha, right. I'd be dancing like a maniac, then the heart would stop and I'd hit the floor. It wouldn't be so bad, fading out to Bernard Sumner's voice."

"'How does it feel?'" Walter quoted the song.

"Oh my God, perfect death lyric. How 'bout you, Walter? What's your collapse-on-the-dance-floor song?"

Wendy was just about to down her glass of wine in order to give herself an excuse to walk away, but Walter turned to her and said, "Let's hear Wendy's first."

"'Into the Groove,'" Thom quickly said.

Wendy frowned. "No Madonna. I mean, I love her, but not while I'm dying. I'd say 'Sinnerman' by Nina Simone."

"Oh, good one," Walter said, then while he was trying to figure out which song he'd like to go out on, Wendy did chug her wine and slide away.

At the bar she realized she was getting tipsy, but instead of that making her decide to order a water she asked for a vodka and soda with a splash of cranberry. Kerry, Marcia and Jim Lever's youngest daughter, whom they'd hired to bartend, made the drink while Wendy turned to look at the party from this new vantage point. She knew everyone here, this strange hodgepodge of a lifetime's worth of friends. Daniela was her oldest friend. Who was her most recent? Probably Mike and Louise, that boring couple. Not that Thom and she weren't their own version of a boring couple. Maybe Mike and Louise had dark secrets of their own.

"Here you go, Mrs. Graves," Kerry was saying, placing the tall drink on the shellacked surface of the bar.

"Call me Wendy, please," she said.

As she took her first sip Daniela rushed over from the dance floor. "What are you drinking?"

"I asked for a vodka and soda, but this tastes like a vodka and vodka."

"Yay. I'm joining you," Daniela said. "And I need you drunk enough to start dancing."

Two hours later, Wendy *was* drunk, now sitting snugly on a vinyl couch between Daniela and Caroline, her boss at Saltwick. Caroline and Daniela were talking at the same time, which gave her the opportunity to ignore them both and concentrate on how delicious her current cocktail was. It was a concoction delivered to her by Walter, of course, some kind of mule with rye whiskey. She heard Jason say into his microphone that per the bureaucratic regime of the VFW, he was forced to play the last song of the night. "This one's for you, Mom," he said, and the rat-a-tat drums of "Sinnerman" began. Wendy laughed, whiskey dribbling down her chin.

"What's funny?" Daniela said.

"Oh, earlier I said I'd like to die while dancing to this song, so it's a little eerie that it's being played."

"Let's get up and dance, then."

She and Daniela began to dance, and Wendy felt twenty again, the room spinning but in a good way, Daniela twenty again too, at least looking like she was. Walter shimmied over, dancing with his elbows locked in close to his sides, and whispered into her ear, "Please stay alive."

"I know, right?" Wendy said, laughing hard enough that she stopped dancing for a moment. Then she was moving again, wondering where Thom was, surprised he wasn't back on the dance floor. Then she spotted him leaning up against the bar talking with Ellen Larson. Thom was gesticulating with his hands, Ellen leaning a little back, but she had a relaxed half smile on her face. Just flirting, Wendy told herself, but she kept an eye on them for the next ten minutes. Who even invited Ellen? And hadn't she had a baby recently? What was she doing out in the middle of the night?

Daniela grabbed her hands and they swung around, the song tailing toward its conclusion, Nina Simone singing "power" again and again. When it finally ended and Daniela and she stood there, breathing hard, sweating, both laughing, Wendy swung her head around to see who was still at the party. Someone turned on the overhead fluorescent lights and the room was bathed in a harsh glow, illuminating the ragged tackiness of the VFW hall and the motley assortment of the party's remaining guests. Thom was coming toward her, a glass of something in his hand. Ellen was gone all of a sudden.

"Here, drink this," Thom said.

"Are you crazy?"

"It's water."

"Oh." Wendy drank, the water tasting better than anything she'd consumed that night, even though she was a little annoyed that Thom was trying to take care of her.

They were driven home by Jason and Laura in Jason's Kia. They sat together in the backseat like two kids while Jason continued to play music from his phone that was somehow coming out of his car speakers. Jason dropped them off then pulled out of the gravel driveway to take Laura to her home on the other side of town.

When they got into the house Thom asked Wendy if she'd like a nightcap in the living room.

"God, no. I need to get into bed."

She went upstairs, surprised that Thom followed her, talking about the highs and lows of the party.

"Aren't you drunk?" Wendy said.

Thom laughed. "Strangely, no. I told myself to alternate every alcoholic beverage with a glass of water and then I actually stuck to my own plan, and now I'm completely sober."

"That makes one of us."

"Good, I'm glad you had fun."

"I'm not sure I did." Wendy had stripped off all her clothes and crawled under the covers.

"You looked like you were having fun."

"I had fun with Daniela. I had fun dancing. What was going on with you and that mousy girl from down the street?"

"Who, Ellen?"

"Yeah, Ellen. Didn't she just have a baby?"

"She only came to the party for an hour. Didn't she say happy birthday to you?"

"If she did, I don't remember. She clearly came to see you."

Thom pulled on the flannel pajama bottoms he liked to sleep in and got into his side of the bed, propping himself up on his pillows. "Are you jealous of a twenty-five-year-old new mom?"

"Jesus, Thom. Of course not. I'm just scared you're going to get drunk and decide that whatever teenager you're obsessed with should hear all about how you married a monster."

"I don't think you're a monster. You know that."

"Maybe you *should* think of me as a monster."

"Why is that?"

"You're not the only murderer in this family, you know. You're just the only one who can't move past it." Despite how tired she was, her spoken words felt cathartic, like the beginning of something.

"Sure, sure," Thom said. "We were in it together."

"That's not what I meant," she said. "It's . . . never mind. It's late. I'm drunk. Jason will be back soon."

She was quiet for a moment. Thom reached over and touched her shoulder. "Disregard everything, okay?" she said as she turned to her side.

Thom leaned over and kissed the side of her neck. He'd forgotten to brush his teeth. As he slid back to his side of the bed, he said, "Fifty years, darling. Fifty years we've been twins in this world."

She fluttered a hand toward him, not sure if he noticed. The room spun a little when she closed her eyes so she opened them again. The spins made her feel like she was in her tiny dorm room at Rice. Had it been that long since she'd had this much to drink? She was worried she might be sick but decided to try closing her eyes again. This time they stayed closed.

iv

Wendy was snoring gently and Thom was thinking about getting up, pulling on a sweater and a pair of socks, and drinking a whiskey by the fireplace. But that just seemed like an inordinate amount of work. Instead he stared at the ceiling and thought about what Wendy had just said about her being a murderer. It felt like a confession, a rarity from his buttoned-up wife these days, but then again, it was a sentiment she'd professed before. Everything they'd done, they'd done together. That was what she had always said. It's what he'd said as well, parroting her, even though down deep he felt as though the blood was still on his hands and his hands only. That unfortunate metaphor brought it all back for a moment, the blood pumping from the knife wound in a woman's neck, her shocked eyes. He sipped some water and told himself to think of something else. He thought of the party and how he'd felt strangely detached during the whole affair, which was unusual for him. He liked parties, as a rule. And he liked birthday parties even more, especially since his wife seemed to loathe them. Maybe he couldn't have fun tonight because Wendy seemed to be the one having fun, drinking too much and cutting it up on the dance floor. Meanwhile he'd been sober, and he kept remembering that scare he'd had earlier in the day when he'd been out shoveling, his heart skittering in his chest like a small dog having a bad dream. Thinking about it now his heart seemed to respond by aching a little. He took several long breaths. Dying at fifty was a perfectly reasonable age to die if you looked at the entire history of humans. Fifty would be ancient to a caveman. Still, despite the lucky life he'd led, it suddenly seemed tiny to him. Like his whole life experience added up to one of those nothing-much-happens *New Yorker* stories. Something by Ann Beattie, maybe. Which was ridiculous, because his life had been full of events, his life had played out in part the way he'd only dreamed of when he'd been a teenager, obsessed with film noir and adventure stories and fatalism. He'd murdered for love and he'd murdered for money. He'd published several essays. He'd had a beautiful son. He had friends. He lived right on the ocean. Why did his life seem so constricted?

He curled onto his left side, his sleeping side, even though he knew it would be at least an hour until he fell asleep. He thought of Ellen Larson. All they'd talked about at the party was parenting, Thom relating to her that Wendy had secretly felt no love for their son until he'd first smiled at her while making eye contact, and then she had felt more love than she'd ever felt before. It wasn't his story to tell, of course, but he'd sensed it was something Ellen needed to hear.

"I can't wait," Ellen said, "but childbirth was an amazing experience."

"I wouldn't know about that."

"But you were there."

"Well, yes. Feeling enormously relieved that the baby wasn't coming out of me, while also feeling completely left out from the experience. A strange day."

Ellen had only stopped in for one drink and then she left. He'd watched her exit the VFW hall, feeling an undefined longing. It wasn't sexual, so what was he longing for? Maybe that she'd come over for coffee dates and she'd confess to him that she, too, had committed cardinal sins. Maybe she would need saving, or she would recognize that he needed saving. Thom pushed her out of his mind and instead began to play out the most frequent fantasy he indulged in, one in which he woke up transported in time. He was always sent to one specific day, during his junior year abroad at Mather College's Rome campus. Jill Ringgold, same year as he was in college, came to visit the campus from her own semester abroad in Paris. Thom had been acquaintances with Jill prior to her arriving in Rome. They'd taken a class together on William Blake, and they'd chatted at parties, but nothing more than that. But on the day that Jill arrived at the Rome campus, Thom was the only person she knew there, and the two had spent it together, walking through the city, drinking coffee, then switching to wine. She told him about the eating disorder she'd had in high school. He told her how he'd forgotten to bring any pictures of his girlfriend with him to Rome and now he was having a hard time picturing her face. Late that night they strolled back to campus along the Via di Santa Prisca, the night having cooled enough that Jill had her arm interlocked with Thom's. Their hips bumped as they walked. Thom remembered that it had felt like a movie, that at any moment they might lift slightly off the sidewalk or break into song. Instead, they hesitated outside of Thom's dorm-room entrance, then Jill asked if he was going to see his girlfriend Maggie soon. He told her he was and that she was due to join him in Florence in a week. She kissed him on the cheek—he could still sometimes feel her lips almost touching his—and that was that. Thom knew then how easily he could have pulled her into his room with him, and he'd been regretting not doing it for years. Lately, at night, he played out different scenarios in his mind. In these time-travel fantasies, he'd be returned to that moment outside his room, that dilapidated hallway with its broken floor tiles. Instead of the chaste kiss that had actually happened, she'd wind up in his room. And it wasn't just a sexual scenario that he imagined, although that was a large part of it. Sometimes they stayed together. In those scenarios their lives were completely changed. But mostly they just spent the one night together, and Thom imagined that a simple act like a one-night stand might alter their lives as well. Jill's fate would be different. And maybe Thom would never have reconnected with Wendy, a thought so complicated that Thom would return to that night in Italy, fantasize about what might have happened if they had truly kissed. And that pleasant thought was usually enough to gently prod him into the semiconscious state that passed for sleep these days.

2013

NOVEMBER

i

On the day before Thanksgiving, Wendy took the cordless phone into the living room and called her mother.

"Just checking to make sure you have plans for tomorrow," she said, after her mom asked if there was a reason she'd called.

"Going to Alan's. Didn't he tell you? Although it's going to be too many people for me. Mindy's whole side of the family will be there."

"Well, I'm happy. I didn't want to think of you being alone on Thanksgiving."

"I knew that's why you called. I don't see what the big deal is. I'm alone today and I'll be alone the day after Thanksgiving. Doesn't bother me at all."

"Mom, when did you get so folksy?"

"I'm just being practical."

"I know you are."

"Who's coming to your house tomorrow? Thom's parents?"

"They're coming, yes. Just for the day, like they always do."

"How's my Jason doing?" It was a new phrase of her mother's, calling her son "my Jason," and Wendy had decided she liked it.

"He's in a detective phase. A detective reading phase, I should say. Lots of crime novels."

"No more comic books?"

"A few, but, no, he's all about the dark adult books right now."

They talked some more about Jason, and then her mom talked about her dogs, telling stories about them like they were her children. Before ending the call, Wendy told her to have a nice Thanksgiving.

"Alan's invited me over. I'm sure you were worried about it."

"Yes, you told me, Mom."

"I know I did. I just wanted to make sure you didn't fret."

After ending the call, Wendy sat on the couch for a while, trying to figure out what to do next. When the doorbell chimed its five-note tune, she was confused for a moment. All of their neighbors came around the back and knocked on their door. Who would be at the front door?

It turned out to be a police detective, shockingly young, skinny, and nearly completely bald. He showed her his badge—his name was Michael Elo—and asked if he could come in.

"Of course. I was just about to make coffee," Wendy said, even though she hadn't been. "Can I get you something?"

"I'm fine, ma'am. Thank you, though. I just have a few quick questions."

Wendy heard a creak on the stairs and remembered that Jason was home because of the half day. She wondered if he'd come halfway down the stairs and was eavesdropping on the conversation.

"It's not about our cat, is it?"

Detective Elo laughed and said, "No, it's not about your cat. Is there something I should know?"

"One of our neighbors calls the police if our cat kills a bird. It's happened before."

"No, I'm here about Alexander Deighton."

"Oh yeah?" Wendy was surprised. Alexander Deighton had been the chair of her husband's department. His death over the summer had been ruled an accidental drowning.

"I have a few questions about your husband's relationship to him that I was hoping you could answer."

"Sure. Are you . . . My husband isn't here."

"I spoke to your husband this morning at the university. He was very helpful. I'm just following up on some of his answers."

A strange sense of unreality went through Wendy—not that a detective was in her house but that her husband had been interviewed already, that there was some sort of formal investigation into his part in Alex Deighton's death. "Okay?" she said. "Are you sure I can't get you a water?"

"Sure, I'll take a water."

Wendy got a glass from the cabinet as the detective stood awkwardly on the other side of the kitchen island. "Ice?" she said.

"Sure."

She cracked one of the trays and dropped two cubes of ice into his glass and passed it to him. "Please sit," she said.

He took a sip of water then settled onto one of their kitchen stools. He really did look young to her, and he seemed a little nervous, as though he were here to be interviewed instead of the opposite.

But after putting his glass down on the island, Detective Elo took a breath through his nostrils and said, "How would you characterize your husband's relationship with the deceased? He'd been his boss for how long?"

"Over eight years, I think. Since right before we moved here."

"Did they get along?"

"In a literal sense, they did. They worked together for eight years."

"Did your husband like him?"

"No, but I'm not sure anyone really liked him."

"You didn't like him?"

Wendy, striving for as much truthfulness as possible, said, "I avoided him, mostly. He worked with my husband, so it wasn't always easy. I mean, I'd see him at parties, but I didn't have a personal relationship with him."

"What was he like when you saw him at parties?"

"He was mainly very arrogant. He liked to talk about himself and he didn't ask questions of other people. And he was one of those men who are completely unaware of how physically unattractive he was."

"He hit on women?"

"Well, yeah. He had three wives, you know, and, yes, he was pretty inappropriate at times."

"Physically?"

"What do you mean?"

"Did he ever touch you inappropriately?"

"Lingering hugs, I suppose, but nothing else. But he flirted and leered and said gross things."

"And how did your husband feel about this?"

Wendy thought for a moment. "I don't suppose he liked it, but it was more something we laughed about. He wasn't jealous or angry or anything like that. Alex Deighton was gross, but he wasn't a threat in any way."

"Okay, Mrs. Graves. What about your husband's working relationship with Mr. Deighton? How would you characterize that?"

"I'm confused. Is there some issue around Alex's death? I thought it was ruled an accident."

"It hasn't been ruled anything yet. There were some indications that Mr. Deighton might have been in a physical altercation before he died, so we're just following up with some of the people who knew him best."

"You mean, some of the people who might have wanted him dead."

"Your words, not mine, Mrs. Graves."

Wendy laughed. "My husband didn't like him, but there's no way he would have done anything to harm him. It wouldn't make sense."

"What about the fact that Mr. Deighton was holding on to a position as chair of the arts department that your husband might have liked to have for himself?"

"Who told you that?"

"He was the chair, yes? If he retired, or died, then that position would be open, right?"

"Thom didn't put himself up for that job."

Detective Elo finished his water and put the empty glass back onto its coaster. "Why didn't he, do you think? I spoke to two of his colleagues, who said that your husband was the most qualified."

"Do you know anything about academia?"

"A little bit. My mother was a biology professor at the University of Maine."

"Well, then, maybe you know that rising to chair of a department is a mixed blessing. I think Thom decided that it was just too much of a headache to be in charge."

"That's pretty much what he told me. Okay, Mrs. Graves, just a couple more questions."

"It's Wendy. And can I get you some more water?"

"No, no. I'm fine. I just have a few more questions. What can you tell me about Tammy Joo?"

"Alex's wife. Uh, is she a suspect as well?"

"No one is really a suspect here. We're just trying to get a complete picture."

"Um, Tammy. I know her less than I knew Alex. When they were first married, she used to come to department parties, but that didn't last long. They'd separated, hadn't they, about a year ago?"

"Is that what you've been told?"

"Something like that."

"He was living in their apartment above their garage."

"Yeah, not surprising. She was fine, I guess. I can't tell you much more about her than that, except that we were all wondering why she was with Alex."

"Why was that?"

"I don't know. Because she seemed a relatively normal, attractive human woman. But really, I didn't know her well."

"Did your husband have a closer relationship with her?"

"With Tammy? Probably. He saw her more than I did."

"I hope I'm not causing trouble by saying this, but your husband said that he and Tammy are close friends."

Wendy laughed to cover up the sinking feeling that another one of Thom's infatuations was about to be uncovered. "That doesn't exactly surprise me," she said. "My husband is pretty social, especially around work. And he has lots of female friends. Are you implying that there was something going on between him and her?"

"No, no. Just that they had a relationship of sorts. You had no suspicions around that?"

"Well, now I do." She made the laugh again, for real this time. "Just kidding. No, I have never suspected that my husband was involved in any way with Tammy Joo. But I'm not surprised they're friends."

"One more thing, Wendy. Can you tell me where your husband was on the morning of July eighteenth?"

"Was that the morning Alex drowned?"

"Yes."

"My husband was in bed with me."

"Are you sure of that?"

"Yes, of course. I remember that day well, getting the news of the death. I'd remember if for some reason Thom went somewhere that morning."

"What time do you normally get up in the morning?"

"Well, I get up around seven most days. Thom gets up about an hour later."

"Could Thom have left the house early that morning while you were sleeping?"

"Not without waking me up. At night I sleep deeply, but in the morning . . . not so much. If sleep was a pond, Thom's on the bottom in the weeds and I'm sort of just under the surface. God, that's an inappropriate metaphor, considering."

Detective Elo laughed himself, not the laugh she'd been expecting, more of a spasmodic cough. "No, that's okay. So your husband was home all morning?"

"Yes, my husband was home all morning."

After letting the detective out and promising to call him if she remembered anything that might be important, Wendy stood for a moment and listened to the house. It was quiet. She went upstairs and knocked on Jason's door.

"Who was that?" her son said after she entered his tidy bedroom. He was lying on his bed, one of his Ian Fleming Bond novels open on his lap.

"Police detective. I thought I heard you on the stairs."

Jason seemed to think for a moment. "Nope. I was just in my room. Why was a police detective here?"

"He had some questions about Alex Deighton, your dad's co-worker."

"Seriously?"

"Nothing that important. Pretty routine stuff."

"Is Dad a suspect?"

"You mean, do they think your father murdered Alex? If they did, they don't now. He was here sleeping when Alex drowned."

"But that means that they think that it was a murder."

"I don't know about that. Maybe. I think they're just making sure."

"Interesting," Jason said, and raised his eyebrows dramatically.

Walking back downstairs, she thought about what a strange age Jason was at, halfway between being a boy and becoming a teenager, although he was running pretty late in the teenager department. Most of his friends already had cracked voices and fuzzy upper lips, and Julia, Jason's best friend, had recently sprouted into a supermodel, while Jason seemed stuck in his gangly child's body. But he wasn't really a child anymore, and she was pretty sure he'd just lied to her about not knowing the detective had come to visit. It didn't bother her, but she felt a little bit sad about it. Once upon a time Jason told her everything.

ii

Thom offered to help Wendy with the big meal, was turned away, and happily went to his office. His parents had told him they would be there at noon, which meant eleven thirty, and that gave him two solid hours to write. He opened up his laptop, went to Word, and clicked on "open recent" in order to get back to the crushingly awful novel he'd started at the beginning of the summer. There it was, tentatively called *The Ghost in You*, but it wasn't at the top of the list of recently opened files. There were two files above it, one titled "Letter of Resignation" and one called "From Paris to Berlin." Thom, confused, hunted his memories from the previous day. Had he gotten so drunk last night that he had somehow opened up two old files with no memory of doing so? It was true that he'd had a few whiskeys in front of the television while watching his DVD of *The Shawshank Redemption*, but he'd stayed relatively sober. After the film was over, he remembered guiltily eating the rest of the mint-chocolate-chip ice cream over the sink, then he'd gone straight to bed. Who had opened these files on his computer?

He couldn't even remember what "Letter of Resignation" was, so he opened it up first. It was vaguely familiar, something he'd written years ago, a joke letter that he had no intention of sending. It read:

To Professor Deighton,

This letter is to formally notify you that I'm resigning my tenured professorship at New Essex State University, effective immediately.

Thank you for this opportunity. All it has cost me is my sanity, my sexual potency, my sobriety, and my will to live.

And I want to thank you personally for the guidance and patience you have showered on me in my tenure under your supervision. Without it, I would have maintained the view that human beings, especially of the subspecies Universitus Administratus, were essentially benign in nature. I now know that this is false, that one human being, namely you, can embody every single terrible trait known to man, you flatulent, small-fingered, wobbly-necked, greedy, unfunny, pigeon-toed, pigeon-brained exemplar of the worst generation at the end of fucking civilization as we know it.

With sincerest regards,
Thom Graves

After rereading it with mild amusement, Thom opened up the other file. It was a story, one he'd started many years ago. He hadn't gotten very far with it, so he read the whole thing.

From Paris to Berlin
a short story
by T. E. Graves

The train, after a seesawing start to the journey, had smoothed out just as the sprawling exurbs of Paris had been precipitously replaced by a series of yellowing fields under gray skies interspersed with stone farmhouses. Nick was about to light a cigarette, then remembered that he'd purposefully chosen the nonsmoking car so that he could stick to his wholly unrealistic goal of only smoking half a pack a day.

Instead, he removed the Julian Barnes book he'd been struggling with and cracked it open. The book at least gave him the opportunity to gaze just above its top edge at his neighboring travelers. Weren't French people supposed to be attractive? Just as that thought went through his head, the nearest door hissed open and admitted a tall, possibly French but definitely attractive woman of indeterminate age.

Nick used all his powers of suggestion to will her to sit in the empty seat across from him and couldn't quite believe it when it worked. She tucked one leg under the other and pulled out a paperback copy of Len Deighton's *Berlin Game*. It was one of Nick's favorite books and now he knew that this meeting was fated.

Awful awful awful awful awful awful awful awful awful awful awful awful

That was all he'd written. Three mediocre paragraphs plus his own review of them. Besides feeling disgust in himself that he ever thought he could be a good writer, something else nagged at him. He suddenly realized what it was. Both the files had the name "Deighton" in them. Was that why they had been opened?

He passed Jason's closed door on the way down from his office and found Wendy peeling potatoes in the kitchen, listening to NPR. "I have a very strange question," he said.

"Okay."

"Have you been on my computer recently opening Word documents?"

"No."

"You're sure?"

She smiled her mean smile, the one she saved for when Thom had just said something stupid. "Of course I'm sure. Why are you asking?"

He told her about the two opened files and how the only connection they seemed to have was the name Deighton.

"I think I know what happened," Wendy said. "I didn't mention it because I wasn't sure, but I think Jason was on the stairs listening to my whole conversation with the detective yesterday. I heard a creak, and then when I went up afterwards he was acting shifty."

"Did he do the thing where he pretends to be thinking about his answer?"

"He did. You know he's in a detective phase right now. He's probably investigating you to find out if you killed Alex."

"Jesus. Well, at least I'm not going insane."

"You should change your password."

"Okay," Thom said, knowing he probably wouldn't. "That turkey smells good."

"Yes, it does."

Thom went and got himself another half cup of coffee, and while he was pouring it Wendy said, "He wouldn't find anything incriminating on your computer, would he?"

"What do you mean?"

"I don't know. He's a thirteen-year-old boy."

"Are you talking about porn, or are you worried I typed up a confession to all the murders I've committed in my time?"

"Okay, okay. I didn't mean to upset you. We just need to remember that we don't have a little kid in the house anymore. He hears and sees everything."

Back upstairs Thom wondered what else Jason might have looked at on his computer. He opened Chrome and checked the history. Not surprisingly he saw a recent search for Alex Deighton, but alarmingly he also saw a search for Alexandra Fritsch. How could Jason possibly know that name? He was dizzy all of a sudden, like he'd been lifted up really fast and set back down, and he did his breathing exercises, trying to calm his mind. Then he had a thought and typed "Alex" into the search bar on the browser. A menu of possibilities presented itself. Not just Alex Deighton and Alexandra Fritsch but also Alexander Hamilton and Alex Kingston and Alexis Bledel and a local pizza place called Alexander's. Jason must have put the name Alex into his search bar to see what had come up and Alexandra Fritsch, a name that Thom frequently entered, had appeared. But it looked as though Jason had clicked on the name and read one of the accompanying news articles. Thom opened the article himself, a story archived from the *Lubbock Avalanche-Journal*. He'd read it before but glanced through it again, trying to see it through his son's eyes. It began by referencing the unsolved stabbing death of Alexandra Fritsch, over twenty years ago, then connecting that crime to the scandal that swept Caprock College when it was revealed that some of the Texas college's female students were part of an amateur prostitution ring.

Thom leaned back in his chair and thought for a while. He decided that he didn't really have much to worry about. What bothered him the most, in a way, was that his son had read both his stupid letter to Deighton and his embarrassing European travel story. It seemed like only a couple of years ago that Jason had seemed to idolize Thom, impressed by his job, by his sense of humor, even by his mediocre tennis game. There was a period when Jason wore shorts late into the fall with button-down shirts and sweaters just like Thom did. But those days were over. It was only a matter of time until Jason saw Thom the way that Thom saw himself: a failed, out-of-shape writer who drank too much and who was barely tolerated by his wife. A wave of self-pity swept through him, making him feel even worse about himself. His only hope was that Jason would never ever find out about his more cardinal sins. He remembered what

Wendy had said about his password and decided he ought to change it, even though he'd had the same one for the whole time he'd had the computer.

iii

After Thom's parents had left (they always came too early, but they always left early as well), Wendy finished the dishes and went to her office just to have a little bit of time for herself. Samsa was in there as well. Wendy had left a shoebox on the floor a week ago and he'd turned it into his new favorite afternoon sleeping spot; she hadn't had the heart to throw the box out yet.

She logged onto her computer to check her emails. Her brother had sent her a photograph of his Thanksgiving dinner, their mom with a particular grin on her face that meant she wasn't all that happy to be there. Wendy made a note to herself to book a trip to Wyoming soon, maybe over Jason's February break. Thinking of Jason, she clicked the button that showed recent browsing history, but there was nothing suspicious. She opened up Word and checked to see if any files had been opened by someone other than her. Even though she was prepared it was still a shock to see that several documents had been looked at by Jason. Two were poems, both unfinished. One was called "A Murder of Sparrows" and the other "Too Much of Water," both picked because Jason, the boy detective, seemed to be investigating the drowning death of Alex Deighton. She looked at the poems again just to see what he had read and imagined he was more bored by them than anything. "A Murder of Sparrows" was an attempt at a comic interrogation of bird taxonomy, and "Too Much of Water" was actually about her father's death when she was fifteen, but written in a way that there was really no way Jason would ever have figured that out.

But the third document Jason had opened did concern her a little. It was called "Money Stuff" and it was a list of assets and accounts that she'd put together over a year ago. She'd only made it because Thom had no idea about how much money they had, where it was kept, or how to get to it. She'd sent him the document after she'd written it, but he hadn't seemed particularly interested. She wondered sometimes if it was an innate failing of his, or if he felt guilt about the money. Either way, money was simply something he had no interest in thinking about, although he didn't seem to feel too bad about the enormous DVD library he'd amassed or the yearly trips to Europe or the single malt he drank. Wendy opened up "Money Stuff" and looked at it. It was a pretty rudimentary list. She hadn't included account numbers, just the names of banks and institutions, and roughly how much was in each. It was funny. They'd spent a lot of money since Wendy had inherited her first husband's trust fund, but they seemed to have more now than they ever had before. Money made money.

She wondered if Jason understood the numbers he'd looked at. Probably better than his father did, she thought. It was a lot of money, mostly because she had been careful about spending it. She and Thom were basically academics and for that reason neither of them wanted to be driving around in Italian sports cars or wearing designer clothes. They had their house on the sea. They had traveled the world. They'd donated huge sums to multiple charities. Locally, they'd probably single-handedly kept both the New Essex Art Cinema and Mother Hen Cat Rescue in operation. Most important, Wendy was able to make sure that her mother would never have to worry about money for the remainder of her life. Her brother, also, although he was less inclined to take money from her unless it was for something related to his kids (she paid the fees for their sports clubs and contributed to their college funds). Even now, after so many years, just knowing that she had access to money was an enormous weight off her shoulders. When she'd been young her parents had mostly tried to hide just how precarious their situation had been, but both she and her brother knew from a young age that they were poor. She had a childhood habit, one she continued to this day, in which she lay in bed each morning and counted her worries, telling herself to worry about them quickly and get it over with for the day. Her primary worry back then, besides her father and what he might do when he drank too much, was when the money would run out and what would happen then. She'd never really shaken that feeling, and maybe that was the real reason she'd made a list of how much she and Thom had in the bank. People like Thom, who had never really worried about money (even though he loved to talk about his down-and-out days as a video-store employee), were the type of people who would say how money wasn't all that important. But Wendy knew its importance, not in buying things but in making sure that you and your family were safe from the wolves.

After deleting the "Money Stuff" file and changing her password as well, Wendy shut down her computer and went to see what Thom and Jason were up to. They were on either side of the couch in the TV room, both glassy-eyed (Thom from booze, Jason from his grandmother's pecan pie), staring blankly at the screen. Wendy sank down between them. Roger Moore was on screen, wearing a safari suit, in some kind of jungle hideout. "James Bond marathon," Thom said, and Wendy, tired suddenly from a day of cooking and entertaining, stretched out to watch for a while, her head on Thom's lap and her feet up against her son.

2013

JULY

i

"He's dead," Thom said.

"Who's dead?"

"Alex."

Wendy turned away from her computer to face Thom, who was standing in her office doorway. He'd been there five minutes earlier, talking about his rejected American-lit-survey syllabus, when the phone rang and he'd gone to answer it, saying that it was no doubt Alex, calling to explain his decision. Instead, he was back in the same spot, shirt untucked, telling Wendy that Alex was dead. He seemed shocked, dazed almost.

"Wait, what? Alex Deighton?"

"I know. We were just talking about him. He drowned on one of his swims. This morning. That was Linda on the phone."

"Oh my God," Wendy said, standing up and walking toward her husband. "He *drowned*?"

"Apparently. I'm . . . I don't know what I am. I mean, as you know, I hate the motherfucker, but I also thought he'd be in my life forever, you know?"

"Of course. Of course."

"I can't . . ." Thom brought his fingers to his mouth, tapping at a lip, a habit he'd developed since finally quitting smoking just under a year ago.

"What else did Linda say? When did it happen? How was she told?"

"Um, she just said, 'Thom, I have some terrible news,' and you know what I instantly thought? I thought that I was being fired. Which is ridiculous, of course, because I can't be fired, but my first thought was that Alex had found some way to do it. And then she said that Alex was dead, and I think I said the words 'Our Alex?' which is strange, right, since who else would it be?"

"He drowned?"

"Yes, you know how he swims every morning over at Blood Stone Quarry?"

"He never shuts up about it."

"He never did, did he?" Thom smiled, and the act of smiling seemed to relax his whole body, his shoulders lowering, his hands returning to his sides.

"Who found him?"

"I don't know. I didn't even think to ask. Linda just told me that he'd been found dead at the quarry, and that—"

"Who's dead?" Jason had wandered into the room, holding a comic book in one hand.

"Alex Deighton," Thom said.

Jason made a face, keeping his lips together and lowering his chin, then said, "So . . . you're happy?"

"No, I'm not happy, Jason. He died."

Jason put up a hand and said, "Sorry. I mean . . . it's not like you liked him, though. Right, Mom?"

"You can keep me out of this," Wendy said, although she thought her son had a point.

"Just because I didn't like him doesn't mean that I'm happy he's dead, Jason."

"Yeah, yeah, I know." The book he was carrying was a threadbare copy of *Tintin in Tibet*, his favorite. Wendy noticed that he was carrying it with a finger slid between its pages as though he'd come into her office to show her something, probably an illustration he loved or a joke he thought was funny. At thirteen, Jason had suddenly started rereading all his childhood favorites, despite the fact that he was on the cusp of puberty. It was a strange reversion.

"Is Linda calling everyone in the department?"

"That's what she said."

"You should call Marcia."

"I should, shouldn't I?"

"How'd he die?" Jason said.

"He drowned."

"Are you serious? Where?"

"I didn't get a lot of details, but you know the swimming quarry?"

"Which one?"

"Blood Stone. We went there once with Justine and her kids, remember?"

"He was five years old," Wendy said.

"I remember," Jason said. "There's a car at the bottom of it."

"I don't know about that—"

"No, there is. Timmy said he saw it. He went there with a snorkel once and told me that he saw it."

"Okay, well, Alex swims there every morning, used to, anyway, and I guess he drowned."

"How'd he drown?"

"I don't know. I just heard about this myself. Jason—"

"Will you get his job?"

"Jesus H, I haven't even thought about that. Who knows? Maybe. Maybe not."

"Why'd you come in here, Jason?" Wendy said.

"Oh, I was going to show you something, but it doesn't matter now."

Thom noticed the book in Jason's hand and said, "Aren't you too old to be reading that?"

Jason shrugged and said, "Never too old to revisit the classics, Dad."

Wendy laughed, more loudly and longer than the joke warranted.

"You okay there, hon?" Thom said.

"Yeah, fine. I think I'm a little in shock about Alex. Like you said, we didn't like him, but that didn't mean he wasn't a huge part of our lives. It's strange to think he's just gone."

"Yeah," Thom said. "I'm going to go call Marcia. I'm surprised she hasn't called here yet."

Thom departed and Jason asked if he could stay in her office and read. She told him it would be fine, and he threw himself down on the throw rug and cracked the book open where his finger had been. Wendy turned on her computer and did a quick search to see if there was any news online about Alex's death. There wasn't, of course, not if he'd just been found that morning. Still, she read his Wikipedia entry, surprised he even had one, despite the fact that he'd written two well-received novels in the 1980s, one of which had been turned into a TV movie that starred Blythe Danner. She'd read some of that particular book years ago, just after they'd moved to New Essex. It was some typical shit about a college boy who gets a job with a shipbuilder on the coast of Maine for a summer and has a sexual awakening with a young widow in the town. She'd only read about a hundred pages and would have hurled the book into the trash, but she'd borrowed it from the library. What had really bothered her was that its hero, an obvious stand-in for Alex, was presented as this innocent, sensitive kid, when in reality there was maybe a chance Alex might have been innocent once but zero chance he'd ever been sensitive.

Her cellphone rang, the screen telling her that it was Janet Brodie, no doubt calling because she'd already heard the news. She flipped the phone open and said, "Hi, Janet."

"Did you hear?"

"About Alex? Yes, Thom just got a call from Linda. When did you find out?"

"Linda called me as well, about twenty minutes ago." Janet was an adjunct professor, but Wendy knew her from when they took a poetry workshop together, years and years ago. "How do you feel about it?"

"How do I feel about Alex drowning? I didn't like him. You know that as well as anybody, but I'm not dancing a jig." Jason looked up at her from his comic book at the word "jig."

"I wonder how Tammy is doing."

"Now, *she* might actually be dancing a jig."

"I hope she has an alibi."

Wendy began to laugh, then stopped herself. "Who knows how she really feels. Maybe she actually loved him." Tammy was Alex's third wife, half his age, and according to everyone who knew them, they were pretty much separated despite the fact that they still shared a house together.

"Stranger things have happened," Janet said.

"Look, I should go. Can we talk later?" Even though Jason was now back into his book, she knew he was listening to every word of their conversation.

"Of course."

She closed the phone and sat at her desk for a moment. The rotating fan that was on low blew something into her eye and she rubbed at it. Jason, flipping a page, said, "How does someone drown if they know how to swim?"

"Oh," Wendy said, swiveling toward him. "Lots of ways, I guess. He might have gotten a cramp or maybe something else happened to him, like a heart attack or a stroke. He was pretty old, you know."

"How old was he?"

"In his early seventies, I think. I asked him once but he didn't tell me. Vain, I guess."

Jason was reading again, and Wendy found herself thinking about his question, about someone drowning who knew how to swim, amazed for a moment by her powers of compartmentalization. It was something she'd always been good at, putting all the different aspects of her life in boxes and keeping them separated. Different realms, she supposed. It was one of many things that distinguished her from Thom, who saw everything in his life as relating to everything else, one giant mural. She looked at her son, wondered if he was more like her or more like Thom. Right now, he seemed to be like her, asking questions about Alex's death while fully immersed in his book. She could see the page he was looking at, all those little boxes, most of them filled with images of snow. *White compartments*, she said to herself, then remembered that they'd given Jason a biography of Hergé, Tintin's creator, last Christmas. He'd read it in a day then told Wendy all about it. One of the things he'd told her was that Hergé had written *Tintin in Tibet* because he'd been having persistent death dreams that involved snow and empty spaces.

The sound of the dryer's alert from the second-floor laundry room pulled her out of her reverie. "Oh," she said, getting up quickly to make her way to the second floor. Thom never heard the washer and the dryer, let alone helped load and unload, but still, she wanted to make sure she got there first. At the top of the stairs she nearly tripped over Samsa, who must have heard the beep as well and was prowling around in the hopes that he could disrupt her folding by lying on top of a pile of clean clothes.

She swung the door open and pulled out the warm bundle, then carried it into the bedroom and laid it down on top of the made-up bed. Samsa leapt up to sniff the pile, but Wendy scooped him up and put him back down on the floor. It was mostly underwear in this load, Thom's and Jason's, but before she went about sorting those, she quickly pulled out the few items of hers that had been the real reason for running a wash this morning. There was a beach towel, a plain white one, that she put back in the drawer across from the washer and dryer, and then there was her one-piece black bathing suit that had been hung out to dry, which she returned to the same drawer she'd removed it from earlier that morning.

ii

Not knowing what else to do that afternoon, Thom had driven to the university to talk with Linda face-to-face. The English department was located in an old Victorian house on the outskirts of the campus. It was where most of the seminars and smaller classes were conducted, in high-ceilinged rooms with loud radiators and drafty windows. Thom parked on the street right in front of the building and wasn't surprised to see Marcia Lever's rusty Volvo parked there as well.

He could hear Marcia and Linda talking as he walked down the creaky hallway to the offices located at the back of the house. "Thom," Marcia said as soon as he entered Linda's office, then stood up and gave him an awkward hug.

"I still can't believe it," he said.

Linda, who had been in the department longer than any single professor, said, "I won't be surprised to hear it was his heart. You both know how he ate."

"I thought he'd live forever, somehow," Marcia said. "He seemed like the type."

"Too mean to die," Thom said, then instantly regretted it. "God, sorry. Too soon."

"You're among friends," Marcia said. "We don't have to pretend we particularly liked him, but it's still a shock."

Linda's phone on her desk rang and she picked it up, telling whoever was on the other end of the line that the rumor was true.

"Come into my office for a moment," Marcia said, rising from her chair.

Thom followed her into her immaculate corner office and took a seat in the comfy chair across from her desk. "I know it's only July," Marcia said, running a finger across her empty desk, "but it's late July and school starts up again in a little over a month."

"I know. I've already thought about that."

"Alex was teaching two courses this fall."

"Like always."

"Yep. He'd put together that seminar on Shakespeare's contemporaries. All of two students signed up so I think we can safely cancel that, but the department is going to need to find someone to teach his survey course."

"The department is going to need a new chair," Thom said.

"Yes, and I'm assuming that you are going to throw your hat into the ring."

"I hadn't given it any thought yet, but maybe I will. How about you?"

Marcia thought for a moment, Thom knowing that she wasn't posturing for effect but genuinely considering the question. He also knew that if Marcia decided she wanted to be chair of the department, it would have everything to do with trying to make the department run better and nothing to do with personal ambition. "I might," she said at last. "But if you told me that you had your heart set—"

"God, no, Marcia. Besides, I think our friendship could survive a little competition, don't you?"

"I do," she said, and looked relieved.

They returned to the outer office, where Linda was still on the phone. After she hung up, Marcia asked her if she'd like to join them at the Thirsty Hare for a drink. Linda declined, not surprisingly, and Thom and Marcia walked across the empty campus toward the bar. It had been a dry summer, and the lawns were withered and yellow. They walked in silence, Thom already starting to wonder if he really did want to push to be the next chair. It would be between Marcia and him, no doubt about that. Don had been there longest, but he'd made it clear he had no interest in advancement.

At the Hare they each got an Ipswich Ale and made a toast to Alex.

"Shall we both say something nice about him?" Marcia said.

"Okay. I'll start. He had pretty good taste in wives."

"That he did. They were always too good for him."

They drank, and Marcia said, "He could be an excellent teacher, when the subject interested him."

"Yes, that *is* true," Thom said.

"But a terrible department chair."

"True as well."

Midge, the bartender, put a bowl of peanuts between them on the bar, and for a time they silently ate, dropping the shells on the floor, a Thirsty Hare tradition.

When, after a second beer each, they returned to the bright sunshine outside, Thom felt disoriented and slightly drunk. They walked to the department building, and Marcia popped back inside to do some work, while Thom returned to his car. He sat inside its sweltering interior for a moment, sweat creeping out from his hairline, thinking about where he wanted to go next. He knew it was a risk, but he badly wanted to see Tammy, Alex's wife, and he didn't want to call her first. Calling her might look suspicious, but a drop-by, just to check on the well-being of the widow, wouldn't look too strange, he thought.

Alex and Tammy's house was over the river in West Essex, a modest shingled Cape that was a stone's throw from a slice of rocky beach. Thom knew that Alex had spent the last year living in the studio apartment above the garage while Tammy had the house to herself. He thought there'd be cars parked out front, but he spotted only Tammy's BMW in the driveway. Alex's Mustang was probably still parked near the quarry. Feeling empty-handed, wishing he'd brought some food or even flowers, Thom went up the stone path to the front door. Tammy must have seen him coming, and she opened the door before he had a chance to knock. He was surprised to see that she'd been crying.

"Tammy," he said, and she stepped outside to hug him.

When they were in her kitchen, she said, "I don't know why I'm crying, exactly, but I can't stop."

"He was your husband."

"You and I both know how little that particular designation meant."

Tammy had been a graduate student at New Essex in the art department when she'd first met Alex. She still made ceramics, at least Thom was pretty sure she did, but she'd gotten her real estate license two years earlier and had quickly become her agency's top seller. She was rail-thin with dark, straight hair and looked more like an artist than a typical real estate broker, but she was gregarious and well liked. No one really understood why she'd married Alex.

"I didn't think you'd be here alone," Thom said, after accepting a cup of coffee, even though he'd rather have had another beer.

"My sister is on her way from Albany. But basically, I keep shooing people away. Janet came by with a casserole. I made a joke that it was the same temperature as my husband. Still warm."

"God, what did she say?"

"She was confused, and said something like she suspected Alex was probably cold since he'd drowned in cold water."

"Dear lord."

"Dear lord is right. I sent her packing. And the police have been here, of course. I thought they'd take me to see the body, but instead they drove me over to the station and showed me a photograph of Alex's face on the slab. It was him, all right. That's when I started crying. It's just so strange to think I'll never hear his voice again. That's what I kept thinking about. Then they took me back here and asked me where I was at six this morning."

"Seriously?"

"Yeah, of course they did. I'd already told them that Alex was living above the garage, that we weren't exactly husband and wife anymore."

"So where were you at six this morning?"

"Asleep, of course. Alone in bed."

"Right."

"Where were *you* at six this morning?" Tammy said, her lips curling into a strange smile, as though she were trying to indicate she was making a joke.

"Not swimming with your husband. Home in bed with Wendy. Do you think there was something suspicious about his death?"

"I asked them, the police, and all they could say was that they were just following protocol. I believed them. He really shouldn't have been swimming alone at his age. Still, I'm surprised he drowned. I think it's much more likely that he had some kind of stroke while he was swimming."

"They'll perform an autopsy?"

"Are you asking?"

"I guess."

"I'm assuming they will. I'd like to know, even though it makes no difference. Gone is gone, right?"

"Yes," Thom said. "Gone is gone."

They sat quietly together for a moment, then Tammy said, "Wendy know you were planning to come over here?"

"I'll tell her, I guess. No harm in coming to see how you're doing. I was over at the university earlier, had a drink with Marcia Lever."

"Where'd you have a drink? At the Hare?"

"Yes. And we even toasted him."

"God," Tammy said, and looked as though she was going to cry again.

Thom stood and went to her, and they hugged tightly in the kitchen, her body feeling impossibly thin in his arms, her hair smelling of coconut shampoo.

"You're not hitting on the grieving widow, are you?" she said as they separated.

Jokes flitted through Thom's head but he said, "No, I'm not hitting on my friend."

She smiled at him, tears now spilling from both eyes. Thom and Tammy had actually slept together once, five years earlier, two years after she'd married Alex. They'd run into each other one weekday afternoon at the YMCA, then Tammy had invited Thom back to her house for coffee. It was January, dark and unmercifully cold. Wendy was at work. Alex was away at some literary conference in Portugal. They'd skipped the coffee and gone straight to a guest room with drafty windows and a creaky bed. And there they'd had their one and only sexual encounter, ten minutes of ineptness that felt, to Thom, at least, like they were each dancing to a very different tune. Afterward, Thom had felt a wave of desolation pass through him and it was all he could do to not get up and flee from the room.

But then Tammy had said something like, "That was awkward," and they'd both laughed, some of it to cover the embarrassment of the moment, but some of it genuine mutual laughter. They'd stayed in bed together for over an hour, talking about what had brought them there. Tammy told him that as soon as she'd decided that marrying Alex had been one of the dumbest decisions she'd made, that she'd been determined to have an affair, a way to mark the beginning of the end. And then Thom had talked about his marriage to Wendy. He'd said, "I have affairs, but down deep I'm still in love with her. She's faithful but doesn't particularly even like me." He'd surprised himself, because he'd never quite thought of it that way before.

"So why do you have affairs?" Tammy had asked.

"Because I'm lonely, I suppose."

"You and Wendy . . . I haven't spent a ton of time with you, but . . . you seem to have genuine chemistry."

"We talk well together, I suppose. But when we're not talking, I don't know what she's thinking. So I fall in love with other women in the hope that it will solve something but I just end up feeling worse about myself. And more in love with Wendy."

"You've given this some thought."

After that afternoon in bed Thom and Tammy had become confidants, conducting their platonic relationship in secret, as though it were an affair. They met at an Indian restaurant in Beverly to tell each other secrets, and they coordinated their times at the gym, just so they could be close to each other. Sometimes, like lovers, they'd recount their origin story, how their sex together had been so bad that it forced them to become friends.

"You should go back to Wendy," Tammy said after they'd hugged in the kitchen. Her phone was ringing, although she wasn't making a move toward answering it.

At the door Thom said, "Do you think they'll come and question me?"

"Who?"

"The police."

Tammy thought about it, looking at the ceiling. "People must know we see one another. I'm sure they assume it's an affair. Who knows? But like you said . . ."

"I have a solid alibi."

"You still sleep with your wife?"

"You mean, in the same bed?"

"Yes."

"I do," he said. Walking back to his car under the hard blue sky, Thom was possessed by the thought that he'd never see Tammy again, or at the very least that he'd never see her alone again. Whatever they had shared together over the past five years had just come to an end.

He arrived home anxious and sullen, badly in need of a drink. He expected Wendy to question him on his whereabouts but, instead, she was nice to him, even joining him in an afternoon gin and tonic. He waited for a knock on the door, for a policeman to come with questions about where he'd been in the early-morning hours of that day. But no one came.

Two days later, while still waiting, Linda called to tell him that the death of Alex Deighton was being treated as an accident. An autopsy was forthcoming but initial reports seemed to confirm he had drowned. There was a big article in the *Boston Globe* about the incident, most of it centered on the varying swimming holes north of Boston and the dangers they presented. As July turned into August, bridged by the worst Massachusetts heat wave in Thom's memory, he became increasingly depressed. Alex had made him miserable. With Alex gone, things should be better, but they weren't. He found himself haunted by images of Alex drowning at dawn, and he almost brought it up to Wendy but decided against it; she'd think he was dwelling on the past. He did, however, try to express some of his feelings about Alex to Wendy over dinner one evening on their porch, and all she'd said was "Think about how much you couldn't stand him. That's all I heard about all year. 'Alex did this, Alex said that. Alex will never retire, and I'll never be department chair.'"

"I don't even know that I want to be department chair anymore," Thom said.

"Why wouldn't you?" Wendy said, putting her glass down on the coffee table hard enough that the seltzer water sloshed over the rim. "That's all you've talked about for two years."

"I don't know," Thom said, trying not to look directly at his wife. He knew she'd have that expression on her face, the one he'd privately named her Marlene Dietrich stare. "Marcia deserves it more than me."

"What does 'deserve' have to do with it? I'm sorry, I know that sounds awful, but you've been there longer than anyone."

"Not longer than Don."

"Don doesn't count. He's not interested in being anything but a teacher. He never has been. Listen, I'm going to tell you something."

The change in her tone made Thom look up at her. She was on the edge of the outdoor sofa, her hair still damp from her afternoon swim in the cove, and for a terrible moment Thom thought she was finally going to leave him. It was as though a huge wind swept off the inner harbor and tore the house off its roots. Instead, she said, "Never mind. Do what you want. You always do anyway."

2013

JUNE

i

The first time Wendy drove to the quarry, the air outside was so cold that she'd run the heater in the car. It was six a.m., late June, and mist hovered over the lawns and open fields. She'd timed her drive: ten minutes from their house with no traffic. There were two paths that she knew of that led to the swimming hole. One was accessed on the ridiculously named Lane's Lane, but it required parking alongside a narrow road in full view of several residents. The other access point meant a longer walk through the woods, but it also meant parking out of sight, down a dirt road with a few remnants of asphalt here and there to get to an old granite out-building, abandoned when the quarry had gone out of business back in the 1930s. There was space in front of the building to park, and from there she slid past a padlocked fence meant to keep cars from going any farther, then it was a half-mile walk to the southern edge of the quarry, emerging like an artist's rendition of the ideal summer swimming hole, surrounded on three sides by sheer cliffs, the preferred jumping points for successive generations of reckless teenagers, but with one side comprised of long, flat rocks extending into the clear, luminous water like steps made for a giant.

Wendy walked out along one of these rocks, found an outcropping on which she could perch, and stared out at the water, so still that it might as well be glass.

There was no sign of Alex Deighton.

She wasn't particularly surprised. Despite his claim that from April through November he swam at Blood Stone every morning at dawn, she had doubted that was completely true. He was a known exaggerator, the subject of the hyperbole usually himself. He liked to tell stories about the varying literary figures he'd rubbed shoulders with over the years, about his stint in Hollywood ("I could have made a lot of money there, but I missed my blue-collar roots too much"), and about the massive popularity of his one novel in France ("they revere authors there, you know"). But lately he'd been spewing tales of his early-morning cold-water swims at the quarry, cornering Wendy at Marcia's annual Easter party to tell her all about how the solitary, bracing dips had changed his life.

"You go alone?" Wendy said.

"Most of the time. It's why I go so early, to avoid the amateurs. You should come join me sometime. I know your husband wouldn't get much from it, but you might see the magic."

"Maybe I will," Wendy said.

"Just a warning that if you do come, you should know that I occasionally swim *au naturel*."

Anyone else, Wendy thought, would make that statement as a joke, or a genuine warning that nudity was involved, but somehow Alex's intonation implied that his seventy-year-old body in the ice-cold water might be a selling point.

"I can ensure you, Alex, that if I come and join you in a swim, I will be wearing my suit."

That night, back at home with Thom, she told him about her conversation with Alex.

"God, that's disgusting. I wish he'd drown there." They were sitting in the living room, Wendy sipping mineral water, Thom with a tall scotch.

"You're not the only one who wishes he'd drown," Wendy said.

"No, I don't think I am. It infuriates me that someone so unliked goes through life full of the belief that people idolize him. It seems fundamentally wrong. Meanwhile, I go through life believing that every person I interact with walks away hoping to never see me again." After a pause, Thom said, "That's your cue, dear, to tell me how well liked I am."

"Sorry, I was daydreaming."

It was during his second nightcap that Thom monologued about whether anyone in the world would be sad to see Alex die. "No one in the English department, that's for sure. Tammy hates him. He has no kids. His parents are dead. Maybe Midge at the Hare would miss him, but, seriously, who else? Lives would improve. Mine would, for sure."

He finished his drink but stayed seated for a moment, staring into the middle distance as though seeing the life that could be his if Alex weren't in it.

Ever since then, Wendy had been imagining an Alex-free world as well. The thought kept expanding in her mind the way that poems used to, beginning their lives as tiny sparks then blossoming into fully-formed works of art, for better or for worse. Her coming to the quarry was the first step. She needed to find out certain things. First of all, did Alex really swim at dawn? Second, was he truly alone? Third, could she rise early in the morning, go swimming herself, and get back without Thom knowing anything about it?

About that third part, she was fairly sure. Thom, she knew, had difficulties falling asleep, in spite of, or because of, the increasing number of scotches he drank immediately before bedtime, but in the morning hours, he was a deep sleeper. He'd been known to sleep right through piercing alarms and Samsa's howling meows at feeding time, twisted up into a sarcophagus of sheets from a night of trying to get comfortable, his face pressed into a pillow. Most mornings when he'd finally emerge from the bedroom Wendy had been up for hours, bundling Jason off to school, taking a two-mile walk, sometimes grocery shopping. There was no reason to suspect that Thom, or Jason, either, out of school now and beginning to sleep in himself, would notice, or care, that she left the house in the early-morning hours.

She waited twenty minutes on the quarry's edge, the sun rising above the tree line and illuminating the sheet of mist that lay just on top of the water. No sign of Alex. She was fine with that because she'd told herself already that if Alex were actually here, she would need to quickly establish some form of intimacy, at the very least tell him that he should not tell other people that she'd decided to join him on his swims. Despite his big mouth, she thought that the prospect of a sexual union would mean he'd abide by her words. Besides, he already had something to hold over her head, that time less than a year ago when he'd spotted her coming out of the Shoreview Motel.

Before leaving, Wendy told herself that she needed to get into the water. It was the supposed reason she'd come here, after all. For a swim. And if Alex had been there, then she'd have had to get in anyway. She shucked off her shorts and removed her hooded Rice sweatshirt. Underneath she was in her black one-piece, cut high on the sides to show off what she felt was her best feature, her still-youthful-looking legs and hips. She considered wading into the water down the sloping flat rock but decided instead to climb up onto a nearby boulder that jutted three feet out above the water's surface. She stood there for a moment, legs bent at the knee, staring into the deep water below her. Steeling herself, she dove. The water was bracingly cold, but not bone-numbing, and she swam out to the middle and floated a while, staring up at what looked like a pair of crested flycatchers darting in the morning air. She remembered someone telling her, maybe it was Alex, that the quarry was over a hundred feet deep, and an emptiness opened up inside her chest at the thought. She breast-stroked to the edge and climbed out of the water.

ii

She returned the next morning, at six thirty this time. When she'd gotten back home the day before, she hadn't been surprised to find her husband deeply asleep, Jason still in his bedroom. She'd showered off the lake water, wrung out her suit, and hung it in the laundry room, which Thom never went into, then she'd gotten dressed and gone downstairs to make coffee.

He'd never suspected she'd left the house at all.

Returning to the same ledge she'd swum from the day before, she spotted a swimmer on the far side performing what looked like a sidestroke, leaving behind a small wake in the otherwise still wa-ter. She sat down on the rock and watched as he got closer. Some-how she could tell it was a man—maybe it was the lack of a swim cap—and as he got closer she decided it was definitely Alex; she could make out his close-cropped hair and the slack features of his face.

She stripped down to her suit and dove from the boulder she'd used the day before, coming up in a straight line toward Alex, who was now in the middle of the quarry. He'd heard her splash into the water and now was paddling in place, having moved his goggles up onto his forehead.

"Hello, stranger," he said as she approached.

"Is that Alex?"

"It is. Kelly?" he said.

"No, it's Wendy Graves. You invite all the ladies out here to swim with you?"

"Well, hello, Wendy. Kelly is ninety years old and the only other regular swimmer this early in the year. I'm pleased it's you and not her."

"I thought I'd give it a try. You were right. It's invigorating."

They circled each other for a few minutes, chatting. Wendy had no intention of trying to drown Alex on this particular day. She was still fact-finding, still even deciding if this was something she wanted to do, or something she felt she could get away with.

"Not too cold for you?" Alex said. It was strange talking to what looked like a disembodied head bobbing on a misty surface, although she could make out the shifting fleshy abstraction of his submerged body.

"No, I like it, but I don't plan on staying in much longer."

"Have you seen the log?" he said.

"What log?"

"It's been here for years. Come with me."

She followed him to the shadiest area, where an enormous log, the size of a telephone pole, bobbed gently. "The key is to get on top of it and stay balanced. Here, hold it for me."

Wendy, now beginning to shiver a little, wrapped her arm over the slippery, mossy surface as Alex clambered on top and straddled it. She was happy to see he was wearing swim trunks. He placed his hands on the top of the log and stood up in one fluid movement, his stringy body tensing with the effort to stay on top. He was upright for about three seconds, grinning down at her before losing his footing and crashing back into the water.

"Your turn," he said when his head reemerged.

"Maybe some other day, Alex," Wendy said. "I'm cold and I'm going to get out now."

"I can warm you up," he said, propelling himself toward her, one of his hands sliding around the small of her back. His face was alarmingly close, and Wendy somehow resisted the urge to push him off of her. "What happens under the water doesn't really happen, you know? It's another realm with different rules."

He slid his hand off her hip and took hold of her wrist. For a moment she thought he was performing some kind of underwater dance move, then realized that he was placing her hand forcefully onto the rather unimpressive bulge in his swimming shorts. Wendy squeezed, relatively hard, and watched Alex's face flicker through several emotions. Lust, surprise, pain, fear.

"Is this what you had in mind?"

"Um." He was moving his hips backward and she let go of him, then laughed.

"I really am getting out of the water now. Maybe if I come back we can test your water-realm story, but no one knows I've come here this morning. I'd like you to keep it that way, okay?"

"God, of course. I won't tell a soul. I already know that you have secrets, Wendy, don't forget it."

The way he said those words caused a flare of hatred in Wendy, and she knew in an instant that she wasn't just fantasizing about murdering Alex.

"No one," Wendy said one more time.

He mimed locking his lips then throwing the key away.

Wendy, satisfied, turned and swam quickly back toward her rock. After she'd clambered up and wrapped her large white beach towel around her, she turned back to see Alex still holding on to the submerged log. Returning to the path, Wendy saw where Alex had hung his towel, plus a long, thick robe. She kept walking, wondering how long he'd stay in the water.

Back at home she thought about how she'd do it. Maybe she could somehow attach a lead pipe or something like it to the log and then she'd lure him back there, tell him she wanted to try and stand on top of it herself, then get hold of the lead pipe and bash him in the head. Professor Alex Deighton, in the quarry, killed with a lead pipe. A few years earlier Jason had gone through a brief obsession with the board game Clue. She'd been excited at first, remembering it from her own childhood, until she realized what a dull game it truly was. The only good parts were the descriptions of the suspects and the rooms and the murder weapons. Where did one get a lead pipe, exactly? And she couldn't imagine that it would be easy to bash Alex on the head while she was floating in water. She discarded the idea.

What if she simply took him in her arms in the middle of the quarry, wrapped her legs around him, and held him under the water. He was a small man, not much bigger than Wendy, and quite a bit older. How hard could it be? Once upon a time, in another life, Wendy's father had drowned in their bathtub when Wendy was just a teenager. She'd never forgotten her mother, Rose, telling her afterward that drowning was a pleasant way to die, almost like falling asleep. And if Alex somehow fought his way out of her embrace, she could apologize and say she was overcome by passion. He might suspect her, but it wasn't something he would bring to the police. In that way, it was kind of a foolproof plan.

iii

She went back to the quarry two more times that summer, once in the second week of July, a Monday morning, no sign of Alex. She decided to swim anyway. It was a warm dawn, the air still and the light soft. She stripped down to her bathing suit and stepped gingerly out along the flat ledge of a mossy rock. When she was ankle-deep, she realized the water was almost the exact temperature of the air. On a whim she quickly shucked off her suit, throwing it so that it landed on her pile of clothes, then did a shallow dive into the perfect water. She stayed in for close to thirty minutes, slowly making her way back and forth, happy that Alex hadn't been at the quarry, although expecting to see him emerge from the woods at any moment.

When she returned home that morning, relaxed and dreamy, she felt certain that she really did want to kill Alex. He was a loathsome man. Not just that, but a loathsome man who felt as though he had the upper hand on her. Plus, more and more these days, Thom seemed to be beaten down by his position in life, his perceived failures. With Alex gone, the job of department chair would be his for the taking. His life would open up in a way that her life had opened up years ago after her first husband had died.

But there was something else as well, a feeling that was hard to put into words. Taking a life would allow her to cross that boundary that her husband had crossed for her all those years ago. It was an experience she wanted for herself. She'd plotted a murder before, of course, but part of her wondered how she'd fare at the actual moment of death. It was knowledge she didn't have. Very few people did, but Thom, her husband, was one of them. Maybe it would help her to understand him more. Years ago, she felt she understood almost everything about him, that she could see him as clearly as she saw herself. They were bound by their twinhood, after all. But these days Thom's interior life was more and more of a mystery; she was aware that there was a black hole inside him, eating away at his health, his confidence, his sobriety. Maybe killing Alex would give her some insight into that black hole. At the very least it would equalize them.

Just over a week later, as she walked through the cool shadows of the woodland path to the quarry, she seemed to know for a certainty that Alex would be there. It was cool and overcast, the air filled with a dusting of mist, as though she were moving through a cloud. When she reached her rock she could hear him, the rhythmic disturbance of the water his sidestroke made, before she saw him, that dark head slicing out of the fog. A calm came over her. She even gently folded the clothes she'd removed before diving into the water herself. It had only been a week and a half since she'd been here, but the water now seemed warmer than the air. She did a careful breaststroke out toward Alex, now waiting for her at the deepest point in the quarry.

"You've come back," he said.

"Are you surprised?"

"I don't know if I'm surprised or not, but I'm very pleased."

"How pleased?" Wendy said.

"I've been thinking of nothing else." He laughed as though he'd said something witty, the water sputtering where it touched his lips.

She moved closer to him and said, "What was it you were saying last time about what happened under the water?"

"What happens under the water doesn't count above water. That's my theory. I'll tell you about it sometime if you'd like. It's a real theory, not just some kind of joke."

"A theory about water?"

"Well, no. It's a theory about realms. We all exist in several realms throughout the course of our life. When a man goes to war, that is another realm. When a woman has a baby, she enters the realm of motherhood. These realms have different rules and yet we treat them, the young people do, anyway, as though the same rules should apply in different realms."

Wendy had spent enough time talking with Alex at cocktail parties to sense that he was ramping up to a seriously long monologue, so she slid the last two feet to him, took his hands and wrapped them around the small of her back, putting her own arms above his shoulders. He went to kiss her, but she moved her head. "No," she said, but pulled one of her hands back from his neck and slid one strap of her suit over her shoulder, then awkwardly freed her arm. Her right breast was freed of the suit and all of Alex's attention went to it. He was breathing heavily, and she could feel along one thigh that he wasn't wearing a bathing suit. She directed his head down and he pressed his face against her breast, her arms locked around his back. And then she simply stopped kicking and let the weight of her body pull him under the water.

Two minutes later she stood back on the rock, gathering her bundle of clothes and reentering the woods. It had been simpler and harder than she could have imagined. At one point he seemed to have a surge of improbable strength, his arms thrashing, and she wondered if she were going to drown with him. But she took a deep breath and leaned all her weight on top of him, and he'd gone under again. One of his hands pulled at her suit and she could feel the water roiling below him as he kicked to come back up to the surface. She simply pulled him closer. There was one last expulsion of air, and then he was still. Just to make sure, she held him for another minute.

She dried herself off by the car, re-dressed, and got inside. The radio blared on, tuned to Emerson College's radio station, and Wendy turned it down a little, but not off. Halfway home she found herself singing along to Dylan's lyrics. *How does it feel?* She didn't know yet, not exactly. One thing she felt was cold and damp, and she looked forward to showering and getting her clothes into the washer. But what did she feel about Alex? He'd died with her breast in his face, her legs around his waist. Who knew what horrors of old age she'd saved him from? She smiled in the car, the song ending and another song she loved starting up. She didn't know the name of the song but the opening lyrics were familiar, something that Jason listened to: *I want to live where soul meets body.*

She pulled into the driveway of her sleeping house. For a moment she wondered if she'd open the front door to find her husband and son, maybe even the local police, gathered in the living room to accuse her of what she'd just done. But the living room was just as she'd left it, quiet, neat, filled with items she loved. She went up the stairs and began a load of laundry, including her bathing suit and the towel she'd used at the quarry. She heard a thunk, Samsa jumping down from the guest-room bed, where he liked to sleep. He padded sleepily up to her and rubbed against her calf. She started up the washer and made her way back downstairs to feed Samsa and start a pot of coffee.

2012

i

Before leaving, Thom said, "There was a distant past when you would have joined me on this expedition."

"Oh, it's an expedition?"

"You never know who or what you might find at the Tavern."

Wendy knew exactly what he would find there. Several scotches, and the same slurry, repetitive conversations with the other semi-regulars. "I'll pass for now," Wendy said.

"Your loss," Thom said, and went out the side door.

"You can go with him if you like," Jason said, either being sweet or else there was something he wanted to watch on television that he wasn't supposed to.

"Maybe I'll go later," she said to Jason, then finished cleaning the kitchen. There were three bars on Goose Neck, but the Tavern at the Wonson Inn was the only one that was open year-round. It was a dark, wood-paneled cellar bar with portholes that looked out on nothing. The longtime bartender, Howard, was famous for ignoring drink orders, especially from tourists, and simply making martinis or Manhattans, depending on his mood. And it was true that for a time in her marriage to Thom they would often walk down after dinner for a nightcap or two. Maybe she should join him, she thought, or at the very least wander down and peek in at the bar. It was a nice night for late October, a light breeze kicking up the fallen leaves, cold enough that you needed a sweater but not so cold for a jacket. Wendy decided to go.

After stepping down the short stairway to push through the heavy door that led into the cellar bar, she spotted Thom in his usual seat, at the far curve of the bar. He was talking intently to a man whom Wendy didn't immediately recognize. She approached them, and Thom looked both surprised and genuinely pleased. A rare surge of affection for her husband pierced at her.

"Meet my new friend . . . I'm sorry, I know you told me your . . ."

The man reached out a hand and Wendy took it. "I'm Stan. Your husband was giving me the rundown on this area." His hand was very warm and very dry, and he had a faint accent that was familiar.

"You sound like you're from Dallas," she said.

"Aren't you clever? I thought I got rid of that years ago. Yes, I was from Texas, but I like to think of myself as a nomad now."

He couldn't have been older than fifty, Wendy thought, and yet he was putting on an act like he was some kind of old salt. She instantly disliked him and was annoyed at herself for giving in to pressure and leaving the house to meet Thom. She was about to say that she'd only popped in to say hi, but there was a sudden martini in front of her, courtesy of Howard, even though she hadn't ordered one.

"Thank you, Howard," she said, then added, "and don't make me another unless I ask for it."

"How is it that you so quickly recognize a Dallas accent?" Stan said.

Before Wendy had a chance to answer, Thom said, "Her first marriage. You weren't in Dallas, but—"

"I lived in Lubbock for about two years."

"Oh yeah? In college, I suppose?"

"Actually, no. But it was right after college."

"And what did you think of the Lone Star State?"

"It was a long time ago," Wendy said, quickly adding, "Stan, what do you do for work?"

"Well, I'm lucky enough to be an early retiree. I worked for twenty-five years as a police officer in Flower Mound, just outside of Dallas. Have you heard of it?"

"I haven't. What brought you here?"

He hesitated, enough for Wendy to know that he was deciding what to say. "Well, I've always loved to fish, and I was all set to head to Corpus Christi like I usually do, and then I thought to myself, now that I'm a man of leisure, why not travel around America and see what fishing is like in different parts of the country? So I'm on an epic road trip. And New Essex was pretty much first on my list."

His Texas accent, through the course of this story, had noticeably strengthened.

"You should talk to Rick. He should be in here later tonight, and he'll happily bore you with fishing stories."

"Oh, you know, I think I talked with Rick a few nights ago."

"Yeah, that was Rick," Thom was saying, and Wendy realized that Stan had been hanging around the Tavern for a while.

The door swung open and two older couples came in, probably having just finished their dinner at the upstairs restaurant. Stan slid down the bar and back to his seat. Wendy and Thom clinked glasses.

"It's so nice you came," Thom said.

"Jason convinced me. God knows what he's up to right now."

Thom lowered his voice and said, "What was up with you and Stan?"

"What do you mean?"

"You were acting pretty chilly toward him."

"Well, I suppose so. You ever meet someone and instantly dislike them?" After saying this, Wendy realized that Thom had probably never experienced something like that. It was a fundamental difference between them.

"He seems okay," Thom said.

Wendy requested a glass of ice from Howard, poured her martini on top of it, and then asked him to add tonic. She had decided to stick around that night, at least until Thom was ready to go. The door swung open again, and several more people entered, a couple of tourists (the past few years the tourist season had been expanding all the way through November), and then Fred Hayes, one of their neighbors. Wendy asked him to join them.

While chatting with Fred, she watched Stan, who was very slowly nursing what looked like a light beer, a drink he'd been lucky to get from Howard. Now that she was able to study him, she realized he was older than he looked. It was just that he was still fit and had a full head of dark hair. But his hands were ropy and his face was sun-damaged, his cheeks rosy with those tiny broken vessels that hard drinkers sometimes get. Yet he was deliberately not drinking much tonight. And watching him now, she had a strong feeling that he was here—here on Goose Neck, here at the Tavern—because of them. It was a feeling she'd had before, that they were being watched by someone, and even though that feeling in the past hadn't amounted to anything, she was convinced that Stan was an exception.

Fred, like Thom, was a big fan of classic Hollywood, and the two of them were trying to impress each other by naming particularly obscure films that they loved. Wendy asked Howard how the summer season was, and he smiled. "My faith in humanity is diminished, but my wallet is fatter."

"Sounds like an even trade."

"I'd say so. Can I get you something else?"

"Just a plain old soda water, please. With a lemon."

After he'd brought her the drink, Wendy asked him what he knew about the new guy, tilting her head toward Stan's seat, unoccupied for now, although there was a coaster on his beer to indicate he'd be back.

"Been here every night for a week. He's your husband's new best friend."

"Looks that way," Wendy said.

When she and Thom left, the temperature had dropped, and she wished she'd brought at least a light jacket. Walking back along the narrow lane, Wendy scanned the license plates of the nearby parked cars. She spotted what was definitely a rental car, a white Ford Fusion with one of those barcode stickers in the window. "Why are you studying cars?" Thom said.

"I didn't know I was."

Lying in bed that night, Thom downstairs watching the World Series, Wendy wondered why she simply hadn't told Thom her suspicions about his new friend, Stan. Maybe because it would sound like she was being paranoid, but she didn't think that was it. Because, in truth, she didn't think she was being paranoid. When Bryce, her first husband, had died, it had been very clear to her that Bryce's older sister, Sloane, firmly believed that Wendy had been responsible. She'd said as much at the funeral, and she'd also managed, along with a few other members of the Barrington clan, to hold up Wendy's inheritance as long as she could. It wouldn't surprise Wendy at all if Sloane had decided to hire a private investigator to take another look at Bryce's death. Stan—had he told her his last name? She didn't think so—was from Texas, an ex-cop, weirdly interested in talking with Thom. His story didn't exactly add up either. If he was on an "epic road trip" to different fishing areas all around the country, wouldn't he be doing that in his own car? Possibly, but maybe not. Still, she didn't see any cars with Texas plates outside of the Tavern, and she had spotted a very obvious rental car. Who knew if it was his. Still, she felt in her gut that Stan was bad news somehow. The question was: Why now?

The following night Thom was playing trivia at a brewery in Beverly with a few of his work colleagues and Jason was over at his friend Julia's house to watch a movie. Wendy went down to the Tavern by herself after dinner, surprised again by how crowded it was but not surprised to see Stan at the bar. There was a free seat next to him, and she went and sat there. Stan swiveled to face her. "Just you tonight?"

"Just me."

Howard brought her a gin and tonic, unprompted but at least it wasn't a martini, and Stan began peppering her with questions, mostly about the town, how long she'd lived there, what she did for work. Basic stuff. She began to think she was wrong about her suspicions, but after she'd asked for her bill, Stan said, "Thom said you used to live in Texas?"

"Well, a lifetime ago."

"Where exactly?"

"Near Lubbock, like I told you already. It was for a total of about two years."

"What did your husband do?"

Wendy decided that even if this Stan character wasn't somehow sent by some member of her ex-husband's family, he was annoying her with his constant questions.

"He was a musician," she said. "His name was Declan MacManus."

Stan was nodding, but he'd given himself away. She could tell by the expression on his face that he was trying to figure out how to deal with the fact that she'd just lied to him.

"You're either a very nosy person, Stan," Wendy said, "or you're a very mediocre private detective."

He laughed, and she realized it was the first time she'd seen him open his mouth that wide. His teeth were stained yellow by a lifetime of smoking. "Why do you say that?"

"Because you're prying. And because you're being very obvious about it. I'm going to guess that you were hired by my ex-sister-in-law, and that you're looking into the death of Bryce Barrington."

She watched him think about how to answer, and then he said, "Did you know that your current husband was in Austin, Texas, on the weekend that your previous husband drowned in his pool?"

Her chest tightened, and she hoped that her voice sounded normal as she said, "So you are a private detective. Did Sloane hire you?"

"I'm afraid I can't disclose my client, but, yes, I will disclose that I'm looking into the death of Bryce Barrington. My client believes there's significant new information to warrant reopening an investigation."

"Is this new information that Thom, who I didn't know at the time, happened to be in the same state when Bryce drowned?"

"Not just that. And you did know him already."

"Not at the time," Wendy said, alarm rising in her.

"Weren't you at school with him in Ringwood, New Hampshire?"

Wendy, somewhat impressed, said, "Yes, we knew each other when we were fourteen, but I didn't know him at all when I was first married. We met again long after my husband died. Do you think my husband fell in love with me in middle school and then flew to Texas to murder my husband so he could have me all for himself?"

"I don't really think anything at all," Stan said. "I'm just trying to figure out any and all possibilities. For instance, maybe the two of you did stay in contact with each other after you were kids, and because no one really knew that you two knew each other, he was the perfect person to come and murder your husband while you were out of town."

"My husband wasn't murdered. He drowned in his own swimming pool."

"What about Alexandra Fritsch?"

Wendy said, "I don't know who that is."

"She died the same night as your husband did. She was a college student who was stabbed to death in downtown Lubbock. She was also part of the Caprock College prostitution ring. You remember that whole scandal?"

Wendy had been jarred by the fact that this hired detective had figured out that Thom had been in Texas when Bryce had died, *and* knew that Thom and she had attended the same middle school, but now he was talking about a college prostitution ring and she realized that he probably had nothing. "None of this is ringing any bells for me, but it wouldn't surprise me if my husband had some connection with prostitution. It was not a good marriage. I'm sure you know that. He was out drinking every night without me. I'm sure he wasn't faithful."

"So you wouldn't say that your marriage to Bryce Barrington was a happy one."

"I'm not sure any of that is your business, but, no, it wasn't happy. And, no, I didn't kill him. Did you tell my husband who you really were?"

"I thought I'd get to know him first before divulging that. He's a very nice man."

"He is. Look, Stan . . . What's your full name, by the way? Is it even Stan?"

"Stan Benally. Nice to properly meet you, Wendy Eastman." He put out his hand, and Wendy, despite wanting to refuse, found herself automatically shaking his hand again, surprised once more by how warm and dry his palm was.

"Look, Stan. I'm happy you're being paid by one or another Barrington for this fishing trip, but you're not going to find anything, because there's nothing to find."

"You know, Wendy, I'd agree with you about that, except that when I asked your husband if he had ever been to Texas, he insisted that he hadn't."

A surge of annoyance at her dim-witted husband went through her, but Wendy simply said, "Honestly, he's a little forgetful these days."

"Why's that?"

She took a deep breath, hoping Stan could tell how irritated she was getting. "He drinks too much and sometimes he forgets things. Look, I'm getting pissed off at you right now, so I'm going to go home. I assume you'll pay for my drink."

"I'll put it on my expense account," he said as he slid a business card along the bar to her. She almost left it there, but took it just in case.

Walking home under a canopy of particularly bright stars, Wendy considered calling her husband on his cell and telling him to come right home. But he'd already be relatively drunk, and she wanted to talk to him when he was sober. It could wait until the following morning. When she got home she poured herself a glass of wine and went out and sat on their screened-in porch, despite the cold night. She didn't know what was more stupid, the fact that Thom had lied about being in Texas, or the fact that he hadn't figured out that his new friend at the bar was the world's most obvious private detective.

A car pulled into their drive, its headlights passing across the screen of the porch. She heard a door slam and Jason yell out "Thank you!" He came in the back of the house and Wendy shouted out to him that she was on the porch. He joined her, telling her all about the film he'd seen, something called *Once* that was apparently about Irish singers.

ii

Thom's only class on Friday was in the afternoon so he was planning on sleeping in a little, but Wendy had shaken him awake and told him that they needed to have a talk before she left for work. He dressed, his mind flipping through the assorted possibilities of what he'd done wrong.

"Am in trouble?" he said, sliding onto a stool at their kitchen counter. Wendy was eating toast with jam, her everyday breakfast.

"Maybe. I don't know," she said, and something in her face alarmed him. She looked nervous.

"I should get myself a coffee first," he said.

"Stay there. I'll get it."

As she handed his mug over to him, she said, "Your friend Stan from the Tavern is a private investigator. He's looking into Bryce's death."

"What?" Thom said.

"How did you not figure that out, Thom? It was pretty obvious."

"Seriously?" Thom said. "How did I not figure out that the random guy at the bar was investigating me for something that happened twenty years ago?"

Wendy lowered her voice and said, "We always knew we would need to be vigilant our entire lives. We always knew that we needed to assume we were being watched. We talked about this."

"I am vigilant."

"Apparently not."

"I didn't tell him anything."

"You told him you'd never been to Texas."

"Right. What's wrong with that?"

"Because you have been, Thom, and he knows that. Apparently, there are records that you flew there, or else he talked with your friends in Austin. Who knows? It doesn't matter, but he knows that you lied to him."

"Jesus," Thom said. Bile suddenly rose up in the back of his throat and he thought he might be sick. He swallowed some of the bitter coffee. "I didn't even think anything of it. He's from Texas, and when he asked me, I mean, I'd forgotten . . ."

"Look, forget about it. I'm going to take care of this, Thom. Don't talk to him again, okay? Even if he approaches you here, or at your office. Or go ahead and talk to him, but don't say anything. Just tell him you forgot you were ever there. That's what I told him."

"When did you even talk to him?"

Wendy told Thom about the whole conversation the previous night. As she spoke, he found himself fixated on the cords of her neck, particularly prominent either because she was mad, or because she'd aged and he was just now noticing.

"But they won't actually find anything?" he said, when Wendy was done, hoping he didn't sound like a child looking for reassurance.

"Of course not. We always knew the family would suspect me. But they can't prove anything. There's nothing to worry about, so long as you don't say anything stupid."

Thom's stomach roiled and he got up, told Wendy he was going to the bathroom. He felt terrible, although that might have been the result of the celebratory whiskey sour he'd drunk the night before when his trivia team—the Goose Life—had a come-from-behind win. That seemed like a hundred years ago.

When he came back into the kitchen, he apologized to Wendy, who was putting on her coat to go to work.

"Maybe you should drink at home for a while," she said.

"I'll drink less. Or not at all. I need to anyway. What are we going to do about this guy?"

"I'm going to take care of him. And now that we know who he is, we can just refuse to talk with him. There's nothing to worry about. Besides, I don't think it's that big a deal that you were in Texas at the time. To him either. He's more interested in a dead woman that Bryce was probably sleeping with."

"What?" Thom said.

"Sorry, I forgot that part. Alexandra Fritsch, I think. She was a college student who was possibly even involved in prostitution who died the same time as Bryce did. I have no idea what that might have to do with anything. You okay?"

"I'm fine. I drank too much last night."

"I have to go. I'm late for a meeting."

After Wendy had left, Thom went to the bathroom and was violently ill.

iii

The first thing Wendy did when she got to her office was cancel the all-staff meeting—a brainstorming session for the new mission statement—a meeting that could easily be put off for a while. Instead, she closed her office door, opened up her laptop, and tried to remember the name of the woman Stan the detective had been talking about. She put in a search for "Fritsch" and "Lubbock," and the story came up. Alexandra Fritsch had been a student at Caprock College who was stabbed to death on August 22, 1992, the same day that Bryce had drowned. Her mind reeled with possibilities. Was Alexandra somehow with Bryce the night he died? It didn't make any sense. She had died in Lubbock, while he had been home in Happy Lake.

What was most concerning to her was Thom's face when she had mentioned the woman's death. Nothing in his expression had changed, but he'd turned white, the blood just draining away. And in that moment she wondered if he had not told her everything that had happened in 1992. A door opened inside of her, a door to a room that had a hundred possibilities. They were meant to tell each other everything, Thom and her. No secrets. And now she had to wonder if there had been a witness? And if there had been, why hadn't Thom told her about it? She felt her body tensing, so she dropped her shoulders, took a breath, and told herself that it was entirely possible that the bloodless expression on Thom's face had more to do with how much he'd had to drink the night before. She'd seen him on enough hungover mornings to know that he spent half the day fighting nausea until it was time for his first drink. Still, that version of events was not as convincing to her as the version in which Thom had concealed something major about what had happened in Texas. Wendy thought about getting back in her car, driving to the house, and demanding that he tell her everything. That was what she would have done ten years ago. They were in it together, after all, for better or worse. But some part of her was worried that Thom couldn't handle whatever it was that might have happened. And she wasn't quite sure that she even wanted to hear the truth. She'd rather just solve the problem.

She dug into her purse and pulled out the card she'd gotten the night before. All it said was: "Stanley Benally, Security Consultant," and then a phone number. She wondered if he was an actual accredited private investigator. His title seemed to suggest otherwise. She called him and arranged a meeting.

That afternoon, Thom now at the university, Wendy went home early from work and opened their bedroom safe. She took one of their gold bars, a kilogram's worth, then decided to grab two more items she thought she might need. She'd bought the gold bars during the 2008 recession after watching their stock portfolios crater to almost nothing. She'd often thought that the bars were her version of the envelope of cash that her mother used to keep hidden in the back of the freezer.

Stan was staying at the only cheap place left on the peninsula, the Shoreview Motel, room number 19. Wendy parked across the road in the lot of a strip mall that included a convenience store, a dance studio, and the worst Chinese restaurant Wendy had ever ordered food from. She crossed the road, her purse heavy at her side, and knocked on Benally's door. He let her in.

She'd never been inside one of the Shoreview Motel's rooms, but it was exactly as she'd imagined it. Dark, musty-smelling, with ancient seaside prints on the wall. She sat on the single chair and Benally sat on the edge of the bed. He was wearing gray suit pants and a white shirt with a yellow sheen to it.

"I think I know what happened, but your client isn't going to like it," she said, hoping it didn't sound too rehearsed.

"What's that?"

"I was out of town, as you know, on the night that Bryce drowned. I was happy to get away from him, and he was probably just as happy to be alone. He was a piece of shit. And there's no doubt that he was probably involved with prostitution."

"So you do think they're connected?"

"I have no idea. I'd never heard of the woman you mentioned. All I'm saying is it wouldn't surprise me one bit if Bryce had been out that night, in town, drinking. I don't think he was some kind of murderer, that he would have that in him, but maybe she accidentally died and he tried to make it look like a murder. I have no idea. And if that's the case, then maybe he came home and drowned himself in the pool."

Stan smiled at her, showing his terrible teeth. "Yeah, I thought of that. But that's not what my client thinks happened."

"Do I even want to know?"

"My client thinks that Alexandra Fritsch was a witness to what happened to Bryce and that's why she was killed."

"What happened to Bryce was that he stupidly fell into his own pool and couldn't get out. Your client is grasping at straws. And trust me, my husband had nothing to do with this. He can't even remember he ever went to Texas."

"Well, I think he probably can remember," Stan said. "Why don't you tell me why you really came here."

"You can do what you want, obviously," she said. "But I'm here to ask you a favor. I want Sloane Barrington out of my life. She's been dogging me with this for years because I got more of the family money than she did. That's what this is all about. Nothing more. And I don't want my husband, who is going through some tough times right now, to be bothered. That's all I want."

"Your husband seemed fine to me."

"You saw my husband when he was drinking. That's the only time he's fine."

Stan uncrossed and recrossed his legs, then said, "Yes, my client did mention to me that you walked away with quite a lot of what she called *her* money."

Wendy took a deep breath, hoping it wasn't visible. Stan was willing to negotiate. It was what she had been hoping for, and she said, trying to make it sound casual, "So, what's it going to take to get you to return to Texas and tell her you found nothing?"

Back outside of the motel room thirty minutes later, Wendy had to squint her eyes against the bright sunshine. Had it been this sunny earlier? She couldn't remember.

Walking across the tarmac, a male voice spoke to her from her left. "Is that Wendy Graves?"

She turned to see Alex Deighton, her husband's disgusting co-worker, coming from around his midlife-crisis Mustang with an enormous grin on his face.

"Well, well, well, it is you." He turned back to look at the door she'd emerged from. "What are *you* doing here, Wendy?"

"None of your business, Alex, and I could ask the same of you."

"The difference is I'd tell you all about it, if you were interested in hearing."

Wendy shook her head. "Not interested, I'm afraid. And I have to get going."

"Where's your car?" he said, swiveling his head to look around at the parking lot, and then noticing the strip mall across the road. "Oh, your car is over there. You really are up to no good, Wendy. If I was a different sort of man, I could blackmail you with this information."

"Alex, I'm not in the mood right now. I'm late. Goodbye."

As she crossed the road to retrieve her car, she could feel his eyes on her, making her feel helpless and exposed. And by the time she'd pulled back into her own driveway, those feelings had morphed into something else entirely. She'd never liked Alex—no one really did—but what she felt now was pure hatred. And a little bit of fear that he had something on her.

Back at home she fed Samsa, then took her purse with her to the upstairs bedroom. She'd brought along several items she thought she might have to use in the motel room with Benally. The first was a condom she'd managed to find deep in the top shelf of the medicine cabinet, which she returned unopened. Then she opened up the safe and put back both the stun gun and the leather sap. Those had been more for self-defense than anything, although a plan had briefly formulated in her brain that had Stan Benally dead in his shower as though he'd taken a bad fall. But she was happy it hadn't come to that. She had no real issue with the detective, who was just doing his job.

Before shutting the safe, she looked at the remaining gold bars, six of them, and didn't think that Thom would ever notice that one had disappeared.

She was exhausted and lay down on the bed, Samsa sidling up to her, hoping for attention. She closed her eyes while idly stroking his back. What she was thinking about was Alex Deighton and his smarmy smile, the pleasure he'd felt that he'd learned something about her. There had always been a part of her that felt bad that her husband Thom was the one who had to live with the memories of the murder he had committed (that *they* had committed). Now, at least, she had a perfectly good candidate for a murder of her own. Just the thought of it made her feel better.

2011

Judy, Wendy's best friend at work, was moving to D.C. in one week, so they were planning as many lunches as possible in the remaining time. And since it was a Friday, they were currently on the deck of the Rockaway Hotel. It was an ideal September day in Massachusetts, the air warm and dry, the tourists relatively sparse. They each ordered the fish tacos, and they were sharing a bottle of Sauvignon Blanc between them. "It feels like we're on vacation." It was something Judy always said whenever they went to the Rockaway for lunch.

"I can't believe you're leaving me."

"I know. You'll come to visit, though."

"Of course I will," Wendy said, knowing it was a lie. She liked Judy, but she also knew that she was just a work friend, and they'd keep in touch for a little while but would probably never see each other again after Judy moved. Their food arrived, the waiter splashing more wine into both of their glasses. As they began to eat, Wendy watched Judy's eyes go a little big. She was turned away from the sun, facing the inside portion of the restaurant.

"Who did you just see?" Wendy said, beginning to turn.

"It's Thom. He's not alone."

Annoyed by Judy's conspiratorial whisper, Wendy fully turned in her chair. Thom was at the bar with a woman she didn't know, who had to be at least fifteen years younger than he was. Thom's attention was on the menu—probably studying the beer list—and it was clear he hadn't seen his wife out on the deck.

"Looks like he's punching above his weight," Wendy said.

"What do you mean?" Judy said, alarmed, and Wendy remembered that one of the peculiarities of her friend was her inability to understand metaphors.

"Oh, nothing. Joking. I just meant to say that if he's hoping for anything to happen between him and that woman, then good luck to him. She could be his daughter, and she's gorgeous."

Judy leaned across the table. "Does Thom cheat?"

Wendy sighed, hoping to give herself enough time to decide what to say. "No, not really. But he's a vain, middle-aged man, so I'm sure he entertains fantasies. It's no big deal. It doesn't bother me."

"Entertains what kind of fantasies?" Judy said.

"He probably just wants a woman to look at him without knowing all his flaws. He wants a do-over. Doesn't everyone?"

"Do *you* cheat?"

Judy's questions were being asked with increasing disbelief, and it made Wendy want to shock her a little, so she said, "Nothing serious, of course. Thom and I are solid, but marriages these days last a long time."

"Really?"

"Sure."

"I feel a little shocked right now. I don't know why, but I just thought that you and Thom were . . . You're kind of my couple ideal. You're so good together."

"Maybe because we don't get hung up on who we go to restaurants with."

"Oh, I'm not saying . . ."

"Judy, you're fine. Let's not let Thom ruin this lunch."

They changed the subject, Judy going on a long spiel about the girl they'd hired to replace her in the fundraising department She'd already started and Judy was training her. Wendy listened, and drank wine, and realized that her entire relationship with Judy was based on gossip, both about their coworkers and Judy's own calamitous love life. She wondered if in the next week Judy would let the rest of the office know that she and Thom were in some kind of open relationship. It wasn't even true. Thom had had a few flings, of course, and many infatuations, and she'd chalked them up to nothing more than a way for him to keep his life interesting, or hopeful. She knew he dwelled on the past, and that taking out the cute new teaching assistant or whoever it was had helped him to cope. The only thing she ever really worried about was that he'd truly fall in love with someone else and tell them what he'd done. What they'd done. As for herself, she'd had one affair, or sexual encounter, with a man she'd met at a conference in St. Louis three years earlier. He'd been ridiculously handsome, or maybe it was just his English accent. Either way, she'd decided to see what it was like, because she knew at the time that Thom was up to something, showing up at the house every two weeks or so smelling of cheap perfume and alcohol, like some cliché in a country song. The man she'd slept with—Jacob Lambert (even his name was attractive)—had confessed to her after their rather brief coupling that he was struggling with a sex addiction that had wrecked his marriage. It was more than she wanted to hear, and she'd walked away from his hotel room with the knowledge that she would never cheat again. She already had one thin-skinned, needy man in her life. Why would she want another?

"Oh my God, I'm going to miss it here," Judy said, looking out toward the ocean.

"Judy," Wendy said, "can you do me a favor and not mention what I just told you to anyone at work. It's just—"

"God, no, I would never. It's just between us."

"Thank you."

"And since it's just between us, who was it? Anyone I know?"

Wendy considered making something up, but in the end told Judy about the Englishman in St. Louis, and how he cried afterward because of his sex addiction. It was a nice change to their dynamic, actually, since Wendy was usually the one listening to Judy's dating horror stories.

"You said he was good-looking, though," Judy said, then asked if they should order another bottle of wine.

"I should go back to the office, just to show my face. You can do whatever you want because we can't fire you."

"Are you going to go say hi to Thom?"

"I don't think so, unless he's noticed me. Do you think he has?"

"Definitely not."

"I think I'll leave him alone, and see what he tells me this evening about his afternoon."

"Good plan," Judy said, again in the conspiratorial whisper. Wendy was suddenly relieved that her coworker would be moving soon.

When Thom finally arrived home that evening, after eight, he was noticeably very drunk, the raw smell of alcohol seeping out of his skin, plus the fainter smell of cigarettes. "You've had an afternoon," Wendy said when he joined her on the front porch, carrying a large water in one hand and some kind of mixed drink in the other.

"Honestly, I've only had a few ales," Thom said in an English accent. He was quoting from *Withnail and I*, a movie she'd never particularly liked.

"I saw you today at the Rockaway. With your date?"

"You did? When was that?"

"I was there with Judy. She's insisting on daily going-away lunches. Who was she?"

"Well, at lunchtime my date was the lovely Emma Levieva. She was in that summer dance program that Lorraine is running, but you missed the deluge."

"What do you mean?"

"It was the welcome-back party for the arts faculty. And kind of a going-away party for some of the summer staff. It was a scene."

"Who was there?"

"The usual suspects. Alex made a hideous speech."

"To whom?"

"To everyone. I mean, not everyone listened, but he made it anyway."

"What else happened?"

As Thom dug back into his recent memory to tell her about his afternoon, Wendy tried to remember if he'd told her in advance about the event. She thought he probably had, and maybe she'd been uninterested enough to forget about it. But the more he talked, the more she realized just how drunk he really was, repeating himself, slurring certain words. She was glad that Jason was out at the movies with Julia and her parents.

Later that night, together on the couch, watching Thom's new Criterion edition DVD of *The Night of the Hunter*, Wendy found herself studying Thom in the flickering glow of the television. He was sipping whiskey, staring at the movie, occasionally turning to make some comment on what was happening. She felt conflicted, a feeling she'd had for a while now. On the one hand, she wanted her husband to be stronger, to drink less, to have some control over his life. This current state he seemed to be in pissed her off. But she also felt some pity for him, and when she felt pity she could visualize him as the boy she'd first met all those years ago. Thom had only been a few years older than Jason was now. She wondered what would have happened if he'd never sat down beside her on that school bus. A part of her thought that her life would have been worse, and his life might have been better. But she wasn't sure.

Thom turned to her and held out two fists, showing his knuckles, and said, "Look, hate and hate." He was referencing the film they were watching. Robert Mitchum had tattoos on his knuckles, one that said love and one that said hate.

"That's not how you see yourself, is it?"

"Sometimes," Thom said, laughing. "I mean, I am a bad guy."

A few weeks earlier, another night when Thom had drunk himself into a dark hole, he'd come to bed and woken Wendy up to ask her if they were going to hell when they died. He'd seemed deranged, laughing at himself, but with what looked like genuine tears in his eyes. The next day she asked him how he was feeling, and it was clear from his answer that he had no recollection of that night. She wondered if right now he wasn't properly forming memories.

"There's lots of love in you, Thom," she said.

"No, I know. But other people wouldn't see it that way. Not if they knew what I'd done."

She decided not to answer, hoping the topic would go away, but after a moment he said, "Maybe I'll tattoo 'love' on just one knuckle and 'hate' on the others." He was talking too loudly.

"Shhh," she said. "Jason will be home soon."

He pressed a hand to one of his eyes, and she thought for a moment he was going to burst into tears. She slid over to him and put a hand on either side of his face. "You're a good man, Thom Graves. No one is defined by one single thing."

"I know, I know," he said, his jaw tight, trying not to cry.

"Listen to me. You need to keep it together. Not just for me, but for Jason now. The past is the past."

"You've moved on?" he asked her, his voice cracking.

She could see the reflection of the television in his eyes, and she turned to the screen, the children floating down a river at night. She took the remote and paused the film.

"I haven't forgotten," she said. "But yes, I've moved on. We can't go back and change things. And if I could go back and change things, I'm not sure I would. We have a good life now, don't we?"

"We do, we do." He was fully crying now, his teeth clenched, shoulders shaking.

She hugged him closer, feeling his tears on her own cheek, and even though she was dreading hearing the return of Jason, due any minute, she felt a deep surge of love for her husband. "Shhh," she said, and pulled him closer.

"We do have a good life," he said through the tears. "They don't, but we do."

"Who's 'they'?" she said, but he was crying harder now, and he never answered.

Ten minutes later, when he'd finally stopped crying, Thom got up and went to the bathroom. He came back with a new drink, his face wet from splashing it with water. "I'm a mess," he said. "When's Jason getting back?"

"I thought he'd be back already. Why don't you go to bed?"

"Okay," he said, then looked at the whiskey in his hand. He seemed confused.

"Thanks for the drink," Wendy said, taking the glass from him and having a long sip at it, trying not to shudder. "Let's take you up to bed."

He was asleep by the time she heard the car in the gravel driveway that meant that Connie Alvarez was dropping Jason off. She went downstairs to meet him. He had lots to say about the *Planet of the Apes* film he'd seen, but she could tell he was tired and managed to get him into his bedroom with the door closed by eleven. Then she brushed her teeth and went into the master bedroom. Thom was snoring in the way he did when he'd had too much to drink, silences punctuated by explosive guttural sounds. She got onto her side of the bed, slid under the single sheet, and cracked open *The Year of Magical Thinking* by Joan Didion. She had only a few pages left to go, but she couldn't concentrate. Instead, she watched Thom in the oblivion of his sleep. How would she feel if he never woke up, if his heart suddenly stopped in the middle of the night? She'd be upset, of course, but also partly something else. Relieved? Lightened? He was unwell right now, and there was no reason to suspect that he was going to get better. It was true what she'd told him about her husband, how she had no regrets. But sometimes she regretted that she hadn't found a way to do it herself.

She turned off her reading lamp and curled into the position she liked to sleep in. Who's "they"? she thought to herself, remembering Thom's words. Then dismissed it. Tomorrow Thom would be sober. Maybe they could do something as a family. It was a Saturday, after all, and the weather was supposed to be nice.

2009

i

"I'm going to call," Thom said.

"He's probably just walking around in circles somewhere day-dreaming."

"Still." He had the landline phone in his hand. "Do you know the number?"

Wendy checked her cellphone for Connie's number and read it aloud to Thom. She wished he'd give it a few more minutes. Somehow, as soon as the call was made everything was going to change. Jason would be officially missing.

"Oh, hey, Connie," Thom said. "Jason's not still there, is he?"

Wendy could hear the timbre of Connie's nasal voice but not the words.

"No, not yet," Thom said. "He's probably just lollygagging. Do you know exactly when he left?"

After ending the phone call Thom looked up at Wendy. His face had lost all its color. "I'll go look for him."

"Okay," Wendy said. Seeing Thom's face made it even more real somehow than the phone call to Connie, although she was telling herself there was nothing to worry about. Jason had been walking back and forth to his best friend Julia's house for the whole of the summer. It wasn't far, just under a mile, but there was one semi-busy street to cross, and she also knew that Jason sometimes cut across the conservation land up near the ledge, even though Thom had told him not to do it.

"You stay here," Thom said.

"Where are you going to look?"

"I'll just backtrack over to Mount Salem Street."

"You'll check the woods?"

"I told him I didn't want him to go through there."

Wendy shrugged at him.

"Right, I'll check," Thom said.

"I wish you had a cellphone," Wendy said. It had been a constant fight for the past few years, Thom determined to become the last person in the world to get a cellphone.

"I know, I know. I'll get one, okay? But I don't have one right now."

"Take mine, and if you find him, then call me here, okay?"

Thirty minutes later Thom hadn't returned and he hadn't called, and Wendy dialed her cell number from the kitchen phone.

"I haven't found him," Thom said.

"You've been in the woods?"

"Yes, but I'm at Connie's now. Julia said that he left exactly at five p.m."

"Oh God," Wendy said, checking her watch, even though she knew it was almost six thirty.

"Look, Bob's here now and he's going to help me look."

"We should call the police, I think."

"Yes, okay. Let's do it. You'll call?"

"I'll call."

It was a police officer named Sean Berry who finally found Jason in Brimbal Woods. It was just after eight, the sun having set. The officer had taken his flashlight and gone off the trails when he heard Jason yelling out a feeble-sounding call for help. It turned out that their nine-year-old son had climbed one of the larger boulders in the woods, then had fallen off its side and lodged himself down into a crevice between two rocks. His ankle was badly sprained and his head was bleeding. He'd been shouting for help so much that his voice had gone hoarse.

Jason was taken to New Essex Memorial, had his ankle wrapped, and was given a cognition test. Wendy couldn't take her eyes off of him. He looked the same as he had that morning, but somehow completely different. In the two hours he'd been missing she'd somehow already said goodbye to him, convincing herself that he was gone and that the remainder of her life was going to be empty and terrible. She'd even prayed, briefly, something she'd decided to keep to herself. She hadn't been raised with any kind of religion, but in the fifth grade her father had moved the family to Sweetgum, Florida, for a year, and the only friend she'd made had been a girl named Kristi, who convinced her that since she hadn't been baptized she was going straight to hell when she died. Kristi's family had taken Wendy to church, and for about a month after that Wendy had decided that prayer was her only chance at avoiding eternal damnation. It had been a habit that lasted a month, and yet Wendy had prayed that night, begging a god she didn't believe in for a miracle.

After Jason had hobbled off to bed, she and Thom walked back downstairs, holding hands. Thom went out to the front porch and Wendy asked him if he wanted a drink.

"I don't know. Maybe I'm going to quit drinking."

"I would argue that your timing is off. I'm pouring myself a gigantic glass of wine."

"I'll have some wine, I guess. A small glass."

They sat together and stared out toward the cove. On some nights, if there was fog and no starlight, it was like staring out into the abyss, the edge of the world.

"I thought we lost him," Wendy said.

"I knew we lost him," Thom said. "No, that's not true. I didn't *know*, but I felt in my heart that he was gone. That someone had come along with a van and kidnapped him, and we were never going to see him again, never going to know what happened."

"That's what I thought too."

They were quiet for a moment, Wendy trying to savor the fact that the world had returned to normality.

"I thought we were being punished," Thom said.

It took her a moment to realize what he was saying, then Wendy replied, "Even if something horrible had happened, it still wouldn't have been punishment."

"What do you mean?"

"It doesn't work like that."

"How do you know?"

They hadn't had this particular conversation for a long time, and Wendy searched in her mind for a way to end it quickly without getting into a fight. "It's possible, of course, but you know I don't think about the world like that."

"Some people are punished for what they do. And some people are rewarded for being good. That's a fact."

"Of course it is," Wendy said. "I just don't think those things happen for a reason, or not for the reason you think they do. There's no guiding hand in the universe dealing out karma and rewarding humans for their good behavior."

"Lots of people think there is."

"Well, yeah. Religious people. Look, I don't want to fight, but I think you're being argumentative for the sake of it. You believe exactly what I believe."

"Why? Because I'm not religious?" Thom said. "Don't forget I used to go to church."

"Did you pray?"

Thom said nothing, and Wendy continued. "The reason I know you believe what I believe is because you're a logical human being. You know that people do terrible things all the time and get away with them. And you know that terrible things happen to good people. It's random."

"It's not *completely* random, though, is it? If I work hard at being a good neighbor, when I need help then my neighbors will help me. And . . . let me finish . . . if I'm law-abiding, if I don't commit crimes, then I won't go to prison."

"I think you're being naïve, and I think you know that you're being naïve. Yes, we are lucky enough to happen to live in a country with a decent justice system for people who are like us, but that's it. Being a good person is a guarantee of nothing. I mean, it's possible that you can tip the scales, right? I agree with that. Same with health. I can eat my five fruits and vegetables a day or I can only eat cheeseburgers, but it's no guarantee of anything. Healthy people drop dead all the time."

The lights were off on the porch and Wendy couldn't see the expression on Thom's face, but he didn't immediately respond. "Another drink?" he finally said.

"Are we done with this argument?"

"It's not an argument. I think it's a fundamental difference between us."

Wendy felt a pulse of anger go through her. It had always bothered her that every argument they had led to Thom sulking about it. "Look," she said. "It bothers me because I know, down deep, that we are on the same page here. Or very close to the same page. I just think the big difference is that you wish the world were a different place."

"And you don't?" He had leaned forward in his spring chair, and his voice had gone a little shrill.

"Of course I wish the world had more justice and equality and all that stuff. That's not the point. It doesn't."

"If the world had more justice, then you and I would probably be in prison right now."

"Okay," Wendy said. "Jesus. Maybe right now is not the time for this conversation."

"I'm going to get another drink. Do you want more wine?"

"No, I'm fine," Wendy said.

He went to the kitchen and Wendy looked out at the cove, still dark, although she could make out a faint line of lights across the other side of the harbor in West Essex. The wind must have turned, because she could smell the low tide. She heard Thom returning to the porch and turned to him. But it was Jason, in his pajamas. "I can't sleep," he said.

"Come here."

He came and slid onto her lap, something he hadn't done in a year, at least. "You scared us tonight," she said.

"What did you think happened to me?"

"I don't know. Lots of things. That you fell off a boulder and hit your head. Oh, wait, that *did* happen."

"Did you think I was kidnapped?"

"Honestly, we didn't know what had happened, honey, and that was what was so scary. But no, I don't really worry about kidnappers around here."

Thom came back onto the porch and quietly returned to his chair.

"What do you think would have happened to me if I'd been trapped out there all night?" Jason said.

"I think we would have found you in the morning. But I think that all of us would have had a very scary night."

"It would have been a better story."

"What do you mean? If you'd been out there all night?"

"Yeah." Jason had a big grin on his face. "It might have made the news or something."

Thom said, "We can take you back out there if you'd like, stick you between those rocks, and come back in the morning. How does that sound?"

"Eh," Jason said, a new expression of his, usually said with both his hands out with his palms up.

"You're happy here at home?" Wendy said.

"Eh," he said again.

"How's the head?"

"It doesn't really hurt anymore. My ankle does, though."

"That's good. We'd rather have ankle trauma than head trauma."

"Ankle amputation?" Jason said.

"I don't think they amputate ankles, do they? It would be hard to do without also amputating the foot."

"What about head amputations?"

"They do do those, but generally not for medical reasons."

Thom stood again, and Wendy thought he was going to bring Jason back up to bed. "One more of these," he said. He was now holding a lowball glass. Whiskey, she guessed. "Wendy, wine? Can I get you something, Jason?"

"I'll have what you're having."

"One glass of warm milk coming up."

After he left, Jason said, "How long do you think it takes to starve to death in the woods?"

ii

The following morning, Thom stared at his computer, attempting to work on his John Cheever article, but he was unable to concentrate.

Instead, he opened up an empty Word document, wrote "STORY" at the top, then put down one line: "Edgar Dixon, dodging imaginary arrows showering down from the castle ramparts, lost his footing and wound up pinned between a pair of boulders that had existed since before the invention of man." He read it several times before exiting out of the document, opting not to save. After going to stand at his office window and staring out at the cove, filled with one-man sailboats—a class was in session—Thom returned to his computer and looked at his emails. There was a new one from Wendy, letting him know that she would be leaving soon with Jason to go to the quarry with Julia and her mom. Thom wrote back: "I'm right upstairs, you know." Then he stared at his screen waiting for a reply. When it finally came, she had written: "Sorry. Samsa in my lap. We are going in twenty. In or out?"

Thom wandered downstairs, said hello to Jason, who was reading on the living room couch, then popped into Wendy's office. Samsa really was in her lap, but jumped off as Wendy swiveled toward Thom. "I think I'll pass on the quarry," he said.

"Really?"

"Yeah, I have work. You think Jason will be okay to swim?"

"No, but he can lay on a towel and read. He'll be fine."

"He will," Thom said. Samsa rubbed up against his bare shin. Wendy had turned back to face her computer.

After Wendy and Jason left, Thom got the vodka bottle he kept in the freezer and poured himself two shots. He knew that if he was going to break it off with Catalina he needed to do it that afternoon and he needed to do it face-to-face. He called her landline, Cat picking up after two rings. "Hello," she said, her accent always more pronounced before she knew whom she was speaking with.

"Hi, Cat, it's Thom."

"Hi," she said, and Thom heard a question mark in her tone. They'd been secretly meeting for over a year now, the second and fourth Thursdays of the month at a dive bar in Peabody near her apartment. Sometimes they just had a few drinks. Sometimes they wound up back at her place, a tiny two-bedroom she shared with a sister who worked at a daycare in the mornings and waitressed at night. Catalina Soto was a nurse at a local hospital, a divorcée who was younger than he was, but with two grown children. Thom had met her at a reading that his department had put on, four authors each reading a short story. After the event there had been wine and cheese and Catalina had introduced herself to Thom, who had moderated. She told him that she was a writer as well, and without hesitating Thom said that he'd love to read something she wrote. The next day she emailed him a story that chronicled one night in the life of an emergency room nurse. He was relieved that he liked it, and sent her back a couple of notes, eventually suggesting they meet up for coffee.

"You're a married man?" she had said, five minutes into their first meeting at the Peabody Coffeehouse.

"I am," he said. She nodded, slowly, and Thom added, "What?"

"I'm just trying to figure out if you liked my story or if you like me. There's no wrong answer, I'm just curious."

"I did like your story. And I do like you. But yes, I'm married, and I haven't been a perfect husband, but I have no intention of ever leaving my wife."

"Oh, we're already there," she said, laughing. "Please don't leave your wife on my account."

"I'm just saying I'm happy with her, is all."

"Is she happy with you?"

"That's another story."

"Okay," she said. "Sorry to be so up-front about it, but people are so secretive about everything, don't you think?"

"I do. Oh, and I have something for you." Thom reached into his bike-messenger bag and pulled out his copy of *Jesus' Son* by Denis

Johnson. "No pressure, but I thought you might like these stories. He was a nurse too."

"Thank you," she said, and took the book.

They met three more times for coffee, then two times for afternoon drinks, before going back to Cat's apartment. Her sister was sleeping in her own bedroom—she was between shifts—and Cat told Thom that she used a white-noise machine and nothing would wake her. They stayed in bed together for over three hours that afternoon, eventually talking about Cat's failed marriage and then moving on to Thom's relationship with Wendy. He suddenly found himself fabricating a story, telling her that when he met his wife she was married and they started an affair. He told her they were living in Connecticut at the time and the husband found out, got drunk, and drove his car into a tree.

"Oh no," Cat said.

"I keep thinking I'll get over it, but I haven't yet."

"You don't need to get over it, you just need to live with it. He made his own choice, you made yours."

"I guess so."

And now, a year later, face-to-face at the same coffee shop where they'd first met, he told her that he needed to end the relationship.

"Okay," she said, and didn't seem particularly surprised.

"There's a reason, though," Thom said.

"Well, there's always a reason."

Thom told her about Jason going missing the previous night and how sure he was that Jason was dead. And he told her how, when he'd been alone in the woods, shouting out his son's name, he had dropped to his knees, and prayed. "I made a bargain," he said.

"You told God that if Jason was alive, you'd stop seeing me."

"I did."

"And now you're keeping your end of the bargain."

"Yes."

She took a sip of the green tea that she always drank and said, "I think it's time, anyway, don't you?"

"I suppose so. But I'm going to miss you."

"I'll miss you too. Oh, and I have a question for you."

"Okay."

"Did you get what you were looking for from me?"

He hesitated, and she continued. "Sorry, that sounds accusatory or something. I didn't mean it like that. It's just that when I met you, I knew that you needed something from me. I'm wondering if you found it."

"I loved getting to know you, but I'm the same person now as I was when we first met. Unfortunately. What about you? Did you get what you wanted from me?"

"Well, I liked getting to know you as well. And I loved talking to you about writing, and your book suggestions. I do have some news for you, actually."

She dug into her giant purse and pulled out an envelope, its seal torn, and handed it to Thom. He pulled the single sheet of paper out and unfolded it. She'd had a story accepted at a pretty big university journal. "That's huge," he said, and looked across at Cat, who was beaming in a way he'd never seen before.

"I mean, it's one story," she said.

"It's the start of something, Cat, it really is."

Back at home, Wendy and Jason, both still in their bathing suits, were eating peanut butter and crackers in the kitchen. Thom got himself a beer and told them that he was going to listen to the Red Sox game out on the hammock. He walked across the hot gravel of the driveway to the small yellow lawn and climbed into the hammock, realizing once he was there that he'd forgotten his radio. But he didn't have the energy to get it so he just stared at the leaves above him and listened to some nearby crows having what sounded like a contentious committee meeting. He'd done the right thing by breaking up with Catalina. He didn't really believe in God, and he certainly didn't believe that God cut deals for returned kids, but less than twenty-four hours ago he'd been in a state of grief, convinced somehow he'd lost his son forever. And now Jason was back. Something needed to be sacrificed.

He drank half his beer, spilling some of it down his chin, and remembered the other part of his prayer. He'd promised God to give up Cat, but he'd also promised to give up drinking. At the time he'd meant it. But at the time he'd also have been willing to give up anything to have Jason returned to him. Breaking it off with Cat was enough. It was a good thing. Good for him, good for Wendy and Jason. Most likely good for Cat as well. And he'd quit drinking soon enough. Maybe in January, at the start of a new year.

2005

i

"High tide," Thom said, more to himself than to Wendy, although she was in the room, unpacking yet another box.

She came and stood next to him, and together they stared through the bowed bay windows of their newly purchased Victorian and out toward Naumkeag Cove, the water choppy and almost black. "It's different every time I look at it. Can you believe we get to live here?" Thom said.

"Not really, not yet."

"I might go for a walk before it rains."

"Or you could unpack the books in your office," Wendy said.

"Or I could unpack the books in my office," Thom repeated. "That's a possibility."

On his way to his attic study, he peeked into Jason's room on the second floor. Jason had been anxious about the move, so they made sure to unpack his room first, make it look just like his room had looked in Cambridge. It had apparently worked because he was lying on his stomach on his animal-print rug, flipping through *Cars and*

Trucks and Things That Go, one of Thom's old Richard Scarry books that had been unearthed when they'd cleared out their portion of the basement at the Cambridge house.

Thom went into his own study with its sloped ceilings and its ancient metal radiator. His desk had been set up but not much else. Boxes of books lined one wall, and his grandfather's bookshelf stood empty in the middle of the room. Using his thumbnail, he opened up one of his boxes. It was the one that was filled with yearbooks from high school and college, plus an assortment of literary magazines and periodicals in which he'd published a story or some critical piece. He pulled out the Mather College yearbook from 1990 and idly flipped through it, stopping at a page called Study Abroad, finding that group picture he was in, Penelope Harrison and Annie Imbornoni and Jill Ringgold in front of the Colosseum. It was funny because he remembered so much of his time spent with Jill while she was visiting Rome but didn't really remember the four of them making that trip. And who had taken the picture? Still, it didn't matter. He studied the faces. Not really Penelope's and Annie's but his own and Jill's. They'd almost begun a romance the day before, but it hadn't happened. And a month ago, Thom had gotten his Mather College alumni magazine in the mail and read that she'd died suddenly in August. He'd called Annie and she'd told him that Jill had died in a freak accident, hit by a car in a grocery-store parking lot. Apparently she'd seemed fine immediately after it had happened, but had died that night from a brain bleed. Thom booted up his iMac, the only item currently on his desk, and waited for it to power on. He'd had the computer for over a year but they hadn't had an internet connection in Cambridge so he'd only ever used the computer for trying to write stories and articles and for playing *Bugdom*. But Wendy had insisted they get both cable television and the internet at the new house, and now it was all connected. He opened up a browser window and put in Jill Ringgold's name. An obituary came up that included several pictures. It happened so fast and Thom wasn't entirely prepared. It turned out she was married and had just had a baby. Except for the length of her hair she looked the same.

He read the obituary, written by Jill's older sister. Thom wondered, not for the first time, whether spending the night with Jill back in Rome, when it looked like they might have, would have altered her history enough so that she would still be alive. Of course it would have, he thought. Life wasn't fate but a series of tiny accidents. And if they'd spent that night together, it would have changed her life enough that she would never have been at that exact spot in that grocery-store parking lot. Of course, she might have died earlier, or maybe he would have. It was all random.

He stood up and went and stared out the window, down toward their road below. He could see a lone woman out walking a dog. She wore a yellow raincoat, and he wondered if she was a neighbor he would get to know, someone who would become important to him, or to Wendy. Would he attend her funeral? Would she attend his? He thought for some reason that the yellow raincoat indicated she was an older woman, but what did he know? Maybe she was young.

Back at his computer, Thom started a new search. He'd done it once before on one of the computers in the library at his university, but thought he'd look again. He punched in "Bryce Barrington," then "death."

There were two obituaries for Wendy's ex-husband, one from the *Lubbock Avalanche-Journal* and one from Rice University, and then there was a short news article that had been archived, an announcement that Bryce Barrington's death had been ruled an accident. The date of the article was August 25, 1992. Thom wished there were some way to see the whole newspaper from that date, but there didn't seem to be. Instead, he put in the words "death" and "Lubbock" and "1992" and hit Search. There were several results, but not what he was looking for. He added the word "prostitution" and hit Search again. This brought up an online article, "Lubbock Stabbing Prompts Investigation into Caprock College Prostitution Ring." His heartbeat now audible in his own ears, he clicked on the story, bringing up a long piece. He read only the first paragraph.

The still unsolved murder of Alexandra Fritsch, a sophomore at Caprock College, has prompted an investigation into allegations of prostitution at the elite private school. Fritsch, 19 years old, originally from Houston, was found dead from multiple stab wounds in northwest Lubbock on the night of August 22.

It was all he could read. For so long he had wanted a name, and now he had one. It was enough. He quit the browser, then thought for a moment and brought it back up. Then he cleared his browsing history and shut his computer down.

He went and stood in front of the office window again, staring at rooftops. Now that she had a name, everything had changed. A name meant she had a family, a childhood, a history. And a name meant she had truly existed. There had always been a sliver of Thom's mind that wondered if what had happened with her was some kind of awful dream, a manifestation of guilt. A gust of wind spattered rain against the windowpanes. As he turned from the window Wendy was stepping into his office. His body convulsed in fright.

"Jesus fucking Christ," he said.

Wendy was laughing. "You didn't hear me yell that I was coming up?"

"No, I didn't."

She was holding one of his large framed posters, his three-sheet original of *The Maltese Falcon*, the best poster he owned, one she'd bought him for their first anniversary. "Thought you might like this up here," she said.

"Thanks."

He went and got it from her as she looked around the room. "Coming along, I see," Wendy said.

"Ha-ha."

"It's your office. I won't come back up here and judge, but I knew you'd want that poster."

After she left, he leaned the tall frame against a stack of boxes and stared at it. She'd had it framed under protective glass, and its colors were still really good. He remembered how he'd felt when she gave it to him, one year after they'd gotten married at a casino wedding chapel in Las Vegas. It was back when they'd first moved to Cambridge and had rented the apartment that they would eventually buy. He'd slept in and the poster was hanging on the wall when he woke up, replacing the faded *Chinatown* poster that had been in that spot. After thanking her for the gift, he'd asked her how much she paid.

"Fair market value was what the shady man told me" was her answer.

Thom must have frowned, because she said, "We're rich. You know that, even if we don't want the world to know."

"I know," he said.

"Besides, you earned it."

It was that phrase, that he'd "earned it," that haunted him every time he looked at the poster, and that echoed through his head now, the *Maltese Falcon* now relocated to their new house with its views of the water. Thom wondered where they'd be living right now if they were forced to live off his salary as an associate professor and Wendy's nonexistent royalties from her book of poetry that had been published just over a year ago. "What does it matter?" he said to himself, then realized he'd said the words out loud. He checked his watch. It was just past four in the afternoon, but the sun was already sinking over the cove, casting long, pink fingers across the sky. He opened the window and lit a cigarette, even though he'd promised Wendy he wouldn't smoke in the house. Maybe he should finally switch to a pipe, he thought, picturing himself suddenly on a book jacket, that thought filling him with a combination of hope and shame.

ii

Wendy watched the sunset from the front steps of their new house. She wanted to go get Jason to watch with her, but when she'd poked her head into his room, he was fully absorbed in whatever book he was reading. She'd also told herself that this particular view of the sun setting on the inner harbor of New Essex was a view she now owned, one she could look at for the rest of her life. A woman walked past, a small, bedraggled dog dragging her on a leash. "Oh, hello," the woman said from under her hooded coat. "You bought the Derwatt house."

Wendy had heard that the house was sometimes called that because it was in a painting by Philip Derwatt, who'd summered on Goose Neck many years ago. "We did," Wendy said.

The woman nodded slowly, and Wendy wondered if that was the end of the conversation. But then she said, "I'm Janine. We live in the green house on the corner with the white door. I'd come over and shake your hand, but I have a cold."

"No worries," Wendy said, introducing herself and miming shaking a hand from her seated position on the steps. "My husband, Thom, is in his office pretending to unpack boxes."

"Oh," Janine said, looking bewildered. "We'll have you both over soon. My husband, Larry, makes good haddock chowder."

"We'd like that," Wendy lied as Janine moved off.

Back in the house, Wendy turned on some lamps and started to tackle the job of putting the dishes away in the kitchen. Before she got very far, her new cellphone rang. It was her mother, who, after years of almost obsessive independence, was suddenly now calling to check in every other day.

"Hi, Mom."

"You there, Wendy? I can't hear you."

Wendy walked toward the back of the house, where the cell service seemed better, and said hello again.

"Oh, that's better, sweetheart. How's the move?"

Wendy told her all about the movers who refused to bring the sleeper sofa up to the second-floor guest room, and the neighbor who just invited her over for chowder, and how Samsa had explored only half the house, refusing to go into the upstairs bedroom and also the downstairs dining room.

"Haunted rooms," her mother said.

"Looks like it. Do you think you can come visit? You can cleanse the house with sage for me."

"Oh, you're funny. Yes, of course I'll come visit you in your new fancy house. I'll need to figure out what to do with these dogs, and I'll have to check in with Bert to see if he'll feed the chickens. When would be a good time to come? Not winter, I think."

Wendy told her that summer would be the best time to come, knowing that her mother, who'd moved enough for three lifetimes while she'd been married to Wendy's father, would find an excuse not to come.

After the call, Wendy returned to the kitchen, but she kept thinking about her mother, and how she was probably never going to leave the small house Wendy had bought her in Wyoming shortly after Bryce had died. And why should she really? She'd spent twenty years married to an unstable man who had dragged her all over the country so that he could fail at life in the highest number of states possible. Wendy felt the same way. It hadn't been easy moving from their lovely place in Cambridge, but now that she finally had a house by the sea (her lifelong dream), she knew she was never going to leave. She'd most likely die in this house, a thought that comforted her.

She'd unpacked all the dishes they owned and placed them on the marble-topped island. There were far too many, including an incomplete set of Corelle plates with small green flowers along their edges that Wendy suspected came from Thom's childhood. She repacked those in a box and brought the box out to the garage, where she climbed a stepladder in order to slide it onto the highest shelf behind the workbench. He'd never miss them, never even ask her where they went. And Wendy had a sudden strange thought, imagining Jason, a middle-aged man, finding that box still in its exact same spot after Thom and she were dead. Who knows, maybe they'd be genuinely vintage at that point in time. Maybe they'd be worth something.

2003

The self-addressed envelope arrived in the mail, its return address from Kenosha University Press. It was suspiciously thick, although Wendy still assumed it was a rejection letter. She'd entered her manuscript into Kenosha's First Book Poetry Prize back in the spring.

Still, as she teared at the envelope, a tiny pulse of hope went through her. The letter began: "Dear Ms. Eastman, We are very pleased to inform you that your manuscript, SPECIFICS OMITTED, has been selected as the winner of 2004's Jeremiah Hull First Book Poetry Prize." Wendy stopped reading, suddenly possessed of a mix of competing emotions. She'd wanted this for a while—for no other reason than maybe validation—but now that it had arrived, a sense of trepidation took over.

She went with the letter to her favorite reading chair, which sat by the bay window in the front living room of their second-floor apartment. She read the whole thing. The book would come out in one year, the fall of 2004. She would receive $1,500 and she would be flown out to the university for a book-launch reading at a time to be decided upon. Included with the letter was a three-page contract, plus a printout of the deciding judge's citation on why her manuscript had been selected. It was written by Elizabeth Grieve. Wendy took a breath and read the entire piece.

> *Specifics Omitted* is a remarkable book of poems by a young writer called Wendy Eastman. She is a neo-formalist who uses convention to peel away at layers of understanding. Her lines—usually iambic tetrameter—and her rhymes—often slyly slant—take mundane objects and make them glow like bioluminescence across a nighttime ocean-scape. To quote from "At the Sculpture Park": "There is a wagered immortality at work/ that seems to say: We must not be outshone by trees." The title poem, coming as it does at the end of the book, posits a world shed of identifiers, and in so doing refutes its own thesis.
>
> By not being specific these poems become overtly specific. By not naming the dark, darkness imbues every word. Eastman is here to tell us that in the realm of her poems the world will reveal itself through the details of nature, through the constriction of form, and through the simplicity and complexity (not a contradiction) of these startling works of art.

Wendy, after reading the short essay, stood and wandered aimlessly through the rooms of the apartment, trying to order her thoughts. There were so many. On the most basic level, a part of her was still processing that she had won a poetry prize and that she was going to be a published author. And she was also processing that ludicrous essay by Elizabeth Grieve, which made her book sound like the second coming of *The Waste Land*. But she had been chosen, hadn't she? Presumably she was not the only poet to enter this particular contest. And it was even a possibility that Elizabeth Grieve believed what she had written. She found herself back in her chair, rereading the piece.

She stayed seated, now plagued with sheer horror at what she'd just read. In some ways, the judge had understood her perfectly, in itself a discombobulating thought, to the point where she saw her poems as confessional in nature, something that Wendy had never intended. Or had she? The very first poem that Wendy had written had been about her time in Mendocino with her aunt Andi back when she was fifteen. She'd described her aunt's disheveled cottage, the nearby cliffs, the tall pines. She remembered thinking that she should include in her poem the reason she'd been in California but decided against it. And that had been her directive ever since. She'd been appalled when she began to read the poems of her fellow students, all those free-verse confessions that sounded like diary entries that had been chopped up willy-nilly so that they somehow appeared poetic on the page. She'd known at the time that her own poems, with their end rhymes and stanzas and descriptions of nature, must seem equally ridiculous. But she'd stuck to her guns. Well, mostly. She had written one poem about Thom back then, but even then she'd disguised it to make it seem like it was a poem ostensibly about graveyards.

And now she was getting published because a judge believed that she was a confessional poet. Ironic, because she had worked so long to not use the first person in her poetry, to not dissect relationships, to not fall into all those traps that her contemporaries seemed to fall into, with the constant flaying-open of their bodies and lives for public consumption.

She was just starting to read the judge's citation for the third time when she heard Jason call out to her, having woken up from his nap.

A few hours later Thom called to say that he was on his way back from Boston University and to remind her that he was picking up Indian food.

"I'd forgotten all about it," Wendy said.

"You mean you've cooked us a giant meal?"

"Strangely, no. But I do have news."

"You know you can't say that and then not tell me."

"I'll tell you when you get back."

"Are you pregnant again?"

Wendy thought it was an odd thing to ask, since they'd already decided that one child was more than enough. "God no," she said.

"Seriously, you're not going to tell me?"

"It's good news and it's no big deal."

"Should I get Champagne?"

"How about you get a nice bottle of Chardonnay."

An hour later Thom came through the door while she was on the floor sorting plastic dinosaurs with Jason. "I figured it out," he said. "You were offered a permanent position."

Wendy was currently subbing at Cambridge Rindge & Latin for a teacher who was on maternity leave. "No," she said. "Better. I won a book contest."

"What?"

"I won the first-book contest from Kenosha University Press. It'll be published next fall." Just now, saying the words made her realize for the first time that she'd beaten Thom to a dream they both had. But she saw no jealousy on his face, just pride.

"I don't know what to say," he said. "I'm so proud of you. Jason, are you proud of your mommy? She wrote a book."

He held up a pterodactyl and made a roaring sound.

After dinner, and after they'd finished the wine, Thom insisted on going back out to buy an actual bottle of Champagne. "This needs to be a proper celebration."

While he was gone she cleaned the kitchen, and managed to put Jason down for the night by reading *One Monster After Another* twice through. Thom took so much time buying the Champagne that she began to think he'd gotten into an accident and died, which would make quite a story. Get a publishing deal, lose a husband. Maybe that's how it should work. Good things should be balanced by bad things, and vice versa. She supposed that, in the end, it probably did work out that way. We are all equal at the close. Slowly backing out of Jason's room then heading back downstairs, she heard Thom fumbling at the door. She let him in. Instead of carrying a single bottle of Champagne, he had a case in his arms. "I see," she said.

"I told Al the good news, and somehow he convinced me I needed to buy a case of wine to celebrate. There's one bottle of Champagne in there. It wasn't cheap."

They went out onto their front stoop with two glasses and toasted the book. "You'll be next," she said, then immediately regretted it.

"No, your second book will definitely be next. I'm a big fat maybe. But I don't care. Maybe families shouldn't have two writers."

"We do have two writers already."

"No, I know. I mean published writers."

"Well . . ." Wendy said, trailing off.

"So how did you feel when you opened the envelope?" Thom said.

"It was such a bizarre mix of emotions. I felt glad, but also instantly . . . something. Anxiety, maybe. Terror. Mostly, I felt like somehow I'd put something over on them, like I'd gotten away with something. And then I read the judge's citation, and it just got worse."

"What's that?"

"The judge of the contest, she wrote a piece about why I was selected."

"I want to see it."

"It's awful."

"What do you mean?"

"It's so embarrassing. She talks about me like . . . I mean, read it yourself."

Wendy went inside to get the piece. Walking back to the front door, she could smell Thom's cigarette smoke coming through the screen, and as she got closer she heard him talking to somebody. She stopped just inside the door, listening. He was speaking with Lilith York, who would be out walking her Akita. She heard him say, "It's called *Specifics Omitted*. We'll have a huge party when it's published." The words made her heart hurt a little.

When it had been quiet for a moment Wendy stepped back out onto the porch.

"Sorry," Thom said, about the cigarette, flicking it in a high arc so that it landed on the sidewalk, sizzling then dying in a puddle.

"No worries," she said. "You're going to need another one after reading this essay."

"Read it to me."

"Okay," she said, and managed to get through reading it aloud without being violently sick. "It's a lot," she said, at the end.

"What if she's right?"

"What do you mean?"

"Maybe you're a major talent—I mean, I know you're a major talent, but what if the rest of the world is about to find out?"

"First of all, no one will read this book. Elizabeth Grieve is a poet herself, so she knows she has to make it sound like she's selected the next Anne Sexton in order to make her feel better about her own life choices."

"About becoming a poet?" Thom said.

"Exactly," Wendy said, suddenly enjoying herself, even considering smoking one of Thom's cigarettes.

"Still, she might be right."

"She's not. I mean, who knows, maybe I'll sell a million books, but that wouldn't change the fact that everything she wrote is total bullshit."

"Are you sure you're going into this with the right attitude?"

"I'm loading up on the armor. Trust me, no one will read it."

"You sticking with the title?"

"Oh, definitely."

"Okay," Thom said. He'd been trying to convince her for a while to rename the manuscript *The Moth Party* after his favorite poem in the collection.

That night, Thom fell asleep first, a rare event. He would normally toss and turn for at least an hour, while Wendy could recite a few of her favorite poems to herself and be deeply asleep in twenty minutes. But that night she lay there listening to the rotating fan struggling to cool the room. She kept thinking about the words in that citation, and how embarrassed they had made her feel. Why had she wanted to publish her poems in the first place? For fame and money? She didn't want to be famous, and she had plenty of money. Besides, this was poetry. To advance her career? No. She had never had any real interest in academics. Then why? She racked her brain. She'd called her mother earlier in the day to tell her the news, and her mother had been happy for her but hadn't asked any follow-up questions. She did say that Wendy's father would have been proud, and she wondered if that was the case. It probably was. Her father's flaw, well, one of many, was that he had a desperate need to succeed at something and never managed once to do it. Maybe Wendy had a little bit of that in herself as well, a need to win. In some ways she just wanted to see if she could get a book published, but she hadn't even considered the possibility that she would be opening herself up to scrutiny. One of Elizabeth Grieve's lines went through her head: *By not naming the dark, darkness imbues every word.* Jesus, she thought, what have I done? Something close to panic rose from her stomach through her chest. Was this what Thom felt like when he had his little attacks? She sat up in bed, staring at the glow of city light against the pale curtain.

What finally got her to sleep was a strange little fantasy more amusing than anything real. She imagined Elizabeth Grieve becoming obsessed with her, parsing every word to find out everything she had done. Wendy would have to travel across the country, hunt her down, silence her. She imagined multiple gruesome possibilities for doing the deed, finally landing on strangulation, using Elizabeth Grieve's long ponytail as the murder weapon. Wendy began to calm down, just thinking about it. Right before finally falling asleep, she did make a promise to herself: no more poetry.

2000

Wendy was slowly waking up and Thom was watching her while stroking her arm. When her puffy eyes were fully open she smiled up at him, then something changed in her expression, and she said, "Where is he?"

"He's fine. He's in the nursery. I can . . ."

"Oh," Wendy said. "For a moment, I thought . . . He's fine, though?"

"He's fine. He's perfect. How are you?"

"Tired. In pain. But happy."

"I think I've never had so many emotions at once," Thom said. "How is it possible to love someone you've just met so intensely, and then to feel this much terror that you are going to screw it up? Also, I'm so fucking tired."

"You need to sleep."

"I will."

Wendy shifted herself up a little onto her pillows. She smelled like a combination of milk and sweat. "What do you think of the name Edgar?" she said.

"As a rule, not much. Are you talking about renaming Jason?"

"Did we officially decide on Jason?"

"I thought we did. I thought *you* did."

"Yeah, I guess so. It's just that for some reason he's an Edgar now that he's born. I don't know why."

Thom and Wendy had probably spoken five hundred boy names out loud to each other in the previous months, but as far as he could remember, he'd never heard Wendy mention the name Edgar. "Is it a family name?"

"No."

"So is it because of Edgar Allan Poe?"

Wendy looked surprised, her pale eyebrows rising a fraction. "I suppose it is. I just always loved the name. Do you not love it?"

"No," Thom said. "I don't love it. Besides, I've been thinking of him as Jason. I thought we both had."

"Oh," Wendy said, and Thom realized that she was half asleep, or else talking in her sleep, or maybe just really out of it from the birth and the drugs.

"How does it feel to be a mom?" he said.

She seemed to really think about it, biting her lower lip like she sometimes did when she was reading, and said, "I've been a mom for a long time."

"Have you?"

"It feels like it. And you've been a father for a long time."

"About twenty-four hours."

"See what I told you. A long time." She smiled up at him, her face free of makeup, still rosy with exertion, and for an instant it was like she was fourteen again, unchanged by all the years.

Someone swung open the door behind him and Thom turned to see that a nurse had poked her head into the room then quickly retreated. When he turned back to Wendy he saw that she had fallen back asleep.

He left her and wandered back out into the hallway of the maternity wing at Cambridge Hospital. In the waiting room he found Diane, his mother, alone, flipping through a *Yankee* magazine. His father had never been able to sit still for more than about ten minutes, which meant he was probably roaming the halls, or going to check on the car.

"How is she?" his mom said, looking up from the magazine.

"Out of it. She just fell back asleep."

"You must be tired too."

"I can't sleep. Where's Dad?"

"I told him I needed a cranberry juice, because the cafeteria doesn't have it. So he's out on a scouting mission."

"Good one, Mom."

"Should we go look at your son?"

Together they walked down to the nursery, where Jason/Edgar was swaddled and sleeping in a clear plastic bassinet. There were three other babies in the room with him, and Thom had a brief out-of-body experience imagining the different lives of these humans who would forever share a birthday. And he thought of himself, swaddled and helpless, in Concord, New Hampshire, on February 13, 1968, on the same day that Wendy had been born, somewhere in Southern California, the two of them fated to meet fourteen years later. Thom must have swayed a little on his feet, because his mother slid an arm around him that felt more like physical support than emotional. "I didn't much like babies," she said.

"No?" Thom said.

"I like them when they start to talk. Your father was different, though. He was surprisingly good with both you and your sister when you were newborns. He loved comforting you, walking you from room to room. I remember he used to put your sister in the car and drive her around in order to get her to sleep."

"But when we started to talk . . ."

His mother smiled. "Yes, that's when he lost interest."

Thom looked at his son, had a brief panic that he'd stopped breathing, then saw slight movement that caused a flush of relief to spread throughout his body. God, he loved that boy, whatever his name was.

As though she were reading his mind, his mother said, "So it's officially Jason? Or is that still up for debate?"

"Ninety/ten," Thom said.

"What's the ten?"

"Wendy just mentioned the name Edgar when I was with her in her room. First I'd heard of it."

"Edgar. Good God. Sounds like an old man's name."

"We'll stick with Jason," Thom said.

"You should go outside and get some air. It's beautiful this morning. See if you can find your father."

After looking into the hospital room and seeing that Wendy was still asleep, Thom did go outside. It was morning rush hour and the sidewalks were filled with people moving with purpose, their faces grim and determined. Why weren't they happy to be alive? he thought. After all, it was a new millennium and the predictions that the world would end had turned out to be greatly exaggerated. The world still ticked along. Films were being made and books were being written. Babies were being born. The air was cold but the sky was cloudless, its radiant blue full of promise. Thom ducked into a convenience store and bought a pack of Camel Lights, despite having promised Wendy that he was done with smoking. He crossed the street to a small square park with three empty benches and chose the sunniest one. He lit the cigarette, taking too deep of a first drag, then exhaling the blue smoke into the sunlight. It had been a few weeks since his last secret cigarette, and the nicotine raced to his head, making him feel buoyant in the sunlight. But after he'd smoked the cigarette down to its filter, he put the rest of the pack on the arm of the bench, the matches on top of them, and walked back to the hospital.

His father was back with his mother's juice and Wendy was awake again. He wondered if she could smell the smoke on his clothes, but she didn't say anything. Instead she asked, "How's little Jason?"

"Wrapped up like a burrito."

"Oh, good."

One of the nurses popped her head in and said, "Mom's awake, I see. Want to see your baby?"

"I do," Wendy said, shifting herself farther back so that she was sitting up.

The nurse—her name was Shannon, and Thom had secretly decided she was the prettiest of the several pretty maternity-ward nurses they had dealt with—left to get Jason.

"Any new names for our baby?" Thom said.

"What do you mean? For Jason?"

"Don't you mean Edgar?"

Wendy looked confused, so Thom said, "About an hour ago you woke up and said that you thought his name should be Edgar."

"Did I?"

"You don't remember?"

"Maybe. A little bit. But I thought it was some kind of dream."

"You also said that we've been parents for a long time."

Something crossed her eyes. Amusement, maybe, with a little bit of fear. "It feels like it, doesn't it?" she said.

"I suppose so. So you haven't changed our baby's name?"

"No, he's Jason. Jason Edgar Graves."

"Ha-ha."

"Jason Bergeron Graves." Bergeron was Thom's maternal grandmother's maiden name.

"Okay, good. It's settled then."

"It's settled."

1998

i

"I had a thought," Thom said, sidestepping their orange cat, Trimal-chio, who liked to sleep in doorways.

"You did, did you?"

"I did. You won't like it, but I'll ask anyway."

"Okay," Wendy said, suddenly on alert.

"I thought we could go to a Christmas Eve service tonight?"

It was the last thing she expected to hear, and for some reason it made her laugh.

"Why are you laughing?"

"I don't know," Wendy said. "Just unexpected. I thought you were going to suggest we open all our presents tonight."

"We can do that too."

"Why do you want to go to a service? Should I be concerned?"

"No, no. I was just out walking and there's that church back at the corner across from that bar you like—"

"River Styx."

"River Styx . . . and there was a sign out saying they are doing a candlelight service tonight, and I just thought . . ."

"You should go. I'm not sure I'm interested in joining you."

"It's not a religious thing, at all. I hated going to church as a kid, except for the Christmas Eve service. But the songs are nice, and I like the candlelight part . . ."

"What's the candlelight part?"

Thom described the services he'd attended as a kid. She could picture him with his lovely New England family walking across the town green in parkas and scarves to a white church, a spotlit creche blanketed by snow. "Sure, I'll attend," she said, mostly because she could tell how much he really wanted her to come with him, and partly because she wondered if she should be worried about something.

After dinner—Thom insisted on oyster stew for Christmas Eve—they bundled up and walked out into the night, headed for the church. It was a clear, cold night, the weather report predicting snow squalls and high wind. Wendy's cheekbones ached by the time they stepped inside the bustling church and found a pew strategically located toward the rear. Thom showed her the small white candle, skirted by a protective piece of cardboard, that was located in front of everyone's seat, where the hymnbooks were. He was giddy, she thought, or maybe just nostalgic. Wendy, herself, just felt curious. All these neighbors living this secret life of religion right on her block. Ruth Flaherty, their upstairs neighbor, was sitting two rows in front of them, conversing with the couple next to her.

The organist finished playing "O Come, All Ye Faithful," then moved on to that Christmas hymn that had the lines "Snow had fallen, snow on snow." And then the minister stepped up to the podium. He looked like a hip bartender or maybe an aspiring folk singer, and he beamed out at the parishioners before beginning to talk.

All in all, it hadn't been a terrible experience. Wendy listened to the sermon—really just the myth of Christ's birth—and sang along with the hymns, all the while keeping an eye on Thom next to her. She didn't exactly know what she was looking for, maybe some signs that he was having a genuine religious moment, or an epiphany, but while he seemed engaged, he didn't seem particularly moved. He didn't close his eyes during prayers, and he spent much of the service making faces at the young girl in the pew in front of them, who kept turning around. Toward the end of the service there was the candlelight portion, the lights dimmed, and a single candle at the front was lit, its flame traveling down the pews, from row to row, until everyone held a burning candle. Wendy admitted to herself that it was aesthetically pleasing, despite the fact that she got candlewax on her corduroys.

"It's nice, right?" Thom whispered in her ear.

After the service she was surprised that Thom dug out a few bills to put into the donation plate toward the back of the church, and that he stopped and introduced Wendy and himself to the minister and assistant minister.

"Lovely to see new faces," said the minister, named Andrew, who, now that she was seeing him up close, reminded Wendy of David Foster Wallace.

His assistant, wearing a black robe, and a very colorful scarf, was named Ariel, and Wendy thought she was far too young and pretty to be spending her time at this church filled with Baby Boomers and families with small children. Then she reminded herself that these weren't priests, and were presumably allowed to have sex lives.

Back at home Thom mixed them two eggnogs, heavily laced with whiskey, and they sat in front of the television. They watched the very end of *It's a Wonderful Life* and then it started up again. Neither reached for the remote. Wendy was trying to calculate the best way to ask Thom how he felt about going to church, mostly because he'd been unusually quiet since they returned. She knew that the last year had been hard on him. He'd lost his grandfather, whom he'd spoken to every other day for years. He'd also applied to two writers' workshops, Iowa and Provincetown, and been rejected by both. After that he'd seemed unmoored, quitting his job at Harvard Bookstore, briefly taking up watercolor painting, then deciding finally that he was going to apply for a PhD in English literature. Filling out the applications had consumed him, at least, and he had seemed less moody for a while. Her big worry was that he was depressed, and she thought the best thing for him would probably be therapy. But she couldn't suggest it, couldn't risk him talking to anyone about their past—even a person who was sworn to secrecy by doctor-patient confidentiality. For that reason, too, she worried about his drinking. She'd noticed that he always drank a beer, or two, before heading out to a social event, one while he was getting dressed, and usually one in the car if they were driving ("road sodas" he called them). When she'd asked him about it, he'd said, "You think I want to talk to any of our friends while sober?"

"So are you a parishioner now?"

"Huh," he said, turning from the screen to look at her.

"Do you think you'll go back to that church?"

"Oh," he said. "Next Christmas Eve, for sure. But no, probably not. Why? You look worried."

"No, just curious."

"How about you? You said it was okay."

"I thought it was pretty, honestly. But at the end of the day, it's all just nonsense, isn't it?"

"Do you mean celebrating the birth of Jesus, specifically, or just religion?"

Wendy thought for a moment, her eye on George Bailey, who was dancing at the high school dance, about to fall into the under-floor pool. "Both. All of it. It's a nice story, but that's all it is. It's just been made up to give people hope that their horrible lives aren't entirely in vain."

"Cynical," Thom said, also watching the screen.

"That's why you married me, right?"

"Right."

"Look, I don't think it's the worst thing, religion. Whatever gets anyone through this life is generally fine with me. I just don't think it's real. But if you're interested in that church, then I'm not going to stop you. Maybe you'll find something there."

"But you're worried?"

"No. Why do you say that?"

"I don't know. I sense it. I think you're worried that I'll get a conscience and feel worse about myself than I already do."

"Do you feel bad about yourself?" She turned her body and put a hand on his hand that was holding the remote control.

"No, I'm fine. I'm not going to find God and confess everything I've done. I just think something about church is comforting. It's the same way I feel when we walk into a bar and see someone we know. Being part of something."

"That makes sense," Wendy said.

"But being part of you, part of us, that's the most important thing. Now and always."

It was a phrase she'd heard him use before—"now and always"— and she liked the ring of it. She told him.

They finished the movie, rewatching the end again, then went upstairs to bed. Before falling asleep, Wendy said, "Maybe we should have a kid."

"Oh," Thom said.

"You okay?"

"Yes, you just took me by surprise."

They'd talked a little bit about it already—having children—but always in an abstract way, something that might happen in the future.

"We don't have to talk about it now. It's just, I watched you tonight at the church service, and saw the way you looked at kids."

"You were like: Either he's dying to be a dad or else he's a pervert."

"Pretty much what I thought."

"If it's something you want, then I want it too."

"Okay, we can leave it at that for now. I'm tired."

"Good night, darling," Thom said.

Wendy rolled over and looked at her clock. It had ticked over to midnight. "Merry Christmas," she said, curling herself into a ball, wind now rattling the bedroom window.

ii

They'd each had two beers at lunch—that was the first mistake—and now they were on Ariel's threadbare couch in her studio apartment in Somerville, and Thom was pulling off her jeans. It was something he'd been dreaming of doing for a while, during this whole anxious spring, and now that it was happening, he was filled with equal parts joy and an unspecified dread that everything was about to change. He supposed it already had. He was an adulterer now, and always would be.

Naked, they arranged themselves awkwardly on the couch, the double bed just four feet away, but Thom had intuited somehow that the bed was off-limits. Maybe that had something to do with Ariel's boyfriend, a mysterious figure with the unlikely name of Alun with a *u*.

"You sure?" Thom said, holding his body above hers, although it seemed abundantly clear that both of them were quite sure.

"I am."

Afterward, both partially re-dressed, Ariel had made a pot of coffee and they sat together on the same couch, rain tapping on the window, mugs in hand. The day had turned dark since they'd walked back from lunch in Union Square to her apartment up a steep hill that overlooked city hall and Somerville High School. It was Thom's first time in her apartment and now that he could focus on its interior and not just its owner, he found himself looking around for signs of Ariel's calling. All he could see was what looked like a Bible on the bedside table next to her reading lamp.

"What are you thinking about?" Ariel said.

"I thought there might be a giant cross on your wall or something. Above the bed."

Ariel laughed. "I have my master's of divinity degree framed in the bathroom."

"I saw that."

"Are you disappointed?"

"In what?"

"That my apartment doesn't match my job."

"No, no. I was just curious. I mean, I'm curious about seeing where you live."

"What does your place look like?"

"Besides having a wife in it?"

"Ouch."

"Sorry, that was a weird thing to say. It's nice. We have our cat, Malchy, but you know about that. We have lots and lots of books."

"When I picture your apartment, I picture a grown-up place, like something from a Woody Allen movie. I feel like I still live in a dorm room, basically."

"Are you happy here?"

"I'm happy right now. I'm happy you're here with me." Ariel put her coffee down on the glass-topped coffee table and slid in close to Thom. He slipped his arm around her, pulling her in tighter, her head against his chest, trying to stave off the sudden feeling that he needed to flee this apartment as soon as possible. It had been a mistake, but he'd known that even before it happened. It had all been a mistake, really. Ariel was the assistant minister at the Unitarian

Church in Cambridge, close to where Thom and Wendy lived. He'd met her on Christmas Eve, then re-met her two days later at a wine-and-cheese shop he went to frequently.

"You're so familiar," he'd said to her as she was studying a label.

"You came to my Christmas Eve service. You and your wife. Her name was Wendy, but I'm sorry. You're . . . ?"

"I'm Thom Graves," he said. "You have a good memory."

"It's part of the job."

"Right. All those Bible verses."

She laughed, the first of so many times that he was going to see her do that, and he fell a little bit in love with her right then and there. What had Wendy called her after the service? Something like a hot pixie? He couldn't remember exactly, but she was quite small, and also quite pretty. Short, dark hair and big, brown eyes. And her laugh was almost awkwardly explosive.

"Well, yes, Bible verses," she said. "But mostly I need to remember the names of parishioners."

"I'm afraid that Wendy and I are, at most, once-a-year parishioners. I don't want you to waste the brain space."

"Too late," she said.

The encounter at the wine shop would probably have been the end of it, but they ran into each other again in the middle of February at the post office. He was mailing off an application for the PhD program at Cornell, with very little hope of getting in, and she was there on what she said was official business, bulk-mailing a church newsletter. Afterward they went to a coffee shop on Mass Avenue and talked for two hours.

It turned out that Ariel Gagnon was from New Hampshire, as well, but together they determined that their two towns were about as far apart as you could get in that particular state. She came from the northernmost part of the state, both her parents wildlife managers more interested in nature than humans. "When people ask me why I found God, I tell them that it was loneliness, that I had no one to talk to growing up so I started to talk to Him."

"And He talked back."

"He didn't actually. But that doesn't mean I don't think He's there."

"You said 'think' and not 'know.'"

"I did," she said. "Ministers have doubts too. But I'm really in it because it's a form of social work. I want to help people. You know how I said at the cheese shop that I didn't remember your name. I actually did and have no idea why I said I didn't. But I'd been thinking of you. You looked like you were there for a reason, like you were looking for something."

Thom, on the cusp of making a joke, instead said, "I think I'm looking for forgiveness."

"Forgiveness for what?"

"My own selfishness, I guess. I don't know. I just don't like myself very much."

"This is where I'm supposed to say that God loves you, but I think you know that, or at least you know that that's how it is supposed to work. Instead, I'll tell you that I like you, and I'm never wrong about anyone."

"Is that true?" Thom said.

"That I like you?"

"No, that you're never wrong about anyone?"

"So far."

Between the conversation at the coffee shop and the afternoon spent on Ariel's couch in her Somerville apartment, they'd seen each other almost once a week for lunch or for coffee. She'd told him about her on-again, off-again boyfriend Alun, and her wavering belief in her calling to the church. He told her about the constant anxiety he'd been feeling, and how Wendy approached life in a different way.

"You mean she's happy?"

"I suppose that's what I mean."

"Must be hard."

"It is. It is." He reached across the table at the Middle East, where they were sharing a falafel platter and a bottle of lunchtime wine, and dramatically took hold of Ariel's hand.

"But you said you wanted forgiveness, back when we first talked. What do you need forgiveness for?"

"When Wendy and I met, she was married—I told you that already—and I had a girlfriend, a serious girlfriend. I guess I don't feel guilty about her because we weren't meant to be together."

"You were meant to be together with Wendy."

"I was. I believe that. I'll be with her forever. But I feel guilty about the end of her marriage to Bryce. I guess that's what I'm hoping to be forgiven for."

Ariel looked skeptical and poured the last of the bottle of wine into Thom's glass. "I thought Bryce died."

Thom quickly rearranged the features on his face, trying to remember what he'd already told her. "He did, yes. But we had already . . ."

"Right, you told me that. Look, it seems to me like you've followed your heart, and that's the important thing. I don't think you've really hurt anyone."

Toward the end of that lunch—or had it been the time they met in Boston at Cheers, just because it seemed like a funny thing to do?—Ariel said, "I take it Wendy doesn't know about us meeting like this."

"She sort of does," Thom said.

"What do you mean?"

"Remember when we took that walk across Harvard last week? She saw us. She was in her car at a crosswalk and we walked by."

"What did she say?" Ariel sounded genuinely alarmed.

"Oh, nothing much. A little hurt that I hadn't told her that you and I were friends."

What Wendy had actually said, after grilling Thom and getting him to admit that they'd been meeting up for heart-to-heart talks for a few weeks now, was that she'd prefer it if he just fucked her and got it over with.

"You wouldn't mind?" Thom had asked.

Wendy made the face he'd seen a few times in the last year, a face that seemed to say that he was about one and a half steps behind her, and said, "I wouldn't be happy about it, but all I'm saying is that it's preferable to you getting a new best friend that wants to know everything about your life."

Thom, wanting to change the subject from his wife, asked Ariel about Alun, her boyfriend.

"What about him?"

"Does he know about us?"

"No. But it doesn't really matter."

"Why doesn't it matter?"

"Because I'm not in love with Alun."

Less than a week later, Ariel, dressed only in a pair of boxer shorts, her head against his chest on the sofa, said, "We just made a mistake, didn't we?"

"If it was, it was a very nice mistake."

"But you feel guilty, I can tell."

"Are you sure you're not projecting?"

"I'm definitely projecting," Ariel said. "I feel very guilty. I only met Wendy once but I liked her."

"You're not responsible for her. I am."

"I know, but it doesn't make me feel any better about it. And it's not just her, it's me. I didn't cheat on Alun, but I think I just cheated on God a little bit. Does that make sense?"

"Not really."

"Remember when I told you I started to speak to God because I was lonely?"

"Yes."

"Well, I think you made me realize that I'm still lonely, even with God in my life."

"I'm sorry."

"Don't be. It's not your fault. And it's not your fault that this is over."

"What do you mean?"

"We're over, right? Now that we've done this."

Thom felt the lie rising in him, but stopped himself from saying it. "I think so," he said. "I'll miss you, though."

"I'll miss you too."

When he got back late that afternoon, he just assumed that Wendy would be able to see what he'd done on his face, that she would take one look at him and know everything. But she was in a good mood, watering plants, playing her Lauryn Hill CD. After dinner that night she told him that she was three days late in getting her period. "You're pregnant?" he said.

"I might be."

"I'm going out to the CVS to buy a pregnancy test," Thom said, standing, knocking his knee on the underside of their dining-room table.

"No, not yet. We can do it tomorrow. Tonight it will be a mystery."

In bed, later, Thom almost told Wendy about what had happened that day with Ariel, and how it was over, but he could already hear her response. "You know, darling, just because we're married, you don't have to tell me *everything*." She'd said it enough times. So he kept it to himself, another secret, hopefully the last one he'd ever have to keep.

1995

Outside of the Clark County Marriage License Bureau the sun was blinding. Wendy put her sunglasses on, while Thom, having left his pair back at the hotel, shielded his eyes.

"Where to now?" he said. "Straight to the chapel?"

"Which chapel?"

"Any chapel. There are literally two of them across the street."

"Sure," Wendy said. "You pick."

They crossed the avenue. One of the chapels was sort of a miniaturized church, dwarfed by a neon sign of a large red heart pierced by an arrow. The alternative was in a strip mall, and was called the Carousel Wedding Chapel. Thom and Wendy approached it and saw that behind the plate-glass windows there was an actual merry-go-round. It wasn't spinning, but maybe that was because a couple were being photographed standing on the carousel's platform. She was holding up her hand, showing her ring. He had a hand on her back and the other on the mane of one of the plastic horses.

"It seems like a bad metaphor," Thom said.

"What does?"

"A carousel. I feel like riding a carousel is kind of a fickle thing. You can get on and off and pick different partners."

"You mean different horses?"

"Right."

"I don't know," Wendy said, sliding her arm through Thom's and moving closer to him. "Maybe it's a perfect metaphor for marriage. You go around and around, getting nowhere, and you feel vaguely nauseous the whole time."

"Aw, sweet," Thom said.

"You know that there's a chapel in our hotel."

They were staying at the Flamingo on the Strip for three nights. Neither of them had been to Las Vegas before, and Thom had been the one to choose where to stay. Apparently, it had been in *Ocean's 11*, the heist movie with Frank Sinatra. "Is there?"

"You didn't see it? Right near where we checked in. We can go there. It really doesn't matter to me."

They took a cab back to the Flamingo from downtown Las Vegas. While they paid the fare the cabbie slid a card into Thom's hand with a picture of a woman's torso in a glitzy bra. The text simply read "Most beautiful girls on the Strip," and there was a phone number. In the elevator on the way to their room Thom showed the card to Wendy. "There's a phone in the room, isn't there?"

"There is. You should call. We're not married yet."

The room was ice cold, but after the heat of the outdoors neither of them minded. Wendy stripped off the skirt and blouse she'd been wearing and clambered onto the king-sized bed, cracked open the *Fodor's Las Vegas* guidebook that Thom had bought for the trip. "Where should we have dinner tonight?"

Thom lay down on the bed next to her. He was suddenly anxious, and not sure why, a phenomenon that had been happening to him more and more recently. What he really wanted to do was smoke a cigarette, but he'd booked a nonsmoking room, knowing that Wendy would prefer it. "We could just go downstairs, stand in line, and get married, then we could wander down the Strip and look for a restaurant."

"I'll do whatever you want to do, darling," Wendy said. It was a recent pet name she was using for him, and Thom wasn't quite used to it yet. It always sounded vaguely sarcastic.

"I just think that now that we've got the marriage license, I should make you an honest woman."

"That's what we're here for," she said, still flipping through the pages of the Fodor's.

It was Thom who had ultimately convinced Wendy that they should get married, and it was Wendy who had proposed that they elope to Vegas. She told him that she'd already had one wedding ceremony and that it had been one too many. Thom had readily agreed. For one thing, his minor anxiety attacks were getting worse, and the thought of standing up in front of a hundred friends and family and reciting vows made his spine feel like it was made of rubber. And he didn't think his parents would mind, especially after the stress and expense of his sister Janice's wedding on Cape Cod the year before. When he told them, it turned out he'd been right, his mother saying, "I don't care how you get married so long as it's to Wendy. You know how much we've always loved her." His parents, of course, were really the only other people who remembered that once upon a time Thom and Wendy had been childhood sweethearts. Thom and Wendy didn't exactly hide it from their new friends in Cambridge, but they didn't talk about it either. When Wendy had called her mother to tell her that she was planning on eloping with Thom to Las Vegas, she'd offered to buy her mother a plane ticket so that she could be there. "Haven't you always wanted to be the mother of a bride at her second wedding?" Wendy had said. Her mother had responded by laughing, and saying, "I just want to be the mother of happy children. And I am." Alan, Wendy's brother, had just gotten a degree to be a vet tech and had moved two towns away from Rose. Like her, he was engaged. Wendy was glad that Alan would be living close to their mother, but she wasn't convinced it was a necessity. Her mother had made more friends in Lander, Wyoming, than Wendy suspected she'd make in her entire life. It hadn't surprised her when her mother turned down the ticket to Vegas, saying that she'd rather travel to see where they actually lived their lives.

"So here's the plan," Thom said, placing a hand on Wendy's thigh. "You stay here and research restaurants. I'll go down and make sure the chapel can take us this afternoon. Maybe I can even make a reservation, then we'll reconvene and start this marriage off with a bang."

"You promise?" she said.

Wendy had moved his hand from her thigh to between her legs, where she was wearing new lacy underwear he'd suspected she'd bought just for this trip. "We're not married yet," Thom said, rolling off the bed.

Late that afternoon they were married in the hotel chapel. The officiant was a man with a handlebar mustache, and the witness was an off-the-clock baccarat dealer named Joan Webster. Thom asked her if she knew she shared a name with the lead character in the movie *I Know Where I'm Going!*, played by Wendy Hiller. She'd never heard of the movie or the actor. When they were officially a married couple, Thom and Wendy went to the bar at the Flamingo and each had a Champagne cocktail. Then they spent the early evening walking the Strip, popping into some of the glitzier casinos just to see what they looked like. At the MGM Grand they won $50 on a slot machine, then lost it five minutes later on two bets at a blackjack table. They wound up eating at a ridiculously fancy restaurant at Caesars Palace. They'd lucked out on getting a table, having walked up to the hostess a few minutes after there had been a cancellation. They had escargot to start then each had Steak Diane, splitting a bottle of red that cost $250. "Think of the money we saved by eloping," Wendy said.

Thom was going to comment that she'd also recently secured

her inheritance of Bryce's money. There had been some minor legal wrangles, but his estate had cleared probate and Wendy had become a multimillionaire. Thom, too, he supposed. The first thing she did with the money was purchase the house in Wyoming that her mom had been renting, overpaying for it because she knew her mother never wanted to move again. The second thing she did was pay off her brother's student loans. She'd asked Thom if he wanted anything for his own family, and he told her that he didn't, that he wasn't even telling them how much money she'd received. "We won't tell anyone," she said. "I know we're rich now, but I don't want to live like we're rich."

After dinner they returned to the bar at the Flamingo and drank several more Champagne cocktails. They started a conversation with the sole other patron, a recently widowed Englishman named Jason, who was visiting Vegas on his own from his home in Florida. When they told him what they'd done that day, he insisted on picking up their bill; he also gave an eloquent toast on the nature of marriage. He told them all the cities he'd lived in with his wife over their forty-year marriage and shared his advice for marital happiness (turned out it was eating a hot breakfast together every morning, plus separate vacations). At one point Wendy got up to go to the bathroom and both Thom and Jason Adamson watched her depart the lounge. She had a great walk, his wife did, Thom thought to himself, and said it out loud to their new friend. "You're a very lucky man," Jason said. "Don't squander it."

"No, we're in it for the long haul. To the end of the line."

It was just before midnight when Thom lifted Wendy into his arms and carried her into the hotel room, bumping her head gently against the doorframe. Wendy said that she was pretty sure she could fall asleep standing up, but Thom insisted she change into her wedding-night lingerie, while he stripped and got onto the center of the bed. When she emerged from the bathroom she was naked, as well, telling him that the outfit she'd bought was far too ridiculous for him to ever lay eyes on.

"Our new friend told me not to squander my luck," Thom said as Wendy clambered on top of him.

"I won't if you won't," Wendy said. She sounded a little drunk, unusual for her.

"You won't, I won't either."

After making love, winding up on the far side of the bed in a tangle of sheets, they lay side by side, both now fully awake.

"My twin," Thom said.

"My handsome twin."

"It's our wedding day today."

"It is," Wendy said.

"It's weird to exist in a moment that you know will become a lifelong memory. Like right now we are experiencing the first day of our lives together."

"Is that how you see it?"

"First day of our married life," Thom said. "It means something, doesn't it?"

"I know you already think I'm cynical," Wendy said, "but I'm not really. It's just that today doesn't seem any more important or significant than any other day we've had together. I just think ceremonies and milestones and birthdays are pretty much meaningless. Well, it's all meaningless, really."

"Everything is meaningless?"

Wendy paused, then said, "Yeah, it's all pretty meaningless in the big scope of time and the universe and all that. We just get this little scrap of time, and most humans believe that their scrap of time has more significance than some scrap of time that happened five hundred years ago or five thousand years ago or five hundred years from now. It doesn't. Obviously, this period of time is meaningful to me, and to you, too, because we're alive in it. But that's all there is."

"Nice of you to drop your nihilistic worldview immediately after we got married."

"I guess I thought you might already know that I have at least a touch of nihilism in me."

"No, I was just kidding."

Wendy propped herself up on an elbow. "You're meaningful to me. My mother is, too, and my brother. But pieces of paper that say we're married and birthday parties and political movements and people who talk about living a meaningful life . . . I don't know. We live, we die, and in between we need to protect the people we love."

"What about your poetry?"

"What about it?"

"Does it have meaning?"

"Not really. Sometimes. Some of them have meaning for me, some of them don't. I have no idea if they've ever had meaning for someone else. I write them because I like to write. It's a challenge, and it passes the time. What does writing mean to you?"

Thom, enjoying the conversation but itching for a cigarette, said, "I would never say this to anyone else, but I dream about writing something really important. Like a great American novel, something that lasts for years and years. I'm not saying I think I can do it, but that's what I want, if I'm being honest."

"Maybe you'll do it."

"But you think I'm being silly."

"No, of course not. It's just not the way that I think. Besides, what good would a book that lasts forever do you? You'll be dead and won't get to enjoy it."

"So what makes you happy?" Thom said.

"Everything. This, today, but also the fact that we can live our lives without fear. We have money and that means people can't touch us. I think you don't understand that because you never worried about money. But it's important. And we have each other. You're my real happiness. As long as we always tell each other the truth, as long as we are committed to one another, we'll be okay. Just because I don't talk about it maybe as much as you do, doesn't mean that I don't love you fiercely. I do. I think you probably have no idea how much I do."

"I do know. I love you fiercely too."

"Sometimes I think I can really only truly love one person at a time. Growing up, I only really loved my mother. And now I only really love you."

"You've stopped loving your mother now?" Thom had said it as a joke, but Wendy seemed to think about her answer.

"No, of course not, but it's different. She's safe now, and she has her dogs, and she has Alan. And now I have you."

"What about if *we* have children?" Thom said.

"Well, we'll have to wait and see what happens. You might wind up in second place." She was smiling, then slid up against him, her skin cool. "I'm getting sleepy again."

"Do you think we'd get caught if I crack the window and smoke a cigarette in here?"

"Probably, but it's fine with me if you want to. Why don't you go downstairs to the casino and have a cigarette there?"

"I can't abandon you on our wedding night."

"Trust me, I'll be sleeping. You should go. Are you tired?"

"I have a second wind."

"Go. Smoke cigarettes and have another drink. I'll be here."

Wendy was fully asleep by the time Thom had gotten dressed to go downstairs. She'd moved to her side of the bed and curled into a tight ball. He felt strange leaving her, like it would be bad luck or something, even though he knew, down deep, it wasn't. But once he was in the elevator heading for the casino floor he felt flushed with a sense of well-being. It was his wedding day after all, and there are days in life that you are allowed to feel good about yourself. This was one of them. He'd made an honest woman out of Wendy, and she'd made an honest man out of him. Odd phrasing, that, but it made sense with them. As the elevator doors opened silently and he stepped out onto the humming casino floor, he allowed himself to reflect briefly on what they had done to get here. They'd committed grave sins—he knew that—but he also knew how much worse those sins would be had they not been in the service of love, of a grand romance. The well-being returned as he walked between the tables, stopping only to light a cigarette. He was thinking of heading to the same bar where they'd had drinks earlier but watched a roulette table for a while. He'd never played, but knew the basic rules from films and books. The players at this particular table—one couple, one solo man, and one solo woman, from the looks of it—exuded a little bit of the glamour that he thought he'd find in Las Vegas. He'd never been to a casino before this trip and his judgment of them was almost entirely formed by James Bond movies. He'd pictured tuxedos and evening gowns and not fanny packs and oxygen tanks. But maybe because it was late, the inhabitants on the floor of the Flamingo seemed somewhere in between.

"Can I get you a drink?"

It was a cocktail waitress holding an empty tray. Without thinking, he said he'd like a scotch and soda. She hurried off.

He stepped closer to the table to watch the action. The couple were most likely in their thirties and looked as though they were coming from a nice restaurant. Her dress shimmered in the casino's lurid light, and he wore a white shirt unbuttoned to show a gold chain. It should have looked cheesy but he was indescribably handsome and the white shirt and chain showed off his black skin. The lone man at the table was older and was wearing a cowboy shirt with elaborate stitching. He was handsome as well, but in a leathery way, as though Joel McCrea had spent ten thousand hours in the sun. The other woman at the table was Asian, her long black hair streaked with silvery gray.

Thom's drink came and he tipped the waitress well enough to ensure she'd come back and find him. He lit another cigarette and watched how the players spread their chips on the table in seemingly strategic patterns. Only knowing this game from the movies, Thom always thought that you simply picked a number, or else you placed all your money on white or black, and that was that. But up until the croupier spun the wheel the players would spread their bets around the board, often grouping them around a set of numbers. They all seemed to be winning on a fairly regular basis, everyone smiling, including the croupier. Thom finished his drink then took a hundred dollars from his wallet and stepped up to the table, passing the money across to receive chips. He told himself he'd play until the money was gone and then go back upstairs to bed. On his first bet he mimicked what the other players were doing, spreading his chips around in the high teens, making sure to put some of the chips on the lines between numbers. The ball dropped into the slot for Red 18 and the man in the western wear slapped him on the back. He was given what seemed to be about twice the number of chips he'd started with.

An hour later he'd had two more scotches and he'd amassed close to $500. Paul and Jasmine, the couple from Smyrna, Georgia, had taught him basic roulette strategy, although it seemed to be working better for him than it had been for them the last half hour or so. The Asian woman had left, but Jim Smith, the older man with the Sam Elliott mustache, had told them all that he'd just been diagnosed with lung cancer so he was out having a good time before it all came to an end. He was smoking more than anyone else at the table.

At three in the morning, when he was still up about $400, Jasmine convinced him that he should go back to his bride. "You'll want some energy for tomorrow, and then you can take her out on the town with all that money you've made."

"You're right," Thom said, but Tonya, the waitress, had just delivered another drink for him, so he decided to finish it, have one more cigarette, and make one more bet. Thom's favorite number had always been 22, picked because of roulette, actually, that scene in the movie *Casablanca* when Rick tells the young Hungarian couple to bet on 22 so they can get enough money for a travel visa. And it was a number that had seemed to keep coming up in his life, in mostly good ways. It had been the number of the room in Kokosing, Ohio, where he'd rekindled his romance with Wendy. It had been the number of pages in the first story he'd published in the Mather College literary magazine. The twenty-second of October was his mother's birthday.

Drink finished, cigarette smoked, Thom pushed all of his chips, the whole stack, onto 22, knowing he was going to lose it, but thinking of how poetic it would be. He had come here to lose a hundred dollars. He didn't need the money. Jasmine screamed in delight when she saw the bet while Paul groaned. Jim just laughed. The croupier waved her hand over the table to indicate that no more bets were allowed then spun the wheel. Despite the odds, it didn't particularly surprise Thom when the ball bounced twice on the wheel and landed in its final slot, Brenda, the croupier, saying, with a little extra oomph, "Black 22, Black 22."

1993

i

The event was sold out, but they had let in twenty or so ticketless people to stand in the back of the church hall. Thom had found a column to lean against. It obscured his view of the onstage interview but he could hear the dialogue—Martin Amis was being interviewed by the president of the Paulding Book Festival—and it didn't seem to be going very well. The questions were longer than the answers.

Toward the end of the hourlong interview the discussion had gotten a little livelier, maybe because Amis had steadily drunk his way through a bottle of red wine, and maybe because they had moved on from the topic of the novel being discussed, *Time's Arrow*, and were now talking about pinball machines.

After the question-and-answer period, Thom stayed leaning against his column and watched the audience slowly exit the sweltering hall. Everyone seemed to be carrying jackets and sweaters and sporting shiny foreheads.

"Is that Thom?"

He'd been expecting to hear those words, but they still startled him. Wendy Eastman stood in front of him, a half smile on her lips, holding a copy of the Paulding Festival schedule of events. She wasn't alone; a woman around her same age stood next to her, half smiling as well.

"You're so familiar," Thom said.

"It's Wendy Eastman."

"Jesus, of course. My God, hello." They hugged, their cheeks brushing up against each other's.

"This is my friend Becky."

Thom introduced himself and shook the woman's hand. "It's really nice to meet you," Becky said, "but can we get the hell out of here? I need air."

The three of them joined the slow trickle toward the exit, then emerged onto East Fifty-Ninth Street across from Paulding's Bookstore. It was zero degrees outside, with a fierce wind, and Thom and his two companions put on scarfs and coats and gloves.

"Do you live here?" Thom said to Wendy.

"I don't, no. Becky does, though, and I'm staying with her for the weekend. How about you?"

"I live in New Haven, so not too far away. What did you think of the interview?"

Becky intervened to say that she was freezing and maybe they should find someplace to get a drink. They all walked against the wind toward the park, then pushed through the swinging door of the first bar they came to, a grubby, smoke-filled Irish pub that had several empty booths. After removing all their outerwear, they ordered a pitcher of Bass and three glasses, and talked about the book festival. It turned out that they'd all gone to a poetry reading by Sharon Olds earlier that day, but it was even more packed than the Amis interview, so it wasn't a surprise that Thom and Wendy hadn't seen each other. All three of them admitted they were worn out by book talk and were skipping the Sunday-morning panel on the contemporary Russian novel.

"How do you two know each other?" Becky said.

Thom and Wendy looked at each other, neither speaking right away. Finally, Thom said, "Wendy was my middle school girlfriend."

Becky threw back her head and laughed like he'd just said something incredibly clever. "Really?"

"I very briefly lived in New Hampshire when I was fourteen and fifteen," Wendy said, "and Thom was the only saving grace of that time in my life."

"That's the cutest thing I think I've ever heard," Becky said. "And you haven't seen each other since?"

Thom locked eyes with Wendy, briefly, and said, "Wendy had my address, but she never sent me a letter. It broke my heart."

Becky punched Wendy in the arm. "Why didn't you send him a letter?"

"He told me not to."

"Thom, why'd you tell her not to?" Becky refilled her glass, having fun.

"You know. We were just two ships that passed in the night. Two awkward, post-adolescent ships. I was crushed that I never heard from you."

Wendy made a sad face, then said, "But now we've found each other again."

Becky said, "I feel like I'm at this momentous moment in your lives. Should I leave you two alone?"

Wendy gripped her arm, both of them smiling. "No."

"Were you two serious?"

"We were as serious as you can be in middle school," Thom said.

"And freshman year of high school," Wendy said.

"Yes, and freshman year of high school. Becky, how do *you* know Wendy?"

"Rice University. Creative-writing majors."

"Do you both still write?"

Becky turned to Wendy, who said, "Not really. My concentration in college was poetry."

"She was really good," Becky said.

"So what do you do now? You're married, it looks like." Thom nodded down toward her ring.

"Oh," said Wendy. "I was married. He died about five months ago."

"Oh, Jesus, sorry," Thom said, as Becky put a hand on Wendy's back.

"We don't need to talk about it. I came out here—"

"Yeah, we don't need to talk about it," Becky said, suddenly serious. "Not this weekend, anyway. Thom, how about you, were you a creative-writing major in college?"

"Mather didn't have it as a major, so I was English lit."

"But you write?"

"I do. Stories, mostly, nothing very good."

"And what do you do for work?"

"It's not very exciting. I work at a video store."

"Oh, fun."

"It's not bad. It's a pretty cool indie store in New Haven called Penny Farthings Video. I just got made manager so there's that."

Becky and Wendy held up their glasses and congratulated him.

They talked some more about jobs; Becky was an assistant for a big-time editor at Knopf, and had lots of literary gossip. They ordered another pitcher, and Becky took herself off to the restroom. Wendy turned her head to watch her friend cross the now-crowded bar, then turned back to look at Thom. Neither said anything and they just looked at each other across the booth, each smiling. Thom desperately wished they were alone, but he also knew that it was a good thing that Becky was there to witness their reunion. He wondered if Wendy wanted it that way. He thought of asking her, but she hadn't spoken yet and they just continued to look at each other, pressing their knees together under the table.

"It's very nice to see you." Thom had spoken first.

"Yes. Are you all right?"

"I am. You?"

"Yes. I'm good."

Thom saw that Becky was working her way back toward them, and he leaned back in the uncomfortable wooden bench and lit a cigarette. As Becky retook her spot next to Wendy, she said, "God, I wasn't going to ask, but can I have one of those? I quit three months ago."

Thom gave her a cigarette and lit it for her. It was clear that he wasn't going to be alone with Wendy tonight, but that was fine. She was here across from him. She was real. For now it was enough, and some part of him was happy that they weren't alone, that tonight was not the night that he would have to lie to her about what had happened in Texas.

ii

"It's an hour drive from here," Thom said apologetically as he pulled away from the airport's parking lot. They'd been speaking on the phone for the past five months, but it was the first time they'd seen each other in person since New York.

"No problem," Wendy said. "In Texas it's an hour drive to get to your neighbor's house."

"Oh, good. I was worried you'd be sick of traveling."

She'd flown in from Lubbock that morning, leaving just before dawn and watching the sunrise from her window seat on the nearly empty flight to D.C. On the second leg of her trip, a crowded flight from D.C. to Hartford, the plane had hit a pocket of extreme turbulence that lasted fifteen minutes at least. The man next to her had closed his eyes and seemed to be praying. Wendy had looked out the window, wondering if she were going to die. She imagined that it would be a notably tragic story. Her husband drowning in his own swimming pool nearly a year ago, and then the grieving widow going down in a plane along the eastern seaboard. The pilot came on to reassure the nervous passengers that they'd "unexpectedly hit a little bit of rough air" but that the wind wasn't expected to be a problem on the landing. Wendy felt calm and wondered if the money she'd recently secured would automatically go to her mother upon her death.

"How was the flight?" Thom said.

"Bumpy."

Since meeting at the Paulding Festival in January she and Thom had exchanged numerous letters and spoken on the phone at least once a week. They'd talked about Bryce, of course, Wendy's dead husband, but nothing about the specifics of his death. It wasn't that Wendy thought her phone might be tapped, although she supposed it was possible, or that someone might read her letters, another possibility, it was just that they were now playing roles, and it was important to stay in character.

They were driving through Hartford, and Thom pointed out where he'd gone to school, Mather College, its spires visible from the highway.

"You don't want to give me a tour?" Wendy said.

"God, no. I still know people there."

They reached New Haven by early afternoon, parking on a narrow street lined on either side by triple-decker apartment buildings, some beautifully painted and maintained, but most dilapidated, with sloping porches and faded vinyl siding. "Lower your expectations," Thom said. "I live in a dump."

"I don't care. You know that."

They kissed in the car, the bucket seats making it awkward. Wendy could feel Thom's heartbeat through his rib cage. "God, I forgot how much I love kissing you," she said.

"Do you?" he said.

"Of course."

Thom took a breath, seemed to think of something, and snapped his fingers.

"What was that?" Wendy said.

"Nothing. An inside joke. I'll tell you later, but let's go upstairs first."

He got her suitcase from the back of his Taurus, and Wendy followed him into the dim interior hallway of his building, then up two flights to his apartment. He was making jokes about the peeling wallpaper and the loose banister on the stairs, and Wendy was laughing, but they'd been a little awkward together ever since the airport. It was so different from their most recent phone call, just two nights ago, when they'd told each other how much they were looking forward to this trip. And now, as they stepped into Thom's one-bedroom apartment, they felt like strangers. He gave her a tour of his place. It was cleaner than she'd expected, but that was probably because he knew she was coming. The living room was dominated by an enormous sofa in threadbare velvet. There was a coffee table that had been made by putting legs onto an old door. The table was cluttered with books and ashtrays and candle stubs. There was a large television set on top of an old bureau. A collection of videotapes was stacked all along the baseboard. The walls were filled with movie posters, some framed and some just nailed into the plaster. Wendy didn't say it out loud, but it felt like a dorm room. Thom had left a window open, and there was the smell of car exhaust and baking bread.

"I love it," Wendy said.

"It's a dump, you can say it."

"No, it has character. I mean, my house in Texas, it's definitely not a dump, but it's also incredibly boring." As she said the words, she remembered that he'd been to that house, or that he'd seen the outside of it, at least."Where'd you get all these posters?"

"Most of them I get for free from the store, but there's a few that are collectibles." He brought her to two small framed lobby cards from *Dial M for Murder*, one of them Grace Kelly's hand outstretched as she's being strangled. Then he showed her a full-sized poster from a film called *The Killing*. The background was yellow with images that looked like they were from a gangster film. A tough-looking man with a gun. A woman screaming from her bed.

"I don't know this film," she said.

"Oh, it's a masterpiece. I have it. On tape."

"Hey," Wendy said, touching Thom's arm, "I know we're not supposed to talk about it, but how'd it go in Texas? I need to know that you're okay."

"Should we get a drink first?"

"Oh, sure."

Thom brought her into the kitchen. He had a small array of bottles set up on an enamel-topped side table with rusted metal legs. "What can I get you?"

"What were you going to have?"

"Either a beer," Thom said, "or else I'll have some bourbon with ginger ale."

"That sounds good."

"Which one?"

"Bourbon."

He made the drinks and they brought them to the living room. "Do you mind if I smoke?" he said, when he already had the cigarette between his fingers. She told him it was fine, told him that she was always okay with him smoking. They sat on either end of the big couch. Her drink was very strong.

"How was it on your end?" Thom said. "Who found the body?"

"The maid did, just like I thought would happen. Estella comes every other day so she was there the next morning. Poor woman. I didn't hear about it until late that night when Bryce's parents reached me in my hotel room."

"How were they?"

"His parents? His mom was hysterical but she's hysterical if her club sandwich is cut into squares instead of triangles. His father just seemed angry, somehow. Angry at Bryce. I guess he was embarrassed to have a son who would fall into a pool and not be able to get out."

"Was there suspicion that he might have been pushed?"

"There was a perfunctory investigation. I was interviewed twice by the police, but I never got the feeling that they suspected much. They asked a lot of questions about Bryce's drinking habits, and if he could swim, and things like that. They asked some questions about his social life that I wasn't able to answer. They had the names of some women he might have been associated with."

"Like who?"

"I didn't know them. Other girlfriends. Strippers. God knows. But there was no physical evidence that anyone was at the house that night."

"You know that?"

"No one said that to me, exactly, but the death was ruled an accident."

Thom was nodding. Wendy noticed his drink was nearly empty.

"Do you want to tell me what it was like for you?" she said.

He frowned as though he were thinking about it, trying to remember. "Your directions were perfect. I parked at the church and walked to the back of the house. And Bryce was right on time, smoking his cigar out by the pool."

"You pushed him?"

"I did. And it was just like you said. I didn't have to do anything else. It was easy."

"And you're . . . ?"

"I'm okay. It was what it was. We did it."

"Yes, please always remember that. We did it together. You're not alone." She pressed her hand against his cheek and he leaned into it. Her pinkie finger was on his neck and she could feel his pulse, a thrilling reminder that he was alive, that she was alive as well, and that they were finally together.

"Tell me about the inheritance," Thom said.

"That makes it sound so formal," she said. "He died intestate, so the money he had in his account will go to me. I'll be rich, Thom. We'll be rich." She tried out a smile. "We should celebrate somehow. I mean, not make a big deal out of it, but go have a nice meal, drink some wine, start our life together."

"Haven't we already started our life together?"

Wendy put down her drink and slid along the couch so that she could put a hand on Thom's knee. "Yes, we did a bad thing, and now we get a better life. We just need to acknowledge that and then move on."

"I want us to get married."

"I do too. Although as far as I'm concerned, we're already married. We can do the real thing in another year or so. Make it official."

"How long are you going to stay in Texas?"

"I'm going to see my mom next month and stay with her for a while, then I'm going to relocate. How does New Haven sound?"

She had moved closer, and Thom's hand was now on her waist.

"I thought maybe we could both move somewhere new. That way it would be a fresh start, you and me."

"Where were you thinking?"

"Not far. Boston, maybe, or Cambridge."

Wendy had a sudden and complete vision of a brick house on a narrow, tree-lined street. The weather was cold but they were dressed for it, in sweaters and scarves. "That sounds really good," she said.

1992

AUGUST 28

The funeral, like everything else in Texas, was blazingly hot. One of Bryce's multiple uncles, Hollis, had appointed himself Wendy's escort for the afternoon, sitting behind her during the service and repeatedly pressing a hand onto her shoulder, and then bringing her constant drinks and snacks during the interminable reception afterward. She wondered if Uncle Hollis, who'd already had three wives, was hoping that she might be his fourth.

The only thing that made the day bearable had been her brother, Alan, who'd arrived two days after Wendy's husband Bryce had been discovered dead in the pool of their house. Wendy's mother had actually booked a flight to come out for the funeral but at the last moment she'd had an emergency with one of her dogs. Wendy had been relieved but was ultimately glad that her brother had made it. Bryce's family had alternated between over-the-top concern and bouts of chilliness, especially Bryce's older sister, Sloane, who was either pulling Wendy in for long, awkward hugs or staring at her from across rooms like she was a cat stalking a mouse.

After the small service at the burial site, the immediate family plus a few close friends (the family's, not Wendy's) gathered at her in-laws' house. Wendy had known that this moment was going to arrive, Bryce's funeral, and she had wondered how she would feel when it did. That morning, before she got out of bed, she had gone over her feelings about the day. She allowed herself one moment of sadness, thinking back to the first night she got to know Bryce, how he'd seemed almost childlike, desperate for someone to take care of him. And she allowed herself a moment of worry that everyone at the funeral would take one look at her and know what she had done, that the house of cards would come collapsing down and she would spend the rest of her life either incarcerated or penniless. And then she put those feelings away again. She got out of bed and dressed for her husband's funeral. And now that she was at the funeral reception, all she felt was palpable relief. Bryce was gone from the world, and that meant she would soon be gone from his world as well. Gone from Texas. Gone from his soulless, money-grubbing family. Gone from this tacky ranch with its giant rooms and gaudy furniture. She felt no remorse. And, truthfully, didn't feel any real sadness for the family. She knew they hadn't really liked him. No one really had.

"How are you holding up?" This was from Bryce's aunt, his mother's younger sister, one of the more poisonous members of the Barrington clan.

"It's surreal," Wendy said. "I keep looking around and just expect Bryce to walk into the room. I can't quite comprehend that he's really gone."

Aunt Shelby was nodding her head up and down on her freakishly long neck. "Well, look, the only good news is that you're a Barrington now. Just because Bryce is gone doesn't mean that you're not still part of this family. I was talking to Sunny and she said the same thing. The only thing that makes this at all bearable is that Bryce brought you into this family before he died, another daughter, another niece, another sister for Sloane. Goodness, she needs a steady hand in her life."

"I feel the same way," Wendy said, then managed to catch Alan's eye from across the room. He made his way toward them to break up the conversation.

By dusk most of the guests had either departed or, if they were staying at the house, retreated to their rooms. Wendy and Alan sat next to each other on the sofa that had been upholstered to look like the Texas flag. Alan said, "I think Mom really did want to come. But you know . . ."

"It's fine that she didn't. I can't quite imagine her here, can you?"

"These days I can't imagine her anywhere but in her home. She's happy, you know. She's the happiest I've ever seen her."

Wendy was quiet for a moment, taking that in, realizing that with the money coming to her, her mother would never have to change her life again.

"I'll come out as soon as I can, just as soon as everything's settled here."

"How long will that take?" Alan said.

"Hopefully less than a day."

Alan did one of his silent laughs, his shoulders hitching up. "This is quite a family you married into."

"Tell me about it."

"Several of them told me how they hoped you'd keep living here now that you're a Barrington."

"Yes, they've told me that too. I think it has more to do with keeping the money here. They're worried I'm going to take Bryce's money away with me."

Bryce's father's dog, some kind of terrier, wandered by, sniffing along the white carpet for dropped food. "Is it a lot of money?" Alan said.

"Here in Texas it's pocket money. Across state lines I'm a rich woman. It's your money, too, Alan. Yours and Mom's."

"I'm fine. Mom's fine too."

"I know you're both fine, but I also want you both to know that if you need any money, I have it now. I mean, I had it before but now it's all mine."

"Mine, all mine," Alan said, rubbing his hands together. Then his face suddenly dropped, and he said, "God, I'm sorry."

"No, don't be. It was funny."

Bryce's father's girlfriend, Melanie, came flying by, having spotted the dog eating food off a low coffee table. She snatched him up and as she walked past Wendy and Alan, she said, very drunkenly, "Wendy, you and I are going to go out on one epic girls' night soon, okay?"

"Okay," Wendy said. Then turned to her brother and said, "I'm going to go back to the pool house. You want to come, or do you want to go back to your hotel?"

"No, you go be alone, unless you want me there. I'll stay here a little longer and tell anyone who asks that you're taking a sleeping pill and getting into bed early."

She kissed her brother on the cheek. He had long hair now, longer than hers, and it suited him. Once outside in the diminishing light Wendy put her head down to make her way to the pool house. She could smell cigarette smoke in the breeze and knew that someone was around. When she got to her door a voice said, "Wendy, hold up."

She turned to see Sloane, cigarette burning between her fingers, unsteadily making her way to her across the tarmac. Wendy thought, not for the first time, just how much Sloane looked like Bryce. They had the same small eyes, the same jawline, only Sloane tried to make up for it with neon makeup and teased hair that added six inches to her height. "Wendy, let's talk," she said.

"Sloane, I'm exhausted. I just want to get into bed early and try and fall asleep."

"Sure, sure. I get it, honey. Let's just . . . Do you want the rest of my cigarette? It's making me dizzy."

"No, thanks. Sloane, you should go to sleep as well. You're staying here, right?"

"In my old room. Did I tell you what Daddy did? He turned it into a guest room with, like, little"—she was mimicking something with her hands, pinching at the air—"little soaps in the bathroom, and little things on the pillows."

"I'm sorry, Sloane," Wendy said, taking a step toward her house.

"Look, Wendy," Sloane said, lowering her head and flicking her cigarette away. "You don't care about my room, do you? I mean, why should you? You're a rich widow now. You've got the Cooper Bryce, Bryce Cooper trust-fund money. Do you know how much money I got when I turned twenty-one? I didn't get ten thousand million dollars. No way. Because I was born first, right, but I was a girl, so I got a lousy one thousand million dollars. Can you believe that? Because I'm a girl. Do you want to know what my friend Billy said about you? Do you know Billy?"

"I don't think so."

"Well, Billy's my gay friend. And he told me that he thinks you killed my brother for all his money. Can you believe it?"

"Sloan, I . . ."

"I told him, no way, but he was like, bitch, of course she did, and I was like, Wendy wouldn't do that. She loves my brother. But now . . ." Sloane was waggling a finger, and Wendy had a brief thought that if this scene were in a soap opera it would be way over the top. "But now I don't know. Did you love my brother, or did you just kill him for all his money?"

"Good night, Sloane," Wendy said, and turned and went through the door of the pool house.

She could hear Sloan shout out "Bitch!" and for a moment she wondered if she should go back outside, try to talk Sloan down a little, but she just didn't care. Until that moment she'd told herself that she would need to stick around Lubbock for at least a month or so, just to make it look good, but now she wondered if it even made a difference. Everyone was probably thinking what Sloane was thinking, but would that matter? She'd been interviewed by a very friendly police officer after returning to Happy Lake, and he'd asked her some questions in an almost apologetic tone—"Was Bryce seeing anyone else that you know of?"; "Did he have any enemies?"; "Do you think he might have had a problem with alcohol?"—even though it had been abundantly clear to her that there was no evidence of any kind of foul play. Still, it didn't surprise her now to find out that at least one member of the family suspected she'd orchestrated this death. It was a lot of money, after all.

She turned off all the lights in the pool house so that no one would come and check on her, see if she was still awake, and then she got into bed with a flashlight and the Milan Kundera novel she'd been slowly trying to work her way through. She eventually fell into a thin version of sleep, but before that she went over and over both what she'd done to arrive in this moment and what she would be doing next. She thought more about telling the family she was planning on leaving sooner rather than later, that she needed to visit her mother, and then she would be looking for somewhere new to live. If they were going to think of her as a villain, then who was she to stop them?

1992

AUGUST 22

10:23 P.M.

The first stab of the knife, deep into her neck, had probably killed her. Or it would have, eventually, the way that she was bleeding out. But he ended up stabbing her two times more, some small voice in the back of his head telling him to make it look like a crazed killer because that's who was doing this. A crazed killer.

Before getting back into his rental car he looked down at the hunting knife in his hand. He was still wearing gloves. The knife had blood on it and so did his glove. There was a sidewalk grate just behind his rental and Thom bent, slotting the folded-open knife through the narrow grate, and then pushed both gloves through as well. He stood up fast and for a moment he thought he was going to go down again. His head felt loose on his neck, and everything was out of focus. But he recovered and moved to the driver's-side door. He looked around briefly before getting inside. There was no one else on the street, just him, and the woman's body on the sidewalk. He'd rolled her so that she lay up against the side of a brick building, looking as if she were sleeping there, some kind of vagrant and not a murder victim. But that wasn't really what she looked like. Even on her side she looked distinctly dead. Someone would spot her very soon.

Thom drove away. Later, he couldn't really remember how he'd done it, but he managed to wend his way out of the city of Lubbock and back onto Route 84, heading to Austin. He had driven an hour, focusing on maintaining the exact speed limit, when the Please Refuel light went on. He kept driving, the miles sliding by, no sign of a gas station, and began to wonder if this was the end of the story. He'd run out of gas and that was how they'd catch him, a murderer marooned on the side of the road. But he reached an exit that promised gas and food and pulled off the main road, eventually locating an indie gas station called Plangman's Filling Station, which was self-service. There was also a restroom with an outside entrance. He worried it would be locked, but the door swung open and he stepped inside. There was no urinal, just a sink and a toilet, all of their dried-on grime illuminated by a single tube of white fluorescence. He locked the door behind him, and then, without even knowing he was nauseous, he bent over the toilet and threw up violently, tears streaming from his eyes. Then he went to the cracked mirror screwed in above the sink and looked at his face. He was pale, his eyes puffier than usual, but other than that, he looked like himself. He was a murderer now, and would be for the rest of his life. That was a fact that would never change. Suddenly he remembered the blood that had been dripping from his hand in Lubbock and began to check his clothes for other evidence of the crime he'd just committed. He stepped back so he could see himself better in the mirror. There was nothing on his face, nothing in his hair or on his clothes. He ran his hands down the back of his legs to see if anything felt sticky or damp, but they were clean. How was it possible that he hadn't gotten any blood on him at all? Had he imagined the whole thing? Was he in the midst of a lucid dream, all logic suspended? Then he spotted one dark spot near his hairline, a single drop of blood, and he spent a minute rubbing at it with the corner of a paper towel until it was well and truly gone.

Before leaving the bathroom he splashed cold water on his face, drinking some of it from his cupped hands. Inside the gas station he gave a twenty-dollar bill to an old man wearing a straw cowboy hat, then he went and pumped his own gas. The trigger on the pump turned itself off when the meter hit $20.00, and Thom replaced the nozzle. It took him a moment when he was back in the car to remember which direction he was going in, but he managed to get back onto the quiet highway.

Twenty minutes later he began to shake. He noticed it in his mouth first, his teeth chattering if he didn't keep them clamped together. But then his whole body was starting to vibrate, and a deep cold was suffusing his core. He tensed all his muscles, tightening his grip on the steering wheel, but that only made it worse. A sign indicated that there was a truck stop a mile ahead and he told himself he could pull off there. As soon as he made that decision, his shaking got worse, his whole body racked with involuntary movement, and he wondered if he was dying, having a heart attack or stroke. He pulled into the truck stop, managing to maneuver the car around the back of a dimly lit restaurant into a parking space under a busted streetlamp. He cut the engine and curled tightly into himself, still shaking rapidly. Sweat was beginning to build up on his scalp and the back of his neck, even though he still felt impossibly cold. He clambered over the two front seats and lay down on the backseat, curled up. He didn't know how long it was, but he stopped shaking eventually. Maybe that was the worst of it, he told himself, sitting up in the backseat. In the distance he watched a truck driver leaning against the rear of his vehicle, smoking a cigarette. Thom was in a brief period of not smoking cigarettes but knew that as soon as he was back in Austin, he would need to find an all-night convenience store to buy a pack.

He got out of the car to shake out his limbs.

No one will ever know about this, he said to himself. Wendy would know some of it, of course, but not what happened in downtown Lubbock. And not how he felt right now. Somehow this decision calmed him, and he took a deep breath of Texas air. Before getting back into the car he looked up at the enormous sky. That song went through his head again—*big and bright, stars at night.* He'd heard it recently but maybe it had only been in his head.

1992

AUGUST 22
9:55 P.M.

Thom moved forward on the balls of his feet, racing across the concrete apron and shoving Bryce in the lower back. Wendy's husband expelled a sound, a squeal that seemed to come more from being frightened than from the physicality of being shoved. He landed in the water, awkwardly, his arms flailing, his face slapping the surface. For five seconds he churned in place, his head coming up, shouting something unintelligible. Thom had already spotted the pool skimmer used to scoop leaves and made his way to it, thinking that if he could get the net around Bryce's big head he could hold him under that way. But when he reached the skimmer Bryce was still flailing in the water, being dragged down by his waterlogged sweatshirt, now clearly shouting out "Help!" whenever he could get his mouth above the surface. Bryce was so frantic that it wasn't even clear if he knew that Thom was there. Thom crouched, keeping an eye on him, now steadily but slowly working himself to the edge of the pool, trying not to swallow water. He was nearly there when he went under again, quietly almost. Then he seemed to have one last burst of energy and managed to get a hand on the pool's edge, lifting his head one last time above the water and seeing Thom looming above him. Bryce's eyes lit up with hope at the sight of Thom, and he seemed to say something, but his mouth was full of water. In his excitement his hand had come off the pool's edge. Thom went down to his knees and leaned forward, placing his hand on the top of Bryce's head and pushing. There was no resistance, Bryce went under again and Thom held him there for half a minute—or longer; he wasn't sure. When he took his hand away, Bryce had stopped moving. His cigar, snuffed out now, bumped against the edge of the pool. For one absurd moment Thom thought of *Caddyshack*, a film he'd loved when he was twelve, the cigar reminding him of the candy bar floating in the pool that everyone thought was something else.

Thom stayed where he was, watching Bryce bobbing in the pool, his arms outstretched. Another film crept into his mind. A dead man in a pool, filmed from below. *Sunset Boulevard*. The night was quiet again, not even the sound of coyotes in the distance. He kept waiting for a team of police to race in from somewhere, or for Bryce's father to emerge from the big house, but nothing had changed. Except that Bryce had fallen into the pool and drowned.

Thom stood, and as he did, the below-water pool lights turned off. A wave of fear jolted him, but he told himself the lights were on an automatic timer. He checked his watch. It was ten o'clock exactly.

At first, he thought the voice was coming from the pool house, but it was actually coming from the concrete path that led from the front of the main house. A female voice. "Hello," she said again, loudly.

Thom's body went cold and rigid. He could see her walking toward the pool, along a path illuminated by lights that were built into the ground. The fence was behind him, and he could quickly go over the top of it and run back toward his car. But it was too late. She'd see him and then she'd see the body. He and Wendy had already decided that Bryce's death needed to be an accident.

Without even thinking about it, he walked, moving fast, around the pool toward the woman, and said, "Hi there," in a voice that sounded fairly normal in his own ears.

"There you are," she said, and to his relief she stopped walking toward him. She was around his age, wearing a very short skirt and a fuzzy sweater that glowed in the lamplight. Her hair formed a dark halo around her head. Her perfume competed with the smell of chlorine that hung in the air.

"Bryce isn't here," Thom said.

"Oh, you're not Bryce," she said, unclasping her purse, and for a moment Thom wondered if she was going to remove a police badge, or maybe a gun.

"No. I was here looking for him."

"Okay," the woman said. She was now tapping out a cigarette from a hard pack. "This is Bryce's address, though, right?" She had a strong Texas accent.

"It is," Thom said, his mind rapidly calculating how to get her to leave before she noticed the body in the pool. "But he definitely isn't here."

"Okay," the woman said, drawing it out. Thom had no idea what the situation was, but this woman was coming over as some sort of blind date. "You don't think he'll be coming back soon then?"

"Um, I don't think so." Thom was suddenly aware that his right hand and the sleeve of his sweatshirt were wet. He rubbed it against his thigh, and felt this woman's eyes flick down, taking it in. "Hand's wet," Thom said, and laughed.

"If he comes, tell him Holly was here, 'kay?" She dragged at her cigarette and took two steps back, not quite turning around.

"Will do," Thom said, and his own words came out wrong in his head. He suddenly seemed to have a Texas accent as well.

Holly turned and walked back down the path, moving faster than she had when she'd ambled onto the scene. When she turned the corner Thom turned himself, speed-walking past the dark pool,

Bryce's body just visible bobbing in the deep end, then hoisted himself up and over the fence. He quickly checked his compass, pointing it northwest, and began to run, not paying attention to the contours of the ground this time, just running, his mind calculating at an equally furious pace. She'd gotten a good look at him, but did that even make a difference? Would she even hear about the local rich boy who'd fallen into a pool and drowned? And if she did, would she go to the police to tell them she'd been there and seen someone else? *He was acting totally strange, Officer, and I think his hand was wet.* Thom just didn't know. All he knew was that it had gone so right and then suddenly it had gone so wrong. His foot landed hard in a divot in the ground and he stumbled but didn't fall, kept running. The church was now visible, lit only by starlight, but to its right he could make out the headlights of a car skimming through the dark. If the woman, if Holly, had turned right out of the Barrington homestead, then that was probably her. If she'd turned left she'd be gone forever, but why would she turn left? Lubbock was back past the church.

He'd lost sight of the car by the time he got back to his rental, but he jumped into the driver's seat, inserted the key, and started the rental up, backing up into the road, spraying gravel. He had been driving for two minutes before he realized his headlights weren't on. He couldn't remember where the switch for the lights was but managed to flick them on just as he was reaching an intersection, the only car ahead of him taking a left that would lead back to downtown. He followed at a distance. He couldn't be sure that he was following the car being driven by Holly, but there was a good chance it was her. He hadn't seen any other cars on the road since driving back from Happy Lake.

As they neared Lubbock, traffic picked up. Thom had read somewhere, probably in a detective novel, that trailing a car at night was relatively easy because most cars' rear lights were noticeably unique. He found this was the case. The car he was following had thin rectangular rear lights set far apart. He kept his eyes on them, not worried if other cars slid between him and the car he was following. They had entered a busy part of town, a string of bars, college kids coming and going along the sidewalk, then the car took a sharp left down a less populous street, tall buildings on either side. The car was going slow, and he wondered if she was looking for parking. He hung back, but she'd stopped the car and he had to keep going. He took a chance and glanced in her direction as he slowly drove past, almost surprised to find that he was following the correct car. There was Holly, same big hair, a lit cigarette between her lips, beginning to back into a spot just big enough for her compact Nissan.

Thom took the first right he could and immediately parked, partially blocking an alleyway entrance between a college bookstore and what looked like a museum with an enormous sheet-glass façade. Both of the buildings were dark. One moment he was sitting there, overcome by what he believed he needed to do, and the next he was outside of the car, the knife in his hand. Maybe he could simply threaten her, or even beg her, tell her to never mention this to anyone or he would find her and hurt her. But would that really work? He began to move back in the direction where she'd been parking the car. As he was coming up to the cross street, knife in his hand, but still folded, the woman turned the corner and they were face-to-face.

"Oh, it's you," she said, her eyes confused. He jumped on top of her and together they crashed to the sidewalk. The breath must have been knocked out of her lungs, because she opened her mouth to scream but nothing came out. It was like a silent movie.

1992

AUGUST 22

8:02 P.M.

The parking lot at the Happy Lake Baptist Church was a mile from the Barrington Ranch by road, but it was only about a half mile if you walked across a stretch of scrubby desert land.

"Make sure you park at Happy Lake Baptist Church and not Tuxedo Valley First Baptist, which is pretty close to our house as well, but the wrong church," Wendy had told him. He remembered thinking that whenever she talked about Texas things, she did so with the slightest of Texas accents, a barely noticeable drawl.

"Happy Lake Baptist Church," he had said back to her, memorizing the address and also memorizing how to walk from there to the ranch house.

"Bring a compass," she'd told him, "and go exactly southeast and you'll come right out behind the pool. There's a fence but it's easy to climb."

He was in the parking lot now, the engine of his rental Dodge turned off, the lights doused. He'd left Austin at three in the afternoon and it was just after eight now. He stepped out of the car into the warm night. The air was still, and the stars really were big and bright in Texas, casting the stark-white church and the empty parking lot in a sickly yellow glow. He was wearing dark jeans and a gray hooded sweatshirt. All he had on him was a pair of gloves in the pocket of his hoodie, a cheap compass he'd bought a month earlier at an army-surplus store back in New England, plus a less-cheap hunting knife he'd bought with cash in Austin that afternoon. He hadn't planned on bringing a weapon—he didn't plan on using it on Cooper Bryce Barrington—but it felt like a security blanket. A tool that might come in handy if something went wrong.

He used the compass for only a short time, because pretty soon he could see the lights of the ranch house on the horizon. Wendy had told him that the nearest neighbor was about a mile away. It had to be the right house.

He pushed the compass back into his pocket, his fingers touching the handle of the folded knife. He'd heard yipping sounds already that sounded as though coyotes had gathered around a kill, and he was glad to have the knife. Keeping his eyes on the uneven terrain, he kept walking toward the lights of the ranch house.

Wendy had been right about the fence—steel slats, but not even as tall as he was. Still, he stood for a moment outside of the property staring in. He was situated right behind the pool, illuminated by underwater lights so that it gave off an eerie phosphorescent glow. Wendy had told him she was the only one who ever used it, and he pictured her now, doing laps in a white one-piece. On the other side of the rectangular pool was what must have been the pool house, where Wendy lived with Bryce, her husband. As she'd said, it was the size of most people's actual house, a single-story replica of the big house on the property, a monstrous ranch built in the 1980s, its windows dark. The pool house, on the other hand, was completely lit up, all the windows ablaze, and bright spotlights on the front door and all along the pool decking. The darkest area that Thom saw was behind a shed that probably housed the pool equipment.

After putting on the thin gardening gloves, he hoisted himself onto the flat top of the fence and dropped to the other side, landing with a thud, immediately thinking of all those detective novels his mom had given him to read in which the major clue was someone's footprint under a window. He bent and looked at the place where he'd landed, but it was a strip of pebble stone that he doubted would produce a print. Still, he smoothed it out a little with his gloved hand before retreating to the back of the shed. He crouched in its long shadow, with a view of the pool-house entrance. There was a hanging bench under the house's awning, but Wendy had told him that when Bryce came out to smoke his cigar, he always paced along the edge of the pool as he smoked it.

"He surveys his domain," she'd said.

"Oh yeah?"

"Something like that."

"He doesn't smoke the cigar in the house?"

"God, no. I won't let him. It's foul."

"But you won't be there."

"He knows that I would know. Besides, he likes going out to smoke, I think."

"And he'll be drunk?"

"Yes. He always is at the end of the night."

"And he'll be alone."

She'd hesitated. "I think so. We got in a fight a while ago and I made sure to tell him that I didn't care what he did with other girls but not to bring them to our house."

"What did he say?"

"Well, he denied being with other girls at all, but I think I got my point across. I really think he'll be alone. If for whatever reason he isn't, or if he doesn't come out for his end-of-night stogie, then it wasn't supposed to happen. Just call it off."

Still crouching, eyes on the house, Thom wondered if Bryce was even in the pool house. All the lights were on, but he hadn't seen any movement in any of the windows. He scanned the eaves of the house, finally spotting the camera that was secured just below the gutter. Wendy had told him that there'd be a camera there, pointed toward the pool, but that it was just there for show. "There are fake security measures all over the property," she had said. "More fake cameras at the front of the house. One of those signs that says the property is monitored. A sign about a guard dog. You'd think with their money they'd be able to pay for the security, but maybe that's why they have so much. They're cheap." Thom studied the camera, its blank eye visible in the watery light emanating from the pool. He hoped Wendy was telling the truth about it being fake.

Thom listened to the distant cries of the coyotes. The house remained still. Maybe Bryce was out at a bar somewhere or sleeping at someone else's place. That thought caused a brief sensation of relief in Thom's tensed-up body. How would he feel if Bryce never showed up, if he never got his chance? Right now, he thought he might feel okay about it. Wendy would get divorced. They'd still be together. But they'd be poor. Well, not poor exactly, but they wouldn't be rich. According to Wendy, Bryce had received $10 million from his grandfather's estate when he'd turned twenty-one. When she'd told him about it, he'd seen how much the money would mean to her.

Not to mention that Cooper Bryce Barrington was not worth the space he took up in the world. Thom didn't know this personally, but Wendy had convinced him. She'd never said that he deserved to die, exactly, but she did say that his death would not exactly be a tragedy. "Even his parents don't like him," she'd said.

Waiting now for Bryce to emerge, Thom told himself he was here for one reason, to kill Bryce and make it look like an accident. He was doing it for the money and he was doing it for Wendy. It wasn't the right thing to do. He would never try to convince himself of that. They were simply taking advantage of an opportunity that the world had offered up. Murder one douchebag and collect $10 million. And there was something else about what they were doing, something that Thom had thought a lot about, that plotting this act together, getting away with it, made them somehow special. Made them rarefied people, the way that characters from books and from movies were rarefied. He'd always felt that way, ever since that first kiss in Georgetown all those years ago, that he was the protagonist of a special story.

Thom heard a sound from the house and watched as Bryce opened the sliding glass doors and stepped outside. He was wearing shorts and a crewneck sweatshirt. He appeared to be barefoot and there was a long cigar clenched between his teeth. He slid the door closed behind him, then lowered his head. Thom heard the snick of a lighter, then the sound of Bryce pulling on his cigar to get it lit. Then he stood for a moment, shoulders back, puffing away wetly. Thom had seen a picture of Bryce that Wendy had shown him, but somehow, he wasn't prepared for his size. He looked like a college linebacker who hadn't played for a while, which was essentially what he was. He had thick thighs and an emerging beer gut and a large, shaggy head. Once he got the cigar going properly, he did exactly what Wendy had said he'd do, and began to pace, first along the far side of the pool, facing out through the fence toward the dark expanse of land. Then he circled around the deep end, looking down into the illuminated water. Thom could smell the cigar smoke in the air, mixing with the dense waft of chlorine. Bryce stopped for a moment, his legs spread apart, maybe to keep his balance, and stared across the pool into the distance again.

Thom stood up, aware that one of his knees made a popping sound, but Bryce didn't move. He was swaying a little, Thom now realized, and also muttering something under his breath. This was the moment. Bryce was two feet from the edge of the pool. Thom could simply rush him and shove him into the water, then make sure he didn't clamber out. He bent at the knees slightly, like a runner getting ready to sprint. There was another option as well: Do nothing. Stand in the shadows and wait for Bryce to finish his cigar and go back inside. Thom would drive back to Austin, return his rental car, then fly back to Connecticut. He'd meet up with Wendy in two months and tell her he couldn't go through with it. She would tell him that she loved him, and who needs $10 million anyway. These thoughts filled him and then just as suddenly left him. He'd already been through it in his mind, a hundred times at least. He was here because doing nothing was a choice he'd already discarded.

1992

JUNE

i

Wendy had registered in advance for the Tinhook Literary Festival, being held in the Berkshires at a dilapidated inn, but Thom was simply staying in the next town over at a motel that accepted cash payments. It was probably not entirely necessary, this subterfuge, but the plan to murder Wendy's husband was more real now than unreal. Why not be careful?

"Can you tell me where the nearest bar is?" Wendy asked the festival volunteer who was shutting down the registration table.

"To here?" the woman said, startled somehow that she was being asked a question.

"Here in Tinhook. Walking distance, I guess."

"Oh, there's lots," she said. She had heavy glasses and a Louise Brooks haircut. Poet, Wendy thought to herself. "But there will be beer and wine at the reception here."

"Right, when's that?"

"Six o'clock. In the Allingham Room."

Wendy made a show of looking at her watch. The poet said that the next street over had at least two bars on it. "The Ginger Door will be opening soon, I think." It was nearly five. Wendy thanked her and departed the hotel. She'd taken a taxi from Albany Airport to get to Tinhook and had been dismayed that it seemed as though the Lord George Inn was in a residential section of the town. Back when Thom and she had made their plan to meet in Tinhook, they'd decided to meet at the closest bar to the festival site at five o'clock on the Friday. For some reason it hadn't occurred to Wendy that there might not be a bar within walking distance.

But now that she was outside in the cool evening, the sun still high in the sky, she spotted a sign that pointed its way toward the "historic downtown." In five minutes, she found herself on a wide street, brick buildings on either side. Half the storefronts seemed shuttered, but the half that weren't seemed to be either pizza places or bars. She spotted the Ginger Door, calculated that it was possibly the closest bar to the Lord George Inn, and made her way to it. Thom was already inside. He had a full beer in front of him and had just lit a cigarette. The only other customers in the bar were four middle-aged ladies at a booth. All of them were also smoking, and the bar was filling up with smoke, tinged blue by the late-afternoon light coming in through the plate-glass window.

"This seat taken?" Wendy asked Thom as she slid onto a leather-topped stool.

"Do I know you?" he asked, barely suppressing a grin, but she could see the happiness in his eyes. Wendy realized suddenly that she'd been nervous about seeing him again, but now that he was here, all that nervousness dissipated, and she felt something approaching joy as well.

"I don't know. Do we know one another or don't we? Had we already made this decision?"

The bartender, an older man wearing suspenders and a belt, was down the other end of the bar slicing lemons. The women at the table were laughing as though they were already on their second or third drinks. "I don't think there's any harm in our talking together at this bar. God, it's nice to see you."

Wendy squeezed his leg with a hand, surprised to find he was wearing shorts. "Oh," she said.

"I forgot my pants."

"Yes, you did."

"What do you want?"

"To drink?"

"Yes, to drink."

"How about a Tom Collins? That was my father's drink and this bar reminds me of him."

After Thom had ordered her drink, but before it arrived, Wendy said, "I'll just have this one drink. I have to get back for the reception at the hotel."

"What's it like?"

"The hotel?"

"The hotel. The conference."

"I don't know. I didn't notice, and I don't care. I'm just so glad that you are here."

"Are you surprised that I came?"

"A little bit, I think, considering what we talked about last time. I wouldn't have blamed you if you didn't show up."

"That's not going to happen. I mean, I'm always going to show up. No matter what we do or don't do."

Wendy's drink arrived. After tasting it she instantly regretted her choice, because it really did remind her of her father. "Yuck," she said.

"Want to swap? My beer is terrible too."

"Sure."

They swapped drinks, and Wendy tasted the warm beer. "I like this better," she said.

"When can we see one another?"

"I've thought about that. Just come over tonight and spend the night at the inn. There's a dinner but that ends at eight o'clock. There's a bar there and I'm sure all the other participants will be drinking. I'll go to my room and you can meet me there. No one will notice."

"Drink okay, miss?" the bartender said, noticing that they'd switched.

"Oh, fine. Turned out it wasn't what I wanted, but there was nothing wrong with it."

Thirty minutes later, walking back to the Lord George, the sun now casting a long, distorted shadow of her frame along the sidewalk, Wendy told herself that they needed to start being extra careful. It would be fine if Thom came to the hotel and spent the night. No one would see them together. But maybe being together in public was now a mistake. Not that she thought it made any real difference that a bartender had noticed them because they had switched drinks, but it was just the type of thing that could eventually become a problem. *Nobody* should notice them. After Bryce was dead it was important that Thom and Wendy meet again as strangers. Well, not total strangers. They could meet again for the first time since they were kids. That would be okay.

Since the last time they'd seen each other, over six months earlier in Cambridge, Wendy had rented the movie *Body Heat* at their local Blockbuster. She'd actually had Bryce rent the film—he'd brought it home with *Point Break* and they'd watched them as a double feature. He'd insisted on watching his movie first, which was fine, because he'd passed out during the opening credits of *Body Heat*. Thom had recommended it. Well, he had mentioned it, because in Cambridge they had first brought up the idea of murdering Bryce, talking about it as a joke for a while before realizing that they weren't exactly joking. "All I know about killing someone's husband is from *Double Indemnity*, of course, and *Body Heat*." And then he'd told her how it went spectacularly wrong in both those films.

"Why?"

"Because the woman is just using the man."

"If we do it, that won't be the case. I promise that."

"I know. We'll break the mold. We'll kill the husband and live happily ever after."

Wendy ended up watching *Body Heat* twice before returning it. Some actor she recognized from the movie *Diner* gave a great speech about how there were fifty ways to fuck up a crime and that only a genius could come up with twenty-five of them. And what turned out to be the big fuckup for the two murderers in *Body Heat*, besides the fact that Kathleen Turner was only ever using William Hurt, was that they'd been spotted together as a couple before they committed the murder. Wendy decided then and there that Thom and she needed to be virtual strangers until they met again at some undecided literary festival after Wendy was a widow. But for now, there should be no connection between them. That was why Thom wasn't registered here at Tinhook.

Wendy skipped the cocktail reception but went to the dinner, sitting at a table with three other women who were, like herself, simply attendees. But Wendy wasn't surprised to learn that they were all aspiring writers, and two of them had signed up for seminars on small-press publishing that came with a chance to submit work to the editor who was running it. Wendy kept relatively quiet during dinner. She wanted to be forgettable. And normal. That was another line in *Body Heat* that she remembered. Kathleen Turner—or was it William Hurt?—said that nothing out of the ordinary could happen in their lives leading up to the murder.

After dinner she waited in her room, her copy of *Possession* by A. S. Byatt open on her lap, but she found she couldn't concentrate on the words. Instead, she stared at the wallpaper, deep red and intertwined with roses, or maybe dahlias. She studied the pattern, trying to figure out at what point it began to repeat. And she listened to the sounds of the hotel. There was the faint echo of the music being played in the bar, but what she mostly heard were the creaks in the room above her, some guest pacing the floor. And she could hear voices talking but without understanding the words. Maybe they were in the next room, or two rooms down. She reminded herself that when Thom arrived they should be quiet.

At a little after eight o'clock there was a knock on her door and she leapt off the high bed to swing the door inward, Thom quickly entering.

"Anyone see you?" she said.

"Not on your hall. And probably not in the lobby. That was a wild crowd down there."

She smiled. "I'm missing out."

"You are. You could meet a minor poet with a goatee."

"I could move with him to some college in North Dakota."

"Do you think he has tenure?"

"Not yet, but he dreams of it. I will too. We can buy a starter home."

"The real question is: Would he kill your husband for you?"

"Okay," Wendy said. "We're going straight there."

"No, we're going straight to the bed first."

Later, buried under the sheets, the hotel now eerily quiet, Thom said, "I think we should do it. I think we should murder your husband."

They were the words that Wendy had hoped to hear, but now that he'd said them, she felt suddenly reticent. "We don't have to, you know. I could leave him, move to Connecticut to be with you, get a job. Our lives would be good."

"Our lives would be normal."

"What's wrong with that?"

"There's nothing wrong with it, except that it doesn't feel right for us. I feel like something began that first night we kissed, and maybe it was all leading up to this."

"I feel the same way," Wendy said, telling the truth. She had no interest in being normal, not really, although she certainly had interest in appearing normal, considering what they were planning on doing.

"I've thought a lot about this," Thom said. "It's all I think about. But I just keep coming back to this strange feeling that this is fate. We're not supposed to scrimp and save and have uninspiring jobs. We were meant to kill to be together. We were meant to be special."

"What I keep thinking about," Wendy said, "is how, if we do this, and if we get away with it, I'll be able to buy my mother a house for her to live in for the rest of her life. Right now I pay her rent, but if I divorced Bryce, then . . . And when I think about it that way, it's not a hard decision at all. If I could press a button that wiped Bryce off the planet and provided protection for my mom, then I wouldn't hesitate."

"So, let's do it. Let's press that button."

She placed a hand on the side of his neck. "You'd be doing it, of course. The act."

"*We'd* be doing it together, but yes, I know what you mean."

"I need to know you're okay with it. I need to know that it's not going to haunt you forever."

"Tell me the plan again. In detail."

ii

At five in the morning Thom got out of Wendy's bed and dressed as quietly as possible. Wendy slept, curled up in a ball like some small animal in its den. He'd told her just before she'd fallen asleep that he would slip out at dawn, so that he didn't need to wake her and tell her he was going. Still, it was all he could do to not shake her awake, give her one more kiss. It was unbearable, almost, to think about how long it would be until they saw each other again.

They'd talked all night, going over the plan in detail. Wendy had devised most of it. She'd memorized the dates and times, and if everything went perfectly, this time next year they'd be together, starting a new life.

In the downstairs lobby of the hotel, a woman in running gear said "Another early riser" to him as he passed.

"Yes, I am," he stupidly said back to her, and moved quickly for the door. He'd parked on Main Street, and the short walk to his car felt surreal and ghostly. The day was going to be hot and already mist was lifting off the front yards, making everything seem a little out of focus. He was happy when he arrived back at his own cheap motel, where he immediately stripped and got under the sheets, telling himself he might as well attempt some sleep before driving back to Connecticut. Checkout wasn't until noon.

He did manage an hour of deep, dreamless sleep, and then he was awake again, going over the plan in his mind. He'd brought a blank notebook with him, one in which he'd begun to outline a short-story idea about a high school boy who falls in love with an exchange student visiting for two weeks. He flipped ahead to a blank page and considered writing down the details of the plan. He could always rip those pages out later and burn them. But he talked himself out of it. It was important that there be no evidence whatsoever, that it was all only in his mind.

On August 21, Wendy was going to fly to New York City to attend a college friend's art opening. On that same weekend, Thom would visit Austin and stay in some cheap motel. His college friend Samantha was now living there with her boyfriend, Ethan, an aspiring country singer who was performing on the Sunday night of that weekend. His trip could be to see them. It would be easy enough for him to drive on Saturday to Wendy's house outside of Lubbock. She'd told him that every night before he went to sleep Bryce would go outside and walk around the pool and smoke a cigar. All Thom would have to do was push him into the deep end and make sure Bryce didn't pull himself back out. She said that he could barely swim and that pushing him in was maybe all he would need to do. Wendy also told him about the Happy Lake Baptist Church, where he should park, and how to get to the back side of the Barrington property. They both agreed that the most important thing was that it appear to be an accidental death. If it looked as though Bryce had been murdered, then the suspicion would fall onto Wendy, even though she would be away at the time. The Barrington family wouldn't necessarily be able to stop her receiving Bryce's money, but they could try.

The last thing Wendy had told Thom was this: "If something seems off, remember that you don't have to go through with it. If anyone is there with him, then simply turn around and go back. Or even if you have a bad feeling, or decide that you can't do it, then just don't do it. That's more important to me than getting his money. We'll still have each other."

"Okay," Thom had said.

"I mean it. Come end of summer we will be together, one way or another. But here's the thing. If you do succeed, then everything that we do afterward has to be perfect. No signs that you were ever at the house. No getting stopped by the cops on the way back to Austin. No drunken confessions. No remorse. If we're going to do this, then we're going to do this right. We're going to have a good life together, and Bryce is going to wind up exactly where he should wind up. Okay?"

Thom was nodding his head, but the room was dark, and he said, "I won't let you down."

He checked out of the motel. They'd held on to a credit card for incidentals, but he paid in cash. Before leaving, he watched the girl at the reception desk rip up the slip of paper that had his card's imprint on it and put it in the trash. During the long drive back to Connecticut, he kept thinking about what Wendy had said about the end of summer, how they'd be together. If only he could snap his fingers and time would rush forward to that instant, like in a movie, or a book. He tried it in the car, snapping his fingers, but he was still behind the wheel, trapped in this particular moment. *It will happen*, he said to himself. *If we're careful, it will all happen exactly as we planned it.*

1991

OCTOBER

It was a forty-minute walk from Rachel's apartment in North Cambridge to the Harvard Museum of Natural History, but the weather was perfection, and Wendy felt as though she could do this walk every day of her life. Her friend's neighborhood in North Cambridge was a little run-down but still had more character and charm than the nicest neighborhood in Lubbock. After navigating through Porter Square, Wendy began to walk down Oxford Street, lined with trees and Victorian houses and charming brick apartment buildings. The narrow sidewalk was buckled here and there by tree roots and long winters. Wendy wore her oldest, most comfortable jeans and a new sweater she'd bought the day before at Filene's Basement in downtown Boston. There was chimney smoke in the air and the ground was covered with fallen leaves, and Wendy, as she'd felt years earlier when she'd briefly lived in New Hampshire, knew that this was the part of the world in which she belonged.

As she got closer to the university, Oxford Street widened, concrete academic buildings replacing houses, and wide swaths of campus replacing tiny front yards. It took her a while to find the museum, only because there were three museums all in a row, housed in imposing brick structures. She paid her entrance fee and shuffled in between two large families. She was early—their meeting time wasn't until noon—but Wendy genuinely wanted to walk around a little. Before entering the main exhibit she got caught up looking at a display of glass flowers—tiny, delicate specimens. She had never been particularly interested in either glasswork or even real flowers—that was her mother's passion—but something about these pieces, created over a hundred years ago, was fascinating. A voice was speaking to her, and she came out of her reverie. "I've been coming here every day for ten years," he said, and she turned to look into the face of a very old man, dried spittle in the corners of his mouth. She nodded and smiled and left the exhibit.

By twelve o'clock she'd wandered through most of the rooms and wound up in the Great Mammal Hall, feeling as though she'd stepped out of her own life and into Victorian England. There were taxidermied giraffes and great apes, and several whale skeletons hung from the high ceiling. There was a balcony level that ran all the way around the room, displaying hundreds of stuffed birds and allowing a closer look at the whales. She was on the balcony when she spotted Thom, entering the hall below her, his hands tucked into his front pockets, walking slowly, looking like a typical New England college boy in jeans and an unbuttoned peacoat. His hair was longer than the last time she'd seen him.

He pulled his hand out of his pocket and checked the time, then scanned the crowd of other visitors on the lower level, clearly looking for her. Wendy stood still, watching, enjoying the feeling of spying on him. She could tell he was dazed by the majesty of the room, just as she had been. He was slowly moving—he hadn't even looked up yet—then settled in front of a large glass case that contained a stuffed lemur. He bent at the waist to get a better look. Then he mussed his hair a little and she realized that he was looking at himself in the reflection. She was just about to leave the balcony to meet him when he suddenly looked up, his eyes seeing the enormity of the room for the first time. She stayed put and he found her, a smile creasing his face. For a moment she saw herself through his eyes, poised on a balcony, a Juliet surrounded by dead animals. She was about to come to him, but he was already moving toward the steps that would bring him to her.

Later, in the hotel room, he came out of the bathroom and stood naked for a moment just looking at her lying on the bed. She was propped up on all of the pillows, naked as well, a sheet pulled up over her legs and lap. "What are you doing?" she said.

"Memorizing this."

She pulled the sheet off her legs so that he could see all of her, striking a sexy pose, trying not to laugh but failing a little. But he didn't laugh back, just clambered onto the bed and worked his way toward her.

"I keep thinking in clichés," he said, twenty minutes later.

"What do you mean?"

"I don't know. I want to say things like I've never felt so alive as I do right now, and looking at you stops my breath, and how you are the most perfect creation I've ever seen. Do you know what I mean?"

"I know that I will only ever be happy with you," Wendy said.

"See. Clichés."

"I don't care. They're clichés for a reason. And it's not like we'll ever share them with anyone else. Just ourselves."

"How long can you stay here?"

He'd already asked her this as they walked from the museum to the hotel room he'd rented, less than half a mile away.

"I told Rachel I'd be back around dinnertime, but I can call her. She has some new boyfriend she's into, and I can tell that she's not exactly thrilled that I'm here for the weekend."

"Just tell her you ran into an old boyfriend and you're the happiest you've ever been."

"I should. I could. But I don't know, she went to my wedding, she knows Bryce. I don't want anyone to know about this except for me and you."

"No, I know. It's for the best."

"I'll call her, though, and tell her that I'll be back closer to eight. She'll be fine with it. And I can come back here tomorrow."

"I'll be here, waiting for you."

"Can I ask . . . What's happening with your girlfriend?"

"Finito. We broke up. I did it as soon as I came back from Ohio."

"You were living together, right?"

"Yes, but just renting. She had a friend who was looking for a roommate so she moved in with her. I'm still in the same place. I can't afford it, so I need to start looking around myself."

"What did you tell her?"

He rubbed at an eye. Wendy knew that he didn't want to talk about it, but part of her really wanted to hear what had happened. She waited.

"It was awful," he finally said. "It's still awful. I told her that I just felt too young to settle down, that I wanted to experience life as a single person, that it had nothing to do with her."

"Cliché. Cliché. Cliché."

He snorted through his nose. "Yeah, right. She didn't buy it. She was convinced, she's still convinced, that there's someone else. And she just wants to keep talking about it, going over what went wrong. I think what it comes down to is that she can't understand how I was in love with her once and now I'm not. I keep thinking that maybe it would have been easier if I was just cruel to her, told her I had a one-night fling and that I was never that into her in the first place. Then I'd just be the asshole ex-boyfriend. But I tried to be kind about it, and now she wants to keep getting together so we can rehash the whole thing."

"You can't help what you are," Wendy said.

"What do you mean?"

"I mean, being nice, not being an asshole."

"I guess," Thom said, then rolled over onto his side, propping himself on an elbow. "But I am an asshole. I did cheat on her. And I lied to her about it. And if you only knew the dark thoughts I have about your husband . . ."

"Oh, yeah, like what?" She moved onto her side as well.

"Oh, you know, stuff like how we should murder him for all his money."

Wendy surprised herself by how much that made her laugh. "My thoughts exactly. How would we do it?"

"Well, you'd have to be the brains behind the operation. I would be the muscle, of course. You tell me how we'd do it."

"As you can imagine, I *have* given this lots of thought." She realized she was talking a little too loud, in order to sound theatrical, so she lowered her voice and continued. "Bryce is a perfect murder victim for many reasons."

"Because he's Bryce," Thom said.

"Yes, number one, because he's Bryce. Number two, he is a creature of habit. He pretty much does the exact same things every day, at least Monday through Friday. On the weekends it's a little different, but only because he drinks all day instead of just all night."

"So what's his routine?"

"He gets up at seven in the morning and heads to the gym. He's there for an hour, mostly in the steam room, I suspect, and then he goes to work. He eats lunch every day at the same Chinese restaurant. In the afternoon he calls me to check in, and to tell me that some friend of his, Dougie or Shroom or Big Dan, is in town and he's going to grab a few beers with him. I tell him fine, and he stumbles home at around eleven, hammered and incoherent."

"He drives home?"

"Oh God, yeah. Taxies are for pussies."

"And then what?"

"Then he pours himself a big glass of Jack and Coke and goes out by the pool and smokes a cigar."

"Really?"

"Yep. Every night."

"So, we just need an exploding cigar."

"Yes, that would probably work."

"What's your idea?"

"Well, my secret dream is that he runs his Porsche headfirst into a tree on his drive home at night, but knowing my luck, and his luck, he'd drive headfirst into someone else and kill them. Then he'd walk away without a scratch."

"He *is* going to kill someone eventually," Thom said.

"Oh, no doubt. It's only a matter of time."

"I feel like I've seen half a dozen movies where someone cuts the brake lines of someone's car. Is that a real thing?"

"You'd know better than I do, but it doesn't sound like a real thing."

"So what else you got?" Thom said.

"I keep thinking about how I should just push him into the pool when he's smoking his cigar. He'd sink like a stone."

"He can't swim?"

"I don't think he can, at least not well. And definitely not if he was wearing clothes and drunk. The only time I've seen him in the open water is on a Jet Ski, and he wears a life vest. If he gets into the pool at all, he walks into the shallow end and stays there. Or else he lays on a float. Once, some cousin was over with her awful twin boys and they flipped him off his float. He wasn't even completely in the deep end— he was kind of at the midway point where the bottom of the pool starts to slope—but he completely panicked. I asked him later, not that night, but a week or so later, if he liked to swim. He told me he was good at it, but it wasn't really his thing. Which I interpreted as: he can't swim."

"So I think you're onto something. It's kind of a perfect crime if you think about it. Cause of death would be drowning, and they'd test his blood and find out he was drunk."

"Yeah, I just think everyone would know I'd done it. Everyone in his family anyway. I think they know how I feel about him, and they definitely know how much money is involved."

"But there's a prenup, right?"

"Yeah, I can't divorce him. Or, rather, I can divorce him, but I'd get nothing. But if he dies, as far as I know I'd get his money. I mean, there's no house or anything because his parents own that, but he came into a trust fund from his grandfather when he turned twenty-one."

"And how much is that?"

"Ten million dollars," Wendy said. "Give or take."

"Jesus."

"Well, minus what he spent on the Porsche."

"It's still a lot of money."

"It is."

Thom was quiet for a moment. Wendy said, "Maybe we can change the subject."

"Yes, let's talk about what we would do if we had ten million dollars."

It was dark when Wendy walked back from the hotel to Rachel's apartment. She walked along Massachusetts Avenue instead of Oxford Street, past bars and restaurants that were filling up. The night had turned cold, but she didn't mind. She'd already decided that this was where she wanted to live. Here in Cambridge with its old brick buildings and crisp fall weather. Or anywhere in New England, really. Just not Texas. Not with Bryce. And as much as she loved her mother, she had no interest in living in Wyoming. She wanted to be near culture, surrounded by theaters and great restaurants and universities. And she wanted to live near the ocean. This was despite, or maybe because of, the fact that she'd seen the ocean so few times in her life. Her father had moved her mother and her brother and her at least fifteen times in the course of her childhood, all around the country in search of get-rich schemes, or maybe just in search of places where he could start over again, but most of those places were out west. The two years in New Hampshire were an outlier, her father lured there by some shady friend trying to develop condos on an old racecourse. That was the first time she'd seen the ocean. They'd parked in a sprawling gravel lot, just her and her mother, and walked on a boardwalk that took them over a dune. The sight of the ocean, spread out in front of her in all its enormity, had filled her with a peculiar feeling of homecoming. This was where I should be living, she remembered thinking. It was summertime, but her mother and she had driven to the beach without suits or a beach blanket or even hats, since they owned none of those things. But they sat on the sand and took their shoes off and watched the ocean roll in and roll out again.

Back at Rachel's apartment Wendy let herself in with the spare key she'd been given. There was a note on the kitchen table naming a bar within walking distance that said "Join us there!" She wasn't particularly in the mood for Rachel's manic energy that night, but she was famished and went into Rachel's room to change her outfit.

The next day she told Rachel and Josh that she was too hungover to go out for brunch but that they should go themselves. As soon as they left, she got dressed herself and walked the now-familiar route across Cambridge to Thom's hotel. She found him outside on the sidewalk, wearing khakis and a plaid shirt, smoking a cigarette and shivering slightly. "Should we go get lunch somewhere?" Wendy said.

"Let's go back to my room first. I want to talk with you." He seemed serious as he said it, his face tight, and as she followed him up the uneven stairs to his second-floor room, she thought to herself that it was nice while it lasted.

But once they were alone in the room, the door shut, Thom took a deep breath and said, "Let's do it. Let's kill Bryce."

"What?"

"Just hear me out, and I'll understand if you want to turn around and never see me again, but I need to say this. I feel like we've been given an opportunity, this chance for a really remarkable life. It's not just the money, it's the statement we'll be making about ourselves. It will bind us, in a way. Bind us more I mean. We've always been bonded. Since that trip to D.C., since we found out we have the same birthday, and I'm not saying we were meant to do this, but it feels that way to me. It feels like we're special. Let's kill one horrible man and then we'll spend the rest of our lives as millionaires atoning for it." He smiled even though his face was still tight.

Wendy could feel the breath moving in and out of her lungs. "You're serious?"

"I think so." Thom sat down on the edge of the bed and in the dim light he didn't look any different from when she'd first met him.

"You think so?"

"I haven't slept all night. I just keep thinking about it."

"I'll just divorce him. It'll be messy, but I'll be free of him. We won't be poor, exactly, you and I."

"What about your mother?"

Wendy sat down next to Thom on the bed. "I do worry about her. But we'll figure it out."

"Last night when I was in and out of sleep, I kept having this strange half dream, that I knew that one day your husband would do a terrible thing. Like he was a serial killer or a politician; he would start a war."

"Like in *The Dead Zone*."

"Yes, exactly. I think . . . and I know this is ridiculous . . . that we are somehow fated to do this. It's an evil act, but it's for the greater good."

"I don't think Bryce is a serial killer and there is no way he would ever run for political office, but if I'm honest, I think he's someone who makes the world a lesser place. I thought I saw something else in him once, but it's not really there. I just pretended there was more to him so I could justify marrying him for his money."

"Do you want me to stop talking about this?" Thom said.

Wendy pretended to think, then said, "No, we can keep talking about it. It's just hard not to see that we're in some kind of movie and we're about to make a terrible decision and everyone knows it but us."

"If we did this, we wouldn't get caught. We wouldn't turn against one another. We would make something remarkable of our lives. We'd give half the money to charity."

"Half?" Wendy said.

"I'm serious."

"I know."

"And we're special. You know that, right? You feel it, too, don't you?"

And Wendy, honestly and without hesitation, said, "I do."

1991

AUGUST

The crowd around the registration tables seemed to part, allowing Wendy Eastman, eight years older than when he'd last seen her, to emerge into his sight line in all her adult perfection. Thom had already picked up his name badge and schedule and was now standing awkwardly amid a cluster of fellow attendees, deciding what to do next. The weekend retreat was an annual affair at Kokosing College in Ohio called the Aspiring Writers' Conference, designed for recent college graduates interested in a career in creative writing.

Wendy spotted Thom a moment after he'd seen her, and she walked toward him, somehow appearing nonplussed by the coincidence of their meeting. There was a smirk on her face and Thom found himself laughing as she stopped in front of him. "Am I funny?" she said.

"I can't believe it's you."

"Are you going to hug me, or at least shake my hand?"

They hugged, and Thom wondered if she could tell that he was trembling.

"I can't believe it's you," Thom said again.

"I knew you were going to be here," Wendy said. "You were on the list of names in the orientation packet."

"Oh, right. Of course."

"My name is there, too, but you probably didn't recognize it."

"Wendy Barrington," Thom said, remembering that he had spotted the name and even briefly considered the possibility that the attendee from Lubbock, Texas, might be a married version of the Wendy he'd known so many years ago. But he'd discarded that idea as a ridiculous pipe dream.

"Yes, I'm a Barrington now." She showed her left hand, the ring finger circled by a diamond ring that Thom recognized as being abnormally large.

"Congratulations."

"What about you?"

"I'm not married, but cohabitating," Thom said, holding out his hand to show his ringless finger.

"You're in Connecticut now?"

"I am."

"What's the name of your . . . ?"

"Her name is Maggie. We went to college together."

"Same with me. I married my college boyfriend. His name is Bryce."

"Bryce Barrington."

"You are correct."

Neither said anything for a moment then they both laughed again. "Are we all caught up now?" Thom said. "Should we go our separate ways?"

"I mean, if we have nothing left to talk about."

"You live in Texas?"

"Terrible topic, but, yes, I do live in Texas." She said it with a slight drawl, and her eyes flashed, the way they did when she was joking. It brought her back to him as he'd first known her—just a kid, really, but world-weary and sarcastic and his favorite person to talk with.

"Where in Texas?" Thom said.

"Lubbock. My husband's from there, and went to school there, and his whole rich family lives there, so chances are I'll spend the rest of my life there as well. Unless we get divorced."

"Any chance of that?" Thom said.

"Depends on how long we stand here talking," Wendy said, her eyes brightening more. Thom didn't immediately speak, and Wendy laughed. "You look scared."

"I am scared. You've always scared me."

"Have I?"

"Maybe not scared me, but . . . What's the right word? You always stop me in my tracks."

"I've missed you, Thom," Wendy said, lowering her voice.

"I just figured you'd have forgotten me. It was a long time ago."

"Trust me, I haven't forgotten you."

They were silent again, looking at each other, and Thom knew that they were going to sleep together that weekend, that it was preordained. In some ways it was as though it had already happened. And he felt himself reflexively shoving the thought of Maggie, his sweet, trusting girlfriend, to the back of his mind, preparing himself for this betrayal, telling himself he had no choice in the matter.

"Where are you staying?"

"One of the dorms. Isn't everyone?"

"I think so. I am."

Wendy was fiddling with her name tag, which had come pre-packaged, as had his, in a clear plastic case on a lanyard. "Our room number and combo are supposed to be behind our name tag." She pulled out a slip of paper. "Benchley, Room 22."

Thom looked behind his own name tag and found a similar slip of paper. He remembered the woman at the check-in desk saying something about where to find the information about his housing, but he'd already developed his lifelong habit of never listening to instructions the first time they'd been given.

"I'm in a dorm called Robinson. Room 331."

"Let's go look at the wayfinding map and figure out where to go," Wendy said, turning and walking, apparently aware of what a wayfinding map was, and where it was located.

Thom followed her.

They were together the entire afternoon. After dropping off their luggage in their respective dorm rooms they wandered the campus together, steering clear of the conference's other participants. They found a bench down by a murky pond and sat on either end.

"Why didn't you write me?" Thom said.

Wendy pressed her lips together in an amused smile. "You're talking about when we were fifteen? You do remember *you* told me not to write to you."

"I didn't *mean* it. I was very dramatic back then."

"If you didn't mean it, you shouldn't have said it."

"Probably not, but I just figured you wouldn't listen to me. I wouldn't have, if our situations were reversed."

"I did write you. A lot. All the time. I just didn't send the letters. We lived too far apart. There was so much going on in my life, and the truth was that I believed what you told me, that we shouldn't write, that we should only remember one another on our birthdays."

"I was a pretentious little shit. I'm sorry about that. But did you . . ."

"Remember you on our birthday? Of course. How about you?"

"I did. Every one of them I thought of you."

Clouds were gathering in the sky and the air was charged, a rainstorm imminent, but they sat and recounted their birthdays and where they'd been and what they'd done to celebrate. When the first fat drops began to fall, they ran back toward the student union, but it was too late. The skies had opened up and they were drenched by the time they were standing underneath the awning, hand in hand.

"We should go to the opening events, you know," Wendy said.

"We should."

By the time Thom was back at his dormitory, the rain had ceased, and the air was thick with humidity. He took a cold shower then changed for the cocktail party. He no longer had any interest in the conference, in the other writers, in his career. He was only interested in seeing Wendy again, even just seeing her across the room. It didn't matter. She was back in his life.

That night, in the hubbub of the party, they were actually introduced. The moderator of Wendy's workshop—she had signed up for the poetry concentration, while Thom was registered for short fiction—had actually been a professor of Thom's at Mather College, and he introduced the two of them.

"Did you bring a story to workshop this weekend?" Wendy said as the moderator slid away into the crowd.

"I have two possibilities, but I reread them on the train coming here and now I'm in a panic."

"No good?"

"I don't think so," Thom said. "But what do I know? That's why I'm here, I guess."

"What are they called?"

"My stories?"

"Yeah."

"Well, my Raymond Carver rip-off is called 'Let Me Introduce You,' and my Salinger rip-off is called 'Delilah Snow's Ninth Birthday Party.'"

"Hmm."

"What about your poetry?"

"I'm not even going to tell you any of my titles."

"That's not fair."

She shrugged, tilting her head, and then her workshop moderator was back and pulling her away from him.

Toward the end of the party they met again in front of the food table. "In the program, this party was advertised as having 'substantial appetizers.' What do you think that means?"

Wendy said, "I think they're telling you that they are not providing dinner, so eat lots of these mini-sandwiches."

"I will. I have."

"There's a bar near here, apparently, that some people are going to after this. If you're interested . . ."

"Are you going then?"

"I was thinking about it. But if I go, I'm going to drop off this at my dorm." She held up the tote bag they'd been given at registration. "I don't know why I brought it."

"I'll walk with you," Thom said, his voice hoarse, and waited for her to say something like "No, I'll just meet you at the bar," but, instead, she said, "I'd like that," and together they left.

Two hours later, sweaty, naked, and tangled in Wendy's single bed, Thom said, "You haven't changed."

Wendy laughed. "I hope I've changed. Last time we did this I was fifteen years old."

"I guess you've changed a little."

Wendy showed him the groove on her forehead that she called her frown line, and Thom ran the tip of his finger over it, then she told him how her thighs had gotten fat. He ran his hand along the inside of her right thigh, tracing a trickle of sweat. "No, you're perfect," he said. The air in the room was the same as outside, hot and muggy.

"I don't think we've ever been completely naked together, have we?" Thom said.

"What about at Salisbury Beach?"

Thom's mind went back to the two or three images he had from the time they'd snuck up into the dunes to have sex, not for the first time, but for the second. "I'm pretty sure my bathing suit was around my knees the whole time," he said.

"That sounds right."

"And I think your bathing suit was more or less still on as well."

"You have a good memory."

"For some things, yes."

Thom's hand was still on Wendy's thigh. Sweat was pooling where they touched. "Why is it so hot in here?"

"Because we haven't turned the air-conditioning on."

"That might be it."

Wendy got up and walked across the dim interior of the room, the only light coming from the yellow sodium glow of an outside lamp. Thom gazed at her body, her graceful lines as she fiddled with the thermostat. Something about the heat and the yellow light and the distant sound of thunder made Thom think that for a moment he'd gone to some tempting version of hell, a version he hoped never to leave. He briefly pictured his girlfriend, Maggie, in New Haven. She would be curled up on the couch, legs tucked under her, a book on her lap. He put her out of his mind as Wendy returned to the bed.

Later, they made two rules for the remainder of the weekend. The first was that they wouldn't talk about their lives back home, at least not right away. The second was that, since they were cheating on their respective partners, they shouldn't make it obvious. In public they should only act like acquaintances. It was Wendy who made this particular suggestion, and throughout the coming years, Thom would often think about that. They also decided that they would only meet privately in Benchley Hall, the brutalist dormitory on the south edge of Kokosing College that Wendy had been assigned. Her room was cold and utilitarian, but it was large for a single, with its own bathroom. Thom's room, in Robinson Hall, had character—it was high-ceilinged and had two lead-paned windows that overlooked Kokosing's quadrangle—but there were multiple attendees on the same hall and there was a shared bathroom.

Over the course of the weekend Thom called home to Maggie

only once—Saturday after his workshop, using the public phones in the union. She was spending the weekend working on a baby quilt; her older, married sister was expecting a girl in September. He also knew that she'd make an enormous batch of soup for the week ahead, and that she'd spend at least an hour every day talking to her mother. And he knew that at least a couple of her friends would have reached out to her to see if she wanted to grab a drink, and that she would have turned them down. Since college, Maggie had seemed to lose all interest in friends. She only wanted to spend time with Thom.

In bed together on Saturday night, Thom asked Wendy how often she was checking in with Bryce. Despite not having talked much about him, Wendy had explained his name. It was Cooper Bryson Barrington, but he went by his middle name, Bryce. It was family tradition. His father's name was Bryson Cooper but he went by Cooper. His father's father's name was Cooper Bryson, called Bryson. And so on.

"That's the whitest, richest thing I've ever heard," Thom said.

"They *are* rich, and they *are* white."

It turned out that Wendy, like Thom, had spoken to her partner only once, as well. "He's not much for phone calls" was all she said.

On Sunday afternoon, after their final meetings with their respective workshop groups, and two hours before she was getting a ride from one of the local organizers back to the airport, she'd said more about him. "We met at Rice our senior year. Well, we'd already met, but we started dating. He was a rich party kid and I guess I was a scholarship party kid. I took him home from a party while he was having a bad mushroom trip and talked him through it. And that was that. I think I was the first girl he'd seen as an actual human being and not just someone for him to try and fuck. We got married right after college."

"Why did *you* marry him?"

Wendy thought for a moment before saying, "What attracted me to him at first was what attracted him to me. I saw the human underneath his party-kid exterior and I thought that I could bring that fully out. But it didn't take me too long to figure out that he wasn't really going to change. People don't, you know."

"But you stuck with him."

"He proposed to me. It was a shock, but he'd told me once that all the Barrington men met their wives at college and he was all about tradition. I was going to say no, but if I'm honest, I saw his money. That's all there is to it. He's filthy rich and I think you know I grew up filthy poor, and I was sick of it. So a rich boy wants to marry me, and I knew he wasn't the best person in the world, and that I didn't really love him, but . . ."

Wendy paused, her eyes not on Thom but on her suitcase waiting by the dorm-room door. "I hope this won't scare you off, but it didn't matter that I didn't love him, because I still loved you. After we lost touch, I told myself that I might not find you again but that I would never find someone to replace you. That you were my one true love. I think that's why I fell in love with poetry, because that is the great theme of poetry, isn't it? Lost love. So it didn't matter that I didn't love Bryce or his stupid family. I would be rich, and I could do what I wanted. And I could protect my mom. Not protect her but provide for her. I send her money every month to cover her rent, so she can live with her dogs and not have to worry about winding up on the street. Sometimes I think that fact alone made it worth marrying Bryce."

"You're not happy," Thom said.

"Maybe a week ago I might have said that I was happy. My life isn't hard, but Bryce is a worthless human being. That sounds like an exaggeration, but it isn't. Name a bad trait and he has it. Laziness, egotism, stupidity, gluttony, lust. He's got them all."

"Does he want kids?"

"Someday, of course. A boy he can name Bryson Cooper."

"If you're going to leave him, you should do it before you have kids."

"You think?" Wendy said, but she was smiling. "I *should* leave him, of course. I will leave him. Thing is, it's going to be a logistical nightmare for one, just dealing with his family. And here's the rub: there's a prenup. If I divorce him, I get nothing. Even if I divorce him for a good reason. His family is rich for a reason."

"What do they do?"

"They were cattlemen, and they still dabble in that. But the last three Cooper-Bryson-Coopers have been financial advisors for bigger cattlemen. I live in one of those ranch houses with a big gate with the family name on it, like in *Dallas*. Actually, we live in the pool house."

"Seriously?"

"It's a *big* pool house. And we have the run of the actual house. Bryce's father, Cooper, lives there but he spends most of his time at his girlfriend's condo downtown."

"How does Bryce feel about you?"

"I'm his wife. That's all he feels about me. He cheats."

"Really?"

"Yeah, of course he does. Thank God for that. It keeps him out of the house."

"But you won't divorce him?"

Wendy put a hand on Thom's leg. "Of course I'll divorce him. Now that I have a reason. But should we really have this conversation now? What about Maggie?"

"She's a good person," Thom said.

After a moment, Wendy said, "That's it?"

"She loves me more than I love her, and down deep she knows it and it makes her very anxious. She'll be convinced that I had some sort of affair this weekend."

"And she'll be right."

"I know. Part of me, and this is obviously a rationalization, figures that since she already suspects me of being unfaithful, I might as well do the deed."

"You've cheated on her before," Wendy said.

"Not a lot, but there's this woman I work with."

"I don't need the details," Wendy said, laughing.

"Oh, you're jealous."

"Of course I'm jealous. I'm jealous of Maggie too. I'm jealous of everyone who gets to spend time with you, everyone who gets to touch this body." She slid her hand up his stomach to his chest.

"So what are we going to do?" Thom said.

"I've been thinking about that—"

"Let's just each disentangle ourselves from our lives and start over together?"

Wendy bit her upper lip. "I think that's what we should do, too, but don't you think we should meet again first? Give this a little bit of time?"

"Not really," Thom said.

"I'm coming out east, to Boston, in two months to visit a college friend. I'll be staying with her for a week, but she's working while I'm there. My days will be mostly free."

"I'll be there. I'll make it happen. Tell me the dates."

After giving him the dates of her trip and her friend's address in Cambridge, they made a plan to meet up at Harvard's natural history museum on a Tuesday afternoon. "And then we can figure out what to do next, okay?" Wendy said.

"And between then?"

"And between then we have the memory of this weekend."

1991

JUNE

The phone rang and she ignored it. It was either Bryce calling from work because he was bored and needed someone to talk with, or else it was her mother and one of the dogs was sick, and in either case, she was happy to keep reading her book.

But she marked her place with her finger while listening to her own recorded voice tell the caller to leave a message after the beep, and then listened. "Wendy, hi, it's Kerry. Long time no speak—"

She picked up the phone. "Hey, Ker."

"Oh, hi. Screening calls?"

"Maybe."

"How *are* you?"

They lied to each other for five minutes about their lives, but Wendy could tell that Kerry had called for a reason.

"Do you remember that poem you published in the review our junior year? 'Graveyards'?"

"Yeah, of course. But how do *you* remember it?"

"I remember it because we were in class together."

"That's right." Somehow Wendy had forgotten that Kerry had been in the class where she'd first workshopped that particular poem.

"But no, I remember it because it was an *amazing* poem. Really. I could probably quote it to you right now."

"That's okay."

Kerry laughed. "Anyhoo, this is totally random, but it made me think of you and that poem. You know I'm at Kokosing College, right? They do this aspiring writers' conference every August and I'm doing all the admin for it this year as part of my work-study. And one of the attendees is named Thomas Graves from New Haven, Connecticut. Wasn't that the name of . . . ?"

Wendy didn't need to think too hard back to the poem she'd written. The first line had been "I met a boy named Graves out on the sand / By Hampton on the Sea." And in at least one version of the poem she'd dedicated it "To Thom."

"Yes, I did know a kid named Thom Graves a hundred years ago. What makes you think—"

"You told me about him. Don't you remember?"

"Kind of, sort of. What did I say?"

"You told me you lost your virginity to him."

"Yes, that's true. I don't remember telling you that, though. I didn't say it in class, did I?"

"No, but I think the class probably knew. Just from the poem."

"God, that's embarrassing."

"So, do you think it's him?"

"Who's 'him'? The Thom Graves who signed up for your conference? I don't know. I haven't seen him or heard from him since we were fifteen." Wendy was trying to sound blasé about it, but she'd never stopped thinking about Thom and even suspected that was why she'd written the poem about him. The act of putting it out there had possibly brought him back to her. Like a conjuring trick.

"I have his application here. He graduated from Mather College last year, so he's our age. He lives in Connecticut."

"Well, when you meet him, you'll have to ask him if he knows me."

"Didn't I tell you? My dad moved to Italy, so I'm going there for the summer."

"Oh, lucky you."

"It's not as glamorous as it sounds. I'll probably have to work somewhere while I'm there, but hopefully it will be a wine bar filled with cute boys. You'll just have to come to the conference yourself to see if it's the same Thom Graves."

"You know I'm married, right? You came to my wedding, remember?"

"I'm not saying you should have an affair with him, but I thought you might be interested. *Sorry.*"

"Don't worry, I'm just giving you a hard time. And I'm touched you remembered my poem. Maybe it really is him."

"I have his contact information if you want it?"

"I'll pass," Wendy said.

"Okay. I'm done now. You should come visit me in Italy when I'm there."

After ending the phone call, Wendy went up to her bedroom closet and pulled out the cardboard box that contained the few things she'd kept from her four years in college, among them the literary review that had published "Graveyards."

She reread the poem, a slightly modified Shakespearean sonnet. The final couplet of "Graveyards" read "Because the world has gone to bed / I learn to kiss his ghost instead." She remembered how pleased she'd been with it at the time, how clever she thought it was that there was no actual mention of graveyards or cemeteries in the poem, and how excited she'd been when it was picked for publication in the magazine. But mostly she thought about her belief at the time that maybe the poem would bring Thom Graves back into her life. It was why she'd written that uncharacteristic poem. But it had somehow worked. Despite what she'd said to Kerry on the phone, she was certain that the Thom Graves attending the Kokosing Aspiring Writers' Conference was the same Thom, her birthday twin. The future was rapidly unfolding in her mind, and she made herself stop thinking about it. She hadn't written anything since graduation—at least, nothing besides diary entries. How would Bryce feel if she traveled on her own to a writers' conference at the end of the summer?

1984

i

Wendy was relieved, and not surprised, that it was just Rose, her mother, picking her up at Denver Airport. As Wendy pushed through the exit gate, her mother was right there, in the stance Wendy recognized as an anxious one, arms crossed just under her breasts, moving her weight from one leg to the other.

"You look really good," her mother said as they crossed the hot tarmac to the parked car. "How do you feel?"

"I feel fine," Wendy said, realizing as she said it that this brief conversation might be the only words spoken about the actual reason she had been living with her aunt Andi in Mendocino the past four months.

In the car, as they drove toward Tabernash, her mother talked about Alan's summer job taking tourists out horse-riding in Granby, and how he'd decided that he wanted to become a big-animal vet.

"That's a lot of school, right?" Wendy said.

Her mom laughed. "That's what I told him, but he's a new Alan this summer. You'll see."

"How's Dad?"

There was a long enough pause for Wendy to know that something bad was coming. "Unfortunately, he did lose his job last week. Well, no, I shouldn't say that. The job itself fell through. It had nothing to do with your father."

Wendy wasn't surprised, but it did mean that her father was not currently working, and when he didn't work, he drank. Pulling up in front of the small vinyl-sided rental house they currently lived in, Wendy saw that Frank, her dad, was sitting on the front stoop. He wore suit bottoms and a white undershirt as though he'd just come home from work for the evening and was out enjoying an end-of-day gin and tonic. But it wasn't evening yet and he was unemployed.

"The ladies return," he said, standing up to hug Wendy. "Jesus, look at you. Last time I saw you, you were a scrawny kid. What did your aunt feed you out there?"

Wendy was saved from answering by her mother shooting Frank a look, then saying, "Wendy's tired. Let her go get settled again in her room."

Her father wacked Wendy on the ass as she passed him, and said, "I'm not saying anything bad, just that it's been so long since I've seen her. She's a little woman now." Wendy passed through the living room, the smell of gin still in her nostrils, and returned to her room, unchanged since she'd last been there—when was it?—probably the beginning of March. That was when she couldn't hide the pregnancy anymore and her mother had come up with the plan to pull her out of school early and send her to visit her sister in California. Her father was working around the clock at that point, trying to sell some kind of automated rental system to ski areas, so he either hadn't noticed Wendy's state or he hadn't questioned the plan. And neither had Alan, who was mostly high as a kite in those days. The cover story was that Aunt Andi had broken an arm and needed an assistant to help her in her art studio.

Wendy had traveled to Mendocino at five and a half months pregnant. She'd gotten in that particular state on her last day in New Hampshire, Thom Graves and her stealing away into the woods with a blanket to lie on but without a condom. He'd pulled out early, though, and Wendy thought that that was all it would take to ensure there was no chance of getting pregnant. She hadn't even suspected that it had actually happened until December of that year, the family now living in a brand-new state, Thom and New Hampshire a far-off memory.

The first thing Wendy noticed in her bedroom was the mason jar filled with wildflowers on her bedside table, a homecoming present from her mother. Wendy lay down on her made-up single bed and stared up at a cluster of glow-in-the-dark stick-on stars on her ceiling that she'd forgotten about. She hadn't put them there herself; it must have been some other kid who once upon a time lived in this tiny room with the black mold spots covering one whole wall. She swiveled her head from side to side, taking in her bedroom. Except for being pregnant, she hadn't actually minded her time in California. Her aunt was insane, of course, everyone knew that, but she was funny and she lived in a cool bungalow type of house and spent most of her time making pots or dyeing fabrics with mushrooms and things like that. Aunt Andi was the one who contacted the Catholic people who arranged the adoption. All Wendy had to do while she was there was spend her days reading books—her aunt had everything from old Nancy Drew books to Danielle Steel, and a book she read twice called *Even Cowgirls Get the Blues*—and eating weird vegetarian dishes. Her aunt was similar to her mother in one very important way: she could keep up a steady stream of conversation without ever really talking about anything of substance. She never once asked Wendy how she'd gotten pregnant or how she felt about giving the baby up.

It was also nice to be near the ocean, even though it was the

Pacific and not the Atlantic, where Thom lived. She did wonder what he would think if he knew that she was pregnant, but she wasn't even sure she knew what she thought about it, except that she wanted it all to go away.

Aunt Andi had stayed with her in the hospital after she'd given birth. Wendy had held the baby briefly but didn't feel much of anything except the desire to get out of the hospital and pretend that none of this had ever happened. Although after she'd held her daughter for the last time, when she was recovering in her bed, she remembered telling Aunt Andi—this was after some pretty trippy painkillers—that she thought Annabel would be a good name for the baby. Wendy had come up with the name because Andi had a book of poems by Edgar Allan Poe that she'd been reading and rereading. She remembered saying it only because when she did, her aunt had burst into tears and had to leave the room. It was the only time she'd seen her aunt, or her mother, for that matter, cry.

Wendy was glad to be back in Colorado, only because she wanted a return to normalcy. She knew she couldn't spend her whole life drinking herbal tea and reading dirty books at her aunt's house, but it didn't make it any easier watching her father get progressively drunker and drunker throughout the night. It wasn't an entirely terrible evening. Her mom had made shepherd's pie, making Wendy realize how much she'd missed meat the past four months, and Alan, as her mom had said, was somewhat changed by his new job. He wasn't stoned, for one, and seemed actually happy. And for most of the night her father was an amiable drunk, talking about some new idea he had for storing sailboats or something, and actually asking Alan questions about the stables he worked at, but Wendy just waited for him to cross the martini line. That was her and Alan's phrase for the moment that the gin turned her father from corny-joke-telling suburban dad to the blank-eyed evilness that he could become. They called it the martini line because it often came right after their father would switch from gin and tonics or Tom Collinses and decide to have a "good old-fashioned" martini. Then his eyes would somehow empty out and he would go after someone in the family with what felt like true spite. That night he descended on Rose. As always it was like a switch; one moment he was toasting the Eastman family ("the four of us against the world") and the next he was telling his wife he wouldn't have married her if he'd known she would one day look like a fat Midwestern housewife. Alan turned to Wendy and whispered to her, "Go to your room. I'll stick around and keep an eye on him."

"What's that, son?" Frank said, his head swiveling on his neck like it was hard for him to hold it up.

"Nothing, Dad. Wendy's tired, so she's going to sleep."

As Wendy left the room, she heard her father say, "My daughter looks like a whore from California now."

Alone in her room, Wendy listened to the mixtape she'd made by taping songs off the radio at her aunt's house. She fast-forwarded to "King of Pain" by the Police, which was a song that Thom had liked. She decided to write him a letter, one she wouldn't send. She'd written many letters to him, so many that they were more like a diary she was keeping. On their last day together in New Hampshire, the day they'd had sex in the piney woods behind his house, Thom had said that they shouldn't write, that they should just have the memories of their time together. He also said they could think of each other every year on their shared birthday. So she hadn't sent him any of the letters she'd written, even though she knew his address. If he had changed his mind about getting in touch, she wouldn't know about it, because there was no way he'd know where they were now living. But he was probably right. Some things were best forgotten.

She finished the letter by writing "From Wendy, With Love and Squalor," as she always did, and then cracked open the Edgar Allan

Poe book that her aunt had let her keep. Even with her Walkman turned up she could hear her father's booming voice coming through the house's cheap walls, although, thankfully, she couldn't hear the words.

ii

Thom had forgotten the bug spray and the mosquitoes were eating him alive, but it was August 13, his half birthday, which meant it was Wendy's half birthday as well, and he wanted to be in their special place in the woods. He'd brought the same blanket with him that they'd had sex on nearly a year ago, and he was lying half on it and half under it now, trying to shield himself from the bugs, trying to just focus on his memories of Wendy, of what it had been like to actually be in this spot with her, to be able to touch her and hear her voice. He found he could still picture her, for the most part, but he was worried that her voice was becoming lost to him. He knew it was a beautiful voice—everything about her was beautiful—but found he couldn't really remember the specifics of it.

He wondered if she were thinking of him today as well. He knew that half birthdays weren't really a thing, except that they had talked about it together exactly one year ago. Where had they been when they'd had that conversation? Or had it been on the phone? A wave of sadness rolled over Thom, a feeling that life was speeding up and moving too quickly and all his happiness was now in the past. He clenched his jaw, thinking that he might cry, but nothing happened. Maybe his life's tragedy was going to be that he'd met his soul mate when he was fourteen, and now he was doomed to a lifetime of never finding her again. Why hadn't she written him? He knew that he'd told her that she shouldn't, but she knew his address. She even knew his phone number. Maybe she'd forgotten him. Maybe she was with some other boy now, a thought he tried very hard to keep out of his head.

The nubby blanket was making him sweat, so he stood up, swiped away the orange pine needles that clung to both him and the blanket, and walked back through the woods to his house, occasionally breaking into a run because of the cloud of mosquitoes that was amassing behind him. Back in the kitchen his mom glanced at the blanket in his arms and asked him if he'd been reading in the woods. "Just thinking," he said, and she knew enough not to ask him what he was thinking about.

Instead, his mother said, "Did you remember that Mrs. Burke asked you to go swimming at their pool this afternoon?"

He had remembered. The Burkes were two houses down; they had four kids, a senior girl named Kathleen, two middle boys named Kevin and Carter, and a girl that was Thom's age named Kristen. The two girls were okay, but Thom kind of hated the boys, who were always dunking each other in the pool or talking about bra sizes or how you could know the color of a girl's pubes by looking at her eyebrows. But the pool was pretty nice, and Thom had been harboring a strange fantasy for a while, one in which he confessed to Kristen, the girl his age, all about how he was in love with Wendy Eastman, who'd left town and broken his heart. He created conversations between the two of them in his head. She would ask him questions about their romance, and he'd tell her all about it. Sometimes, in these fantasies, he would show her the place in the woods where he had sex with Wendy, and Kristen would kiss him, tell him she wanted to have sex as well but understood he could never truly love her.

"Thom, did you remember?" his mother asked again. He thought he'd answered her but supposed he hadn't.

"Yeah, I'll go," he said.

He wasn't the only kid who had been invited to the Burkes' pool that day. There were about ten teens and preteens, and the Burkes had a few of the parents over as well, although the adults were on the patio drinking tall cocktails.

Thom kept to the deep end, where Kathleen and two of her friends bumped back and forth on floats. Kevin and Carter were in the shallow end, blasting each other with water guns and farting under the water. It was hard to imagine they were basically his age. Later in the afternoon, after drying off, and getting a Hawaiian Punch from Mrs. Burke, Thom got a chance to talk with Kristen, telling her it was his half birthday.

"Is that a thing?" she said.

"Yeah, it's exactly six months from my birthday."

"No, I know what a half birthday is, I just didn't know it was something that people celebrate."

"Oh, yeah," Thom said. "No, I don't celebrate it. I mean, no one gives me cake or a present or anything. It's just that I thought of it. In six months I'll be seventeen."

"You're *so* old," Kristen said, and made a face.

Thom decided not to tell her about Wendy, and wondered why he'd ever even considered it. What happened with Wendy was the most important thing in his life, and he didn't need to share it. Instead, he asked Kristen if her brothers were always creeps, and while she talked, he looked at her summer-freckled skin and her thin, reddish eyebrows, and wondered if it were true what her brothers had told him about pubic hair.

iii

One week before school started again, Rose came and woke Wendy up by sitting gently on her bed. As soon as Wendy looked at her mother's face, composed and serious, Wendy knew that her life was about to change.

"What is it?" she said.

"It's about your father," Rose said. "Alan's already up, so why don't you get out of bed, as well. Get dressed and come straight down to the kitchen."

"What happened?"

"Get dressed and come straight down to the kitchen."

When she walked down the hallway that led to the open living room/kitchen, she could hear her mother talking on the phone. By the time she reached her brother, sitting on one of the kitchen stools, her mother was hanging up the phone. When Alan looked at her, she could tell that he already knew what had happened.

"The police and ambulance are on their way," Rose said. "Your father took a bath last night and it looks like he drowned. I just found him this morning."

"Is he dead?"

"He is, Wendy."

"He's in the house right now?" Her voice sounded hysterical even in her own head.

"Yes, but they'll come and get him. If you want to go somewhere else this morning, I'd understand but I'm going to stick here."

"I'll stay here too," Alan said.

"Are you sure he's dead?"

"He has no pulse, Wendy, and he's cold."

Wendy stayed, but she went outside and sat on one of the two swings on the old rusty swing set that was in the backyard when they'd moved in. Police came, and then an ambulance, but they both left without taking her father's body. Alan walked outside to see Wendy and told her that someone from a funeral home was going to come and get the body.

"Did you look at it?"

"Look at Dad's body?"

"Yeah."

"I did. You don't want to see it, Wendy."

"What happened?"

"He passed out and then drowned." Then, in a louder voice, Alan said, "He was a fucking pathetic drunk and he got what was coming to him. Sorry, Wendy, but . . ." He turned around and Wendy could tell by the way his shoulders were moving that he was crying.

She went into the house, expecting to see her mother in the kitchen, but she wasn't there. She stood still, listening, suddenly convinced that her father would amble through the house, alive again. Where was her mother? Probably in the bedroom, lying down. Wendy decided to go look at her father's body in the tub, maybe not close up, but there was still this part of her that didn't really believe he was gone. She needed to see him.

When she reached the bathroom door, it was slightly ajar, and she put her hand against the door to push it open. But then she saw her mother kneeling by the tub, her knees on the shaggy pink bath mat, her hands on the edge of the yellow tub. From Wendy's angle she couldn't see her father's body. Only her mother, who looked as though she were praying. Wendy, frozen, just watched. And then her mother spoke, looking down into the tub. Her voice was quiet, but Wendy was pretty sure she could make out the words. Her mother said, "I'm sorry, darling. I had no choice. The old you would have understood."

Wendy backed quietly away from the door and went back outside to the yard. She stood still for a while, just going over her mother's words in her mind, searching for a way to feel about them. Eventually, a long, dark car came from the morgue. Wendy didn't see the body being moved from the house to the hearse, but Alan came and told her that their father was no longer in there.

They'd only been living in the town of Tabernash for a year, but Rose arranged a service, and some of Frank Eastman's new friends came, along with a number of churchgoers, who maybe only came for the free buffet after the service. The only person to fly in was her father's brother, George. He came for only one day and stayed at a local hotel. Before leaving he'd given Wendy a hundred-dollar bill, and she thought that she'd probably never see him again.

After the funeral Alan went to visit his new girlfriend, the daughter of his boss, at the horse stables, and Wendy took a walk with her mother. She could feel her mother's tension on the walk, and Wendy waited for her mother to tell her what she'd done. To confess.

"Have you thought about if you want to finish out this school year here in Tabernash?" her mother said.

"It doesn't make any difference to me. But Alan will want to stay."

"Yeah, I thought we'd stay for him. It's his senior year. And then maybe we'd all move somewhere new, or you and I will. It's not like you kids aren't used to moving."

"Where did you want to go, Mom?"

"You probably don't remember, but when you were about five, we all spent a summer in Lander, Wyoming. Your father's friend Nate Rutherford was living there at the time and he offered your dad a job at his hardware store."

"I remember Wyoming."

"Do you really?"

"We lived in a log cabin, like in *Little House on the Prairie*."

"Right. Sort of. Anyway, the point of the story is that I thought Lander was the prettiest place I'd ever been, and maybe we could move back there. I can work, and you can finish school, and if Alan decides to come along, there will be plenty of horse ranches for him to work at."

"He's pretty into Deidre. I doubt he'll leave."

"Well, that will be up to him. But you'd come, right?"

"Of course. It sounds nice," Wendy said.

"Hopefully, you'll have a better year next year than this one has been."

It took Wendy a moment to realize that her mother was not just talking about her father, but also about her time in California.

"Can't be worse," Wendy said, then, to change the subject, quickly added, "Maybe you'll find a new husband in Wyoming?"

Her mother laughed, and said, "I'm done with husbands. But I think I would like a dog."

"Are you sad that Dad died?" Wendy found herself saying.

Her mother laughed, said, "Oh, honey. Of course I'm sad. You don't think I am?"

"I don't know. I guess I know you're sad but maybe, also, things weren't so great between the two of you."

They had turned around at the elementary school, empty on a Saturday, and begun to walk back. Her mother said, "Well, his life wasn't going well for him. You knew that, right?"

"I know that he drank too much."

"He did. That was the biggest part of it. He couldn't hold a job, and sometimes I worried about what he might do when he'd had too much to drink."

They were silent for a moment and Wendy wondered if she was supposed to say something, but then her mom continued: "I want you to have good thoughts about him going forward. He was good to you and Alan when you were young. Sometimes people are only good for part of their lives, and then they move on. Or we move on without them."

"I know," Wendy said.

"The happiest people are the ones who are able to forget the past. Don't be sentimental about people, I guess is what I'm saying."

Back at the house, Wendy went to her room. She thought of writing another letter she wouldn't send to Thom, but decided against it. What she really wanted to say in that letter was that maybe her mom had somehow been responsible for her father's death. It was what she'd been thinking about since hearing her mother in the bathroom. Did she hold his head under when he was drunk? Or maybe she just let him drown? Maybe that was all there was to it. But even though she had these thoughts, she didn't plan on writing them down. Never. Somehow she knew that what her mother did, she did for Wendy more than anyone else. And Wendy knew she would never do anything now to hurt her mother.

So she decided to not write a letter to Thom. Besides, they weren't letters to him anyway. They were to a pretend version of him, or maybe they were just letters to her future self. She picked up her pen and wrote the word "POEM" at the top of a blank page in her notebook in all caps. Underneath she wrote, "By Wendy Eastman." Somewhere between her previous obsession with the poetry anthology she'd stolen from her old school in New Hampshire, a book called *Pictures That Storm Inside My Head*, and her new obsession with Edgar Allan Poe, Wendy had decided that she might like to write poetry herself. She didn't know what those poems would be like, only that it was a way of writing about yourself without writing about yourself. Or something like that. She'd decided to give it a try.

1982

It wasn't a typical yellow school bus, but more like a tour bus, with plush seats and tinted windows. Wendy Eastman, one of the first to arrive for the eighth-grade trip to D.C., decided to sit about three-quarters of the way back. If you sat too close to the front, you looked weak, and if you sat all the way toward the back, the kids tended to be scary. She was only fourteen, but she'd already moved towns ten times that she could count. Being a new kid at a school didn't bother her all that much, but it was good to have some rules for survival.

As the bus filled up, getting louder and louder, she turned so that she was looking out of the window at the middle school parking lot. There was a dissipating layer of dew on the sports fields in the distance, and the sky had a pinkish tinge. She'd tried to get out of this trip, but apparently all the eighth graders were required to go, or that was what her mother had told her. Wendy did wonder about that, because she saw the check that her mother wrote out of her own bank account to send her on this trip. If it cost money, it couldn't be required, right? But it didn't matter. Her mother wanted her to go, enough that she had somehow come up with the money, so Wendy had decided to make the best of it.

Still, it was one thing to keep to yourself in school and another to have to be by yourself on a three-day road trip with other students. There would be nowhere to hide. And it wasn't starting well; she could see in the reflection of the window that the kids now coming onto the bus would reach the empty seat, see that it was next to her, and move on. Maybe she'd luck out and have both seats to herself, and then she could read all the way down, not have to talk to anyone.

But just before the bus began its journey—Mrs. Chappell, one of the parent chaperones, was calling out names from the front of the bus and ticking the names off on her clipboard—Wendy saw a boy running across the parking lot, a plaid suitcase banging against his legs. It was Thom Something—she knew his name because he'd frozen up while reciting "In Flanders Fields" in their shared English class, but their teacher, Mr. Stone, had been kind about it. Mrs. Chappell reopened the bus's door and went down and helped him stow his bag, then Thom was slowly walking down the aisle, looking for a place to sit. He passed Wendy's seat, then came back and sat down next to her. Some kid two rows back made a kind of oohing sound that got a tepid laugh.

"Hey," Thom said.

"I'm Wendy."

"Oh, yeah. I know. We take English class together."

They didn't talk again until they were on the highway, riding along on the hiss of the wet road, the windows blurry with rain. Wendy had decided not to talk unless he talked to her first, but she was intrigued by the book that sat unopened on his lap. It was by Roald Dahl, an author she knew, but the book, a hardcover clearly borrowed from the library, was one she hadn't heard of. *The Wonderful Story of Henry Sugar and Six More*. She asked him about it.

"It's short stories and they're pretty gruesome. More for adults than children."

"Gruesome how?"

He said there was a story about two bullies shooting all these birds and then tormenting another boy. Then the bullies kill a swan and tear its wings off, making the boy wear them. It did seem gruesome, and she wondered if he was making it up to impress her.

They stopped at a Burger King for lunch, and Thom went and found friends to sit with, while Wendy got a table for herself. Mrs. Chappell must have felt bad for her, because when she finally got her food she sat with Wendy and asked her a string of questions about her life. Wendy thought it was probably more humiliating to eat with a chaperone than it was to eat alone.

Back on the bus she thought Thom might find another place to sit, but they wound up next to each other again. She had her own book with her now that she'd retrieved from her baggage; it was *Cujo* by Stephen King, a paperback she'd snagged from her older brother Alan's room the night before. She hadn't started it yet.

"Oh," Thom said when he saw the book. It had occurred to her that she was one-upping him in the gruesome book contest.

"Have you read a Stephen King book before?"

"No, but I saw *Salem's Lot* on TV. Did you see that?" Thom said.

Wendy had heard all about that show, and how terrifying it was, from her brother. "No," she said. "Was it scary?"

She thought Thom might act all brave, but instead, he said, "Are you familiar with the term 'scarred for life'?"

She laughed. "Yeah, I heard it was scary."

"Who told you that?"

"My brother saw it and told me about it."

"He's older?"

"Yeah. He's a freshman at the high school."

"I have an older sister. She's a junior. She tells me about all the scary movies she sees as well."

"Like what?"

"Everything. *Friday the Thirteenth. The Omen* film."

"My favorite is *The Exorcist*," Wendy said suddenly, even though she'd been pretty much traumatized by watching that film at her brother's friend's house.

Thom looked impressed. "My sister told me all about that movie. She watched it at a slumber party. It sounded crazy."

"It's totally crazy," Wendy said, and then they talked about *The Exorcist* for the rest of the ride. It was weird, because even though Thom hadn't seen it, he seemed to know more about it than she did. He'd apparently grilled his sister on every detail, plus he had a subscription to *MAD* magazine, so he'd read the parody version of the film, called "The Ecchorcist." Thom had to spell it for her, and explain to her why it was funny. Then he asked her lots of questions about the green vomit, and even asked her about the crucifix scene, which was something she didn't really like thinking about. What she didn't tell him—because she didn't have the words—was that her favorite parts of the movie were the parts that weren't scary at all. She'd fallen in love with the girl in the movie, with Regan, who got to live with just her mom in this amazing house in the city. The mom was a movie star who had fancy parties and no husband, and Wendy had found herself fantasizing about being her daughter and what that life must be like. Even at the end of the movie it was clear that Regan didn't remember anything about what had happened when she'd been possessed by a demon. So in a way, she'd just get to continue her amazing life. She almost told Thom about this fantasy but thought he might think she was weird, so she kept it to herself. Instead, she told him about the scene where Regan's head twisted all the way around. And she told him about the crazy steps that were outside of Regan's apartment and how the priest fell down them and died. When they were getting close to the end of their trip Wendy said, "You know that this is where it all takes place?"

"What takes place?"

"The movie. It's here in D.C."

Thom looked confused, as though she'd just told him that the film was actually a documentary or something. "It's set in George-town, which is a neighborhood here. We're going to go to it on this trip. Like, I'm pretty sure the steps are really here."

"Really?"

"Really."

"I thought we were just going to go to museums and learn about the presidents."

"I think that's the important part."

One of the teachers was coming down the aisle while the bus was slowing down. "This is it, kids. You need to bring everything with you from the bus, okay?"

"Miss Ackles," Thom said. She stopped and looked at him. "Are we going to Georgetown on this trip?"

"Do you have the schedule, Thom?" she said, leaning forward to talk to him, and Wendy stared at Miss Ackles's incredibly long and shiny hair.

"I guess I forgot it," he said.

"Yes, on the last night here we're having dinner in Georgetown. It's all in the schedule."

"Did you know that's where *The Exorcist* happened?" Thom said.

Miss Ackles frowned. "You haven't seen that movie, have you, Thom?"

"No," he said, and Wendy wondered if he was going to give her up.

"It's pretty scary," the social studies teacher said. "I'm not usually a scaredy-cat about those kinds of things, but that one got to me. And, yes, you're right, it all happened right where we're going." She widened her eyes and changed her voice a little when saying that last part.

Miss Ackles moved on, and Thom turned back to Wendy. His cheeks were kind of red and she wondered if he had a crush on

Miss Ackles, which wouldn't really surprise her. Her hair was really very shiny, and sometimes her sweaters were so tight you could tell she wasn't wearing a bra. Thom said, "Going to Georgetown, I guess. Should we find the steps?"

ii

The trip to D.C. turned out to be maybe the best trip of Thom's life. Partly it was the freedom. His school had booked one entire floor of a hotel, and until nine p.m., when all the kids had to be in their rooms, they were free to be anywhere they wanted in the big hotel, including the game room down near the lobby, or the fitness room up on the top floor. Paul Barbieri and he had gotten into an epic game of spy versus spy, Thom's triumph coming when he ambushed Paul out by the pool area, leaping out at him from one of the bushes that edged the tarped-over pool and making Paul squeal like a little girl.

The trips during the day had been pretty cool as well. They'd been to the Smithsonian Institution (the fossils were the best), and to Arlington Cemetery (just okay, except for the trolley ride). Thom had been impressed with how big the statue of Lincoln was and thought the Library of Congress was more interesting than it had sounded when he first heard it was on their schedule. The first night they'd eaten dinner at some big German restaurant, which seemed like a weird choice to everyone because they were supposed to be celebrating America, but the second night they were taken to a food court at a very fancy mall, and that was where Thom had a chance to talk to Wendy Eastman, the new girl, again. Ever since the bus ride he'd decided that he liked her, even though he was keeping it to himself. But everywhere they went he kept an eye on her, looking for opportunities to maybe say something or even make eye contact, but it hadn't been easy. The Kennedy twins, who were probably the nicest girls in the class, had clearly decided to befriend Wendy so she wouldn't have to do everything alone. Thom was glad about that, but it made it hard for him to make his move. But at the food court, which had about a hundred choices, Thom, having narrowed his options to a Philly cheesesteak or sweet-and-sour chicken, spotted Wendy in line to get a slice of pizza. He went over to say hi and asked her if she was excited about Georgetown. She looked blank for one moment and Thom panicked that she'd forgotten their entire conversation on the bus, but then she was smiling and telling him that they *had* to find the steps.

The next day, that morning spent on a visit to the Supreme Court, Thom could only think about the afternoon and evening trip to Georgetown. It was his big chance to get time alone with Wendy, a prospect that was equal parts exciting and terrifying. He kept playing it out in his mind. Miss Ackles had already told him that in the afternoon they were going to go on a tour of Georgetown University and then they were all going to walk to an Italian restaurant that she said was really good. She knew because she'd been on this trip twice before.

It wasn't raining in Georgetown, but it was the first cool day of the trip, the skies dark and threatening. They'd all been told to bring sweaters or jackets, and Thom wasn't particularly happy with the only sweater he had with him. His mom had packed it; it was yellow and way too tight, and he would have taken it off if it weren't so cold. Wendy was wearing a fair isle sweater and light-blue jeans, and Thom began to wonder if he was going to embarrass himself tonight. She was so incredibly beautiful, with really pretty hair, feathered on both sides, and she'd probably laugh at him if he tried to hold her hand or kiss her. Still, it was all he could think about, and when they arrived at the Italian restaurant—the woman at the door shouting, *"Benvenuti, studenti!"*—Thom spotted an opening. Mary and Ann Kennedy had sat down at the far end of one of the two long tables that had been reserved, and Wendy sat across from them. Next to her was a free seat, and Thom made his move, sidling up and asking if the seat was taken in a voice that didn't even sound like his.

"Help yourself," Wendy said, and Mary smiled at him, even though she probably thought he was being weird. But then the meal turned out to be pretty amazing, Wendy and he were talking just like they'd been talking on the bus, all about horror movies, and Mary and Ann (most people just called the twins Mary Ann Kennedy, like they were one person) listened to their conversation as if it were the most fascinating and terrible thing they'd ever heard. They all ordered spaghetti and meatballs (the house specialty), and the girls got Shirley Temples and Thom had a root beer that was the best root beer he'd ever tasted. Paul Barbieri kept making faces at him from the other table, especially after Thom spilled a meatball down his front, but it was clear that Paul was just jealous. At the end of the meal, Mr. Stone stood up and told the students that after dinner they were going to take a nighttime walk around George-town, plus visit some shops, and Wendy said, "It's our big chance to see the steps."

"What steps?" Ann said.

"When we were on the bus, Thom and I decided that we had to see the Exorcist Steps. They're right near here, and that's where Father Karras dies in the movie."

Thom had a sudden panic that Mary and Ann would want to sneak away with them as well, but one look at their faces, eyes wide with horror, and he thought that it would probably be okay.

"I don't think you should do it," one of them said, the other nodding.

"They're close by, I think," Thom said. "We'll be okay."

But once all the students were back on the sidewalk in front of the restaurant, being given instructions about where they could go and where they couldn't, Thom started to have his doubts. For one, it was dusk, the only light in the sky a line of pink on the horizon, and even though he'd said the steps were close, he didn't really know that for a fact. For all he knew, Georgetown was a massive neighborhood. Still, the important thing was that Wendy was by his side and they were on a mission. It wasn't scary here in Georgetown. It reminded him a little bit of Quincy Market in Boston, where his parents had taken him the previous summer. Except that here in Georgetown the streets were filled with students strolling in and out of bars, smoking cigarettes, wearing scarves. At home, Thom was allowed to watch only PBS so he'd recently seen a long, interesting series called *Brideshead Revisited*, a show that had, among other things, made him want to grow up and be a part of that world. One of cocktails and cigarettes and love affairs. This was what Georgetown felt like to him. It felt classy and adult, and far away from his own life. And Wendy was by his side.

"Which way should we go?" he said as the other students began to disperse.

"The steps have to be that way, right?"

She was looking in the direction she was pointing in, and Thom could see her neck, how beautiful it was, and had a moment of almost dizzying clarity, that his life was going to be filled with the pain of romance. And then Miss Ackles, in a denim skirt and a rainbow sweater, came up to the two of them and said, "Not thinking of sneaking off to find those steps, are you?"

"Who, us?" Thom said, holding out his hands, trying to make it sound like a joke and immediately feeling regretful of that decision.

"Do you know where they are, Miss Ackles?" Wendy said.

"Come with me, you two, but don't tell anyone. I don't want to get in trouble."

Miss Ackles walked ahead, and Thom and Wendy followed. They crossed the main avenue, then kept going down a dimly lit side street. Thom and Wendy were walking close to each other, and

Thom, his heart beginning to thud in his chest, extended his hand so that it brushed up against hers. He expected her to move away, but, instead, she slid her hand into his, interlocking their fingers. The sensation was so intense that for a moment Thom thought he might actually stop breathing, but his legs continued to move, and Miss Ackles, reaching an intersection, hesitated for a moment, then pointed. "There they are."

Thom and Wendy stopped holding hands, and Wendy said, her voice totally normal, "Seriously? Oh my God." It was the most animated Thom had seen her since the bus. She skipped over to the top of the very long flight of steps that seemed carved out from the city around them. Since Thom hadn't seen *The Exorcist*, except for the *MAD* magazine version of it, plus the more vivid one in his own head, the steps seemed both scarier and less scary than he'd imagined. In his mind they were incredibly steep, dangerously so, and while these steps seemed steep, it wasn't exactly like standing on the side of a cliff. But what made them scarier than he'd imagined was how close the building was on one side, the way it made the open steps almost claustrophobic, like a tunnel.

"I'll let you two have your moment," Miss Ackles said. "Don't blame me if you both get possessed by the devil."

Wendy, wide grin on her face, pulled Thom in closer to her. "Are they how you imagined?"

"They're scary," Thom said. "Do you want to run down them and back up?"

"No, I'm happy just looking at them from here," Wendy said.

"Okay. They are pretty scary just to look at."

"Do you need me to hold your hand again?"

Thom opened his mouth to respond, but nothing came out. Wendy whispered, "Sorry. I'm not making fun of you. I like you."

"I like you too," Thom said, and moved closer. Wind was swirling lightly up the steps and Wendy's hair touched the side of his cheek.

He really was dizzy, the stairs yawning in his vision, Wendy's fingers sliding between his again. He turned his head toward Wendy, hoping she would do the same.

iii

Wendy turned to Thom Graves, the boy who was desperate to kiss her. She had decided to let him. It was already such a great night, with Miss Ackles taking them to see the steps, and being in this cool city, and now it even looked as though she had a boyfriend. He didn't move his head, so she moved hers, and their lips met. It was awkward, but it also felt good. Thom put his free hand on her waist and kissed her harder, and she couldn't help it but she giggled and they stopped kissing. "That was really nice," she said, because he was a little pale and his eyes were big.

"That was my first kiss," he said.

"Mine too," Wendy lied.

"All right, you two, I think we should get going now." Thom stepped back and glanced in the direction of Miss Ackles, who was about twenty feet away, her back turned, looking up at one of the brick buildings.

"We should probably go," Wendy said. "I don't want to get Miss Ackles in trouble."

"Okay," Thom said. "These steps are pretty cool, though."

"Yeah, they are," Wendy said.

Miss Ackles was coming back toward them, a smile on her pretty face. "Was it all you hoped it would be?" she said.

"Yeah," Wendy said. Miss Ackles walked ahead of them, back toward the rest of the group. Thom's and Wendy's hands were intertwined again, and Wendy thought about how she'd lied about the kiss being her first. But she hadn't really lied, because tonight had been her first good kiss. The best kiss. She pulled herself closer into Thom, thrilled suddenly to be alive. It was like being introduced to a room in her house that she'd never been shown before. Thom said, quietly, only to her, "I feel like we're in a movie."

Yes, she thought. It's like that too.

iv

Thom was a little embarrassed after he told Wendy he felt like they were in a movie. She hadn't responded, but she'd squeezed his hand. He wanted her to know how excited he was, but he also wanted to be just a little bit cool about the whole thing. He decided to be quiet for a while.

The walk to the steps had seemed long but suddenly they were turning a corner, Miss Ackles in the lead, and Thom could see the other students gathered around the bus. He stopped holding Wendy's hand, and they each moved a little bit apart. Mrs. Chappell, nervously holding her clipboard, spotted the three of them and yelled for them to hurry up. Wendy was suddenly gone from Thom, having been swallowed up by a small group of girls that included Mary and Ann. Miss Ackles was by his side now, and she said, as they worked their way to the sidewalk, "Just so you know, Thom, your romantic escapades were being filmed."

"What do you mean?" Thom said, genuinely alarmed.

Miss Ackles laughed and said, "I'm kidding you. Well, sort of. I asked the clerk earlier at our hotel how to find the Exorcist Steps, and he told me that all these tourists are showing up there now, and how someone fell down the steps and broke his back. He said they had to put a bunch of security cameras around. I spotted one, on the side of a building, pointed right down on you and Wendy. It's a good lesson to remember."

"What lesson?" Thom said.

Miss Ackles changed her voice to make it sound dramatic, like she had on the bus, and said, "You were being watched. You're always being watched. The eyes of God are on you." She held up her hands and shook them dramatically.

"We weren't doing anything wrong," Thom said.

"I know, Thom, I'm just teasing you."

They were quiet for a moment, Mrs. Chappell now letting kids onto the bus, making check marks on her list. Thom's mind was spinning, thinking about the kiss, about his future with Wendy, about when he would talk to her again. He wondered if he should tell her what Miss Ackles said about the camera and decided against it. He didn't know Wendy that well but suspected that she liked secrets. He'd let her believe that the two of them were the only people in the world who knew what had actually begun that night.

Acknowledgments

Martin Amis, Angus Cargill, Emily Dansky, Caspian Dennis, Danielle Dieterich, Joel Gotler, Kaitlin Harri, Jennifer Hart, Patricia Highsmith, Elizabeth Jane Howard, Jessica Lyons, Libby Marshall, Tara McEvoy, Harold Pinter, Josh Smith, Nat Sobel, Virginia Stanley, Liate Stehlik, Keith Stillman, Grace Vainisi, Sandy Violette, Judith Weber, Jessica Williams, Phoebe Williams, and Charlene Sawyer. Special thank-you to the Lake Hopatcong Six (Sarah Reed Carter, Olivia Bingham English, Liz Horn, Peter Lyons, Nina Tiger, Jay Ufford).